# ARE YOU WITH ME?

*Stephen Foster*

D0061674

POCKET
BOOKS
LONDON • SYDNEY • NEW YORK • TORONTO

First published in Great Britain by Simon & Schuster UK Ltd, 2007
This edition published by Pocket Books UK, 2008
An imprint of Simon & Schuster UK Ltd
A CBS COMPANY

3 5 7 9 10 8 6 4 2

Simon & Schuster UK Ltd
Africa House
64–78 Kingsway
London WC2B 6AH

Simon & Schuster Australia
Sydney

www.simonsays.co.uk

A CIP catalogue record for this book is available from
the British Library

ISBN: 978-1-41652-281-2

Printed and bound in Great Britain by
Cox & Wyman Ltd, Reading, Berkshire

For Arthur

Support from Arts Council England, East, gratefully acknowledged.

*There are the mud-flowers of dialect*
*And the immortelles of perfect pitch*
*And that moment when the bird sings very close*
*To the music of what happens.*

Seamus Heaney, *Song*

*One Summer*

For a couple of weeks each August we used to take a holiday in the sun, always a Greek island, each summer a different one. We had visited Corfu when I was nearly six, Paxos when I was nearly seven, Lefkada when I was nearly eight, and now, when I was nearly nine, we were in Kefalonia. In the middle weekend of our fortnight, a huge story broke across the world. It was a Sunday morning. My dad, Ray, was buying two hundred pounds of drachma at the bureau de change. While the cashier counted out the notes, he told him the news.

No way, said my dad. But it wasn't something a Greek person would make up. They weren't like that, they were very straightforward and honest, they gave you things for free, like slices of melon and cakes.

Is that true? he said.

Yes, replied the man. They're talking about it on the radio now. He thumbed at a set on a shelf behind him, but of course the talk was all foreign, so we couldn't understand it.

Next we went to fuel our jeep. We always hired a jeep, a Suzuki, more of a fun car than a genuine 4x4. On Greek islands they have an attendant at the petrol station. This one was a very old man.

EU laws, they're a complete joke, Ray said. Just look at him.

I looked. The man smoked a cigarette with a white filter-tip while he topped us up.

You'd get six months in Wormwood Scrubs for that back home, he said. Still, it only goes to show how stupid the laws are in the first place, eh son, because this bloke's lived to be a hundred and ninety without blowing himself up.

The attendant screwed the cap back on while simultaneously flicking the ash from his cigarette and taking the drachma from my dad. You could see at a glance that he was an old man of few words but, all the same, he told us the same story as the cashier in the bureau de change, about the big news.

Ray took a light from the attendant, and pulled off. A little further down the road we dropped in at Dmitri's roadside café, our regular, where my dad took his morning coffee and his second cigarette of the day, and I took my Coke float and doughnut balls in syrup.

Don't tell your mum, he said. He said that every time we called in at Dmitri's, which was every second day because my parents were on alternate shifts so far as taking a lie-in went.

He meant don't tell on both counts. My mum, Sally, liked me to eat more healthily than that, and she pulled her face at Ray if she caught him smoking before the first drink in the evening. The waiter who served us the coffee and the Coke float and the doughnut balls was talking about the news too. Dmitri himself stood behind the bar polishing glasses and shaking his head sadly. Later in the day the couple selling jewellery from a cart in the town square were talking about it. Even the hippy by the quayside who sold henna tattoos was talking about it. He talked about it as he applied a heart with a dagger to Sally's right forearm, to match the one my dad had, only his was real. I'd already had my tattoo the day before, a skull and crossbones. Versions of events differed considerably, but in this global Chinese whisper one essential fact remained constant: the Princess was dead.

The news was so incredible that my mum broke her holiday rule of 'no newspapers'. Two days later (because of the English press coming in a day late), and out of sequence with their lie-in routine, she and I left our place early in the morning to drive the Suzuki down into the madness of Argostoli town. Our village rooms were in a more relaxed spot up in the hills along the coast, with a balcony, a shared swimming pool, and no nearby newsagent. I was always up and about in the morning whichever of them lay in, because I always wake early if I find myself in a strange bed and the wrong room. After a long time spent scouring empty news-stands on the seafront she finally managed to pick up a tabloid and a broadsheet from a tabac (or whatever a tabac is called in Greek) in a narrow side street. Like the attendant in the petrol station, the old man who served us smoked a cigarette with a white filter-tip throughout the transaction.

These are my last, he said, meaning the newspapers. Very sad news about your Lady Dee, he said. These fucking paparazzi, he said.

Lady Dee was how he pronounced it. He meant Lady Di, of course.

As we crawled back through the shambles of traffic, the Kefalonian drivers honking at the incompetent tourists, and the more so at each other, I cast my gaze into all the souvenir shops. I took in the dinghies, lilos and body-boards, the snorkels, goggles and flippers – all the things that interested me and that I might need. Sally was looking too, but she was seeing something different, she was seeing all the empty carousels.

Not even a *Bild* left, Tom, she said, it's like they've been hit by a plague of locusts.

What's paparazzi? I said.

People who take photographs of famous people, she replied, to sell to magazines and papers.

Why did the man call them 'fucking paparazzi'?

Because it's their fault, the accident, they got in the way of the car and caused it to crash.

What, I said, just for a photograph?

Yes, well, for the money. The photographs can sell for a lot, she said.

We drove out of the traffic, back into the hills, back to the village rooms, where I studied the papers. *Diana, 1961–1997* was printed big at the top of the tabloid front page, *A Nation Mourns* at the bottom, all superimposed over a fuzzy shot of the mouth of a tunnel. The broadsheet had a large picture of the blue-eyed portrait, the one from *Vogue*, I think, the one where she leans forward and rests her chin on the back of her hand. The broadsheet headline was more restrained, more broadsheet, something like *Prince Departs on the Saddest Journey of All*. At the bottom of the page there was a picture of the jet that was to be sent to fetch the coffin. Inside both of the papers there were maps of the route from the Ritz to the tunnel, cartoon frames representing the sequence of events that led to the crash, complete with Roy Lichtenstein Pow! explosions to represent the impact, conflicting accounts of the number of fucking paparazzi who had been buzzing at the car on scooters and mopeds, conjecture about other vehicles involved, accounts of Diana's life and times, testimonials, columns, and all the rest of it.

On the balcony of our village room Sally drank coffee and ate Greek yoghurt with honey as she pored over the coverage. It was a long balcony parted from the other village rooms only by low chain fences. Other British people stopped by to look at the pictures and offer their thoughts. It was a 'dreadful thing'; she was 'in her prime'; what about those 'two poor boys'; and wasn't it 'such a shame', and 'especially ironic', because it had 'really looked as though she was just about to find true happiness at last'.

When Sally had re-read the stuff for a fourth time, my dad took his turn.

Bleedin' Frogs, Ray said, You can't trust 'em an inch, and that's a fact. There you are, minding your own business, ton-up on the autoroute, check the rear view, and what do you see crowding the mirror? I'll tell you what, some irritating little prick in a Peugeot shaking his baguette and flashing his lights like there's no tomorrow – *Vite, vite, out of my way you stinking Rosbif.*

What's that? I said, meaning *stinking Rosbif.*

That's what the French call us, Tom, Les Rosbifs.

Why?

Because we eat roast beef for Sunday lunch.

Well, why do we call them frogs, then?

Why d'you think? he said.

No way, I said, people don't eats frogs for Sunday lunch; that can't be true.

He looked at me in a way that meant to suggest that it was

indeed true. I turned to Sally, who nodded, confirming that he wasn't kidding me on. Only the legs, though, she said.

Oh, that's okay, then, isn't it, Ray said, winking at me. That's fine, if it's only the legs.

Eating *frogs' legs* and flashing their lights like there's no tomorrow, I said, imagining both activities taking place at the same time. (I'd seen Greek people eat squid while driving, but at least that was some sort of a fish.)

And as it turns out, for some, there actually isn't a tomorrow, eh? Ray said. No tomorrow for Dodi boy, no tomorrow for Lady Di, and no tomorrow for this Henri Paul bloke either. Goodnight Vienna . . .

. . . farewell cruel world, I said. (That was the way we always did it, in a canon.)

I thought about the weird French, and I thought about the crash, and it gave rise to a question: Why isn't it Goodnight Paris, Dad?

It's always Goodnight Vienna, he said.

But why?

There's no why, son. It's just the way it is.

He discarded the paper. C'mon, he said, I think we've had enough carnage for one day.

He lifted me up onto his back, stepped to the edge of the pool, and asked me was I ready. Yes, I said. I stood and braced my feet against his shoulder blades, launching myself clear of him as we double-dived in together. Then we climbed out, and we'd do it again and again. *Encore une fois,* I shouted, *encore une fois*. Encore une fois means 'one more time', it was the lyric of the song they were playing in every bar that summer.

Later, in the early evening, we'd do our lengths. After ten,

I'd had enough, so I'd get out, wrap myself in a towel, and occasionally shout to ask how many he'd done now, as he completed his routine, forty every day, fifty on Mondays.

Why d'you swim so much, I asked.

Because swimming is a journey to nowhere, he said. The rhythm of it empties my mind.

A journey to nowhere. I thought about that as I picked up more of the abandoned newspapers which were littering the poolside, splashed and wrinkled on the sun-loungers and tables. I supposed that a journey to nowhere would at least be safe.

Henri Paul, the baguette-waving Frog who drove the Mercedes S280 and wrote off all but one of its occupants, was the concierge of the Ritz hotel. He had been drinking beforehand, according to all accounts. Lucky for him that he didn't live – he'd have had to kill himself anyway, with all the flak he'd have copped once he'd failed the breathalyser. I looked at the pictures of the smashed-up car. I found it hard to believe that anyone had done that to a Merc. Makes and models of cars and bikes were amongst my principal fixations; ever since the age of five I could name any marque just from the grille badge. I had ranks of Corgi and Vanguard die-cast models back home in Balham, set out in grids and formations on window sills and shelves, and lined up in a jam right around the skirting boards of my bedroom.

In my mind's eye I picked up my S280 saloon and guided the three-pointed star into the side wall of the Pont de l'Alma tunnel approach then smashed the vehicle into the unlucky thirteenth support column. Henri Paul's entry speed was estimated at all sorts, a different mph according to each paper, but none of the figures were low. I conducted an experiment.

I cast off my towel, ran to the pool's edge, and side-bombed as hard as I could (knowing that the water would take the breath out of me anyway since I'd already warmed through under the late sun), in an attempt to recreate the impact of a crash. Ray was at the other end of the pool. He disappeared underwater, swam beneath me, lifted me, and launched me in the air. I landed with a back-flop, which came keen, but I didn't think that the sensation of either back-flop or side-bomb would be anywhere near what it felt like to crash in a tunnel.

Sally had struck up a deal with the old man in the side-street tabac. Over the following days she forfeited her share of the lie-ins, and she and I went down there every morning, because the old man had promised to hold back two papers under the counter. She can be a flirt, if needs be. The whole world was totally hooked, of course. One of the new arrivals to our village rooms told us about a family they knew who had cancelled their holiday because 'they couldn't travel, not with all this going on'.

Nutters, Ray said.

But with my mum, at least there was a point of reference to her obsessive newspaper hunt because she used to work at Claridge's in central London, at the time when Diana and Charles got married. She was a young girl then, she said, working as a chambermaid, and Claridge's was the official hotel for the great Royal Wedding. She told me all about it on our daily journeys into Argostoli town and back. Prince Charles held his stag night there too, she said, in a pair of suites specially knocked together on the first floor. It was quite a small do, she said, there were maybe twenty of them. She helped the florist deck the place out, even though that wasn't part of her job.

Did they tie him naked to a tree, I asked. I'd seen that done to a man once, on Wandsworth Common.

I don't think so, she said.

When it came to the wedding, all the guests – all the royalty and the heads of state, the visiting overseas dignitaries – filled up the rooms of the hotel. There were no vacancies for anyone who wasn't someone, none at all. It was exciting and crazy, with all the waiters and pageboys running up and down trying to sort out requests for novelty English things that all these overseas guests had to have – bubble-gum and Tizer and Mr Kipling slices – items Claridge's didn't sell.

Sally looked after the rooms allocated to King Hussein of Jordan and his entourage, on the fifth floor. Twice a shift one of the room-service waiters, called José, ordered a bottle of champagne on the King's tab. At the end of the week he had ten bottles. The King never noticed, she said, nobody was counting. Late in the evening of the big day, while the guests danced to a live band in the grand ballroom, a group of the younger staff smuggled the champagne out under their coats and jackets and walked a block away, where they sat on the soft summer grass of Grosvenor Square toasting the happy couple. The champagne was Dom Perignon. The hotel sold it for more than fifty pounds a bottle which was a lot of money back then, Sally said, though evidently not to King Hussein of Jordan. The party of waiters, chambermaids and valets drank it out of plastic cups. When the champagne had all gone they lined the bottles up on a ledge as a memorial to their great night, and sang, 'Ten green bottles standing on a wall.' They returned to the hotel and watched as the royal stragglers in their royal clothes fell out into the night, tipsy, like any other guests at any other wedding. On the road outside a fleet of Daimlers stood waiting for them, with chauffeurs leaning their elbows on the roofs, smoking cigarettes. When the young staff had watched enough they went round the back to the kitchens in the basement where a sous-chef handed out kedgeree from a big metal tin.

Is Dom Perignon nice? I said.

It's very nice, Sally replied, the bubbles go right up your nose.

Does it get you drunk?

Any alcohol can get you drunk if you have too much of it, Tom.

Did you drink too much of it?

No, she said.

Is kedgeree nice?

I don't think you'd like it, she said. It's fish with rice, and for some reason to do with a special request they cooked it with kippers as well as haddock.

What! They ate *kippers* at a royal wedding?

Yes.

I shook my head. Did you know Dad then?

No, I met him a couple of years later.

Was José your boyfriend?

No, she said, I never had any boyfriends until your dad.

Really? I said.

Of course not, she replied.

Did you see Lady Di wearing her crown, and her wedding dress?

No, she said, Charles and Diana never went to the reception . . .

They never went to their own wedding reception?

. . . strange but true, Tom. Once they'd finished waving to the crowds after the service they flew straight off on honeymoon – to a place called Ithaca, as a matter of fact. I've only just remembered that, she said. And she went quiet and thoughtful.

Because as it happened, Ithaca was another Greek island, a small one, right next to Kefalonia, just a short ferry crossing away.

We could go visit, for a day trip? my dad said, when my mum mentioned this detail later.

Sally looked at him. He looked at his watch.

We could go on Saturday, he said, Catch a bit of the funeral on television in a café.

Ray! she said, as if this suggestion was sick or something. She pulled her hair into a band and I watched all the bangles on her wrist slip towards her elbow.

Being there at the beginning and the end, though, he said, it'd be a sort of circle for you, hmm?

Sally adjusted her kimono and continued to look at him, as though she didn't understand him at all. I could see why. Because she wasn't really there at the beginning, and she was no more there at the end than anyone else – she was just a bystander at a part of the middle, dusting and polishing and arranging flowers and changing bed linen; drinking Dom Perignon on the King of Jordan and eating kedgeree for supper.

I often noticed that puzzled look pass between them, when one made a suggestion that the other didn't buy, but they understood each other somehow. I hardly ever saw them argue, and as on most occasions after those looks, we ended up doing whatever it was that had been suggested. On the final weekend of our holiday we took a day trip to Ithaca. We missed the first ferry, so we sat waiting on the sea wall for the next one, watching all the old fishermen sort through their catches while they smoked their cigarettes with their white filters. It was while we were on that second ferry that the funeral started. There was a television behind the bar, the picture was terrible, full of snow, but the sailors took off their caps and pressed them against their chests and held a minute's silence all the same. The only thing you could hear was the lapping of the waves and the fizzing of a coffee machine. The captain rang a bell to break the silence, then an old lady moved around handing out free cakes and little thimbles of raki. My mum lifted me and held me next to her. I was a bit big for that, for being picked up, but I said nothing; behind her shades I could see that there were tears in her eyes. You always learn something on holiday, and it was this that I learned on that one – that it's possible to cry about people you don't personally know.

She put me down. I looked about and I remember helping myself to a raki from a round table, then coughing and spitting, and my eyes watering. A Greek man laughed, and clicked his fingers to get me a bottle of lemonade to wash it away. I wondered if Dom Perignon really *was* very nice, like Sally had said. If it was anything like raki, it would be absolutely rank. Sometimes adults weren't to be trusted about the things they said, even your mum. Perhaps I thought I'd learned that too.

As the last week of our holiday slipped by, the newspapers gathered in our village room. They were full of it, page after page of speculation and pictures, it was the only story in town. I wondered how long it would be before they found the driver of the white Fiat Uno which was supposed to have been weaving about erratically ahead of the S280. Some of the journalists were trying to pin the blame for everything on this little car (to take the heat off their friends, the fucking paparazzi, no doubt). Fiats were absolute rust-buckets, and the Uno was such a box too. I had a scale model of one, but only to keep my collection intact. Fiat was a marque in total decline. It was amazing to think they had once produced a beauty like the Spyder.

On the flight home they gave us even more papers, the Sundays with the funeral pictorial pull-out supplements. Pictures taken by the paparazzi. There are two images I particularly remember, two that stand out.

The first is the wreck of the Mercedes.

I could already drive, even though I wasn't yet nine years old, because my dad was into wheels, it was how he earned his living, and he'd taught me, down on his friend Tyler Hamilton's farm in Devon. Additionally, I owned a few remote control cars, one a model of a Mercedes Gull Wing that I'd occasionally guide round our flat in Balham, and sometimes crash into walls. But neither the Gull Wing nor any of my other remotes ended up in the state of that S280 after their accidents. This was practically folded in half. As we thrust up the runway building up groundspeed for take off, I imagined the occupants folding in half with it, and I decided there and then that no paparazzi was ever going to chase me, taking pictures, and getting me killed.

The second image I remember is of the princess sitting at the end of a diving board, on a yacht somewhere, soon before the incident. She didn't look at all like my mum, except in age, but she looked like *somebody's* mum, relaxed in the moment, in a way in which mums usually aren't. It was a picture that made me happy that we were a normal family, all alive. You may recall the shot: she's wearing a swimming costume, the sky is perfectly blue, and there's a seagull flying beside her. She has her head slightly tilted to the bird, and some trick of perspective brings it close up to her, so that she might even touch it, or tell it a secret.

# 1.

*Here is what I felt: I felt the silence, the silence of the crowd, the crowd who were all raising their mobiles and camcorders and flashing them off like they were at Jay-Z in Docklands. I dropped the window a touch but all I heard was the whisper of the wind. It didn't last long, the dead moment, but I will always remember it. They'd start talking soon enough, wondering what it was supposed to mean, they were bound to, but by then they had receded from view, and all I took away with me was quiet.*

*I imagined the sound they would make once it kicked in, the trickle of murmur, the plethora of squawk, the flood of words flowing in all languages, coating the air like vomit on a pavement, and I was glad I wasn't there to hear it, that for now, at least, I was out of sight and on my way.*

*So; what exactly went on? I hear you ask.*

Well, as Mark Twain said, *When in doubt, tell the truth.* I've never actually read Mark Twain – I picked that quote up from off a website when I was doing a project in Citizenship. It was from a site about trees, in fact, rather than one about Twain. I was trying to find out why little terns breed on sandy beaches, rather than in the relative safety of a nest in branches. In the way it often goes with searches, I found myself on a tree forum. Someone in the forum was giving the quote, and someone else in the forum was saying that Twain told too much truth, that was his problem, that for instance he could go on and on and on and on for pages just describing the whitewashing of a fence. A third contributor asked what the hell was wrong with that. For him, lengthy description of fence-whitewashing was a good thing. If you can't go on at length about that in a novel, where else will you get the opportunity? he said.

Fair point, I thought, as I studied the forum – it *was* an arborists' message board after all, and fences are made from trees: it's not as if there's no connection. But, all the same, it wouldn't be for me, reading about whitewashing, and it only encouraged me to give Twain a miss.

Still, leaving this whitewashing business aside, I intend to follow Mark Twain's advice. Telling the truth is simple and uncomplicated, much the more so than making things up, I can tell you that for free.

What I've tried to do is to work out how I've fitted in to the whole scheme of everything. At times I have thought of myself as just a simple catalyst. But it's a definition that won't do, because a catalyst only facilitates a reaction, it does not, of itself, undergo any change and I *have* undergone a change – a *makeover* of a sort, to use the idiom (which is a word I like). I might say that I was a conduit, were it not for the fact that conduit is a word I do not like; conduit is to words what the Fiat Uno is to cars.

So I'll try an analogy, instead, as follows: I'm not like Bob Geldof.

My dad knew Bob Geldof, from the old days, from race

tracks. He stopped off at our flat a couple of times for coffee and a cigar. I'm not like Geldof in this specific way: while he made big things happen and was world famous, his own music remained as terrible as ever. I know this because old records were played when he visited, and afterwards my dad would put on a burn of some recent song that Geldof had left behind for a present. It was all dreadful, new and old alike. My dad admitted as much himself.

Tom, he'd say, he's a nice guy, old Bob, but he couldn't hold a tune if you gave him ten grand.

So, this is how I'm not like Bob Geldof: If *I* was him, *my* music would have either improved, or stopped. Something would have changed. Simple as that.

It follows from this that I need to find a specific way of thinking about myself, and I have done so. I have come up with the proper form of words, I am a *live catalyst*. There may be plenty of live catalysts out there, for all I know, not only is it possible, it's likely. The truth is that it's an honest description; that's the important thing.

If there's one single fact of which I'm proud it's that it's taken until now for me to become even vaguely notorious. Another way in which I'm unlike Bob Geldof is that I like to keep my head down. I practically make a religion out of it. That I've managed to remain incognito for this long in today's circumstances is an achievement. Any fame that comes my way will not change me either, I know that – like I said, I've already done myself over once. It won't be necessary to repeat a process that is, in any event, more difficult than people think. Often, when you hear someone say they've reinvented themselves, all they've really done is changed their clothes and hairstyle and maybe had a couple of implants. There's more to it than that.

I hope none of this sounds on the cultish side. I can assure you it's not meant to. Everything is intended just to explain what it's been like.

But anyway, to get some idea of how we got here, with the crowd looking on in silence, I have to go back, to a place I knew so well in my youth, as it says in the song. *Catch me if you can, I'm going back*. My mum had some original Dusty Springfield, signed too, on the Philips label. She had a pile of 45s in her vinyl collection, singles without middles, that she picked up from a juke box in a café called the Four Laps, which was right next to a circuit in the north. Dusty Springfield's real name was Mary Isabel Catherine Bernadette O'Brien, by the way (I found that out by accident in a search too), so there's nothing much new in the idea of reinvention. I'm going back to the place where the school picture was taken, the picture I hear they've been using in the papers, the only shot of me they seemed to be able to come up with. I'd forgotten about that photo.

If I looked at that boy, sitting in front of the blue backdrop with the badly painted clouds, would I wonder whatever happened to him? Of course I would.

What follows, more or less, is the answer.

# 2.

The moment when it all began was when this Luke character pulled up round the back of the school gates at the end of lunch break one Friday, sounding his horn.

If I had not been standing where I was standing that day, things might have all turned out differently.

It was late winter, 2003. I was fifteen. I'd been at the school for just two weeks. I was a beginner twice over because as well as being a new boy, I was an incomer. I knew I was an incomer because I'd overheard a woman in a shop describe me as such, to another woman. They were in the next aisle, the gossiping women. Maybe they thought I wouldn't hear.

Luke was a friend of this other boy, Gelling; they used to be neighbours, I later found out, though they lived in different parts by then. I was just getting to know Gelling, who was in my new class. I'd never seen Luke before. The car he pulled up in was a Talbot Alpine, a more or less forgotten '70s saloon with a notorious tappet-rattle, not the '60s sports convertible you might be thinking of, the model most people bring to mind when they hear the word Alpine. They ran a rare fleet out there in Norfolk, you could say that for sure. Apart from this Talbot there were old Rovers, Consuls, three-wheelers, all sorts, it was a proper time warp. You wouldn't have been surprised to see a plumber idling along in a sign-written Morris Minor with a timber roof-rack, so when you did see precisely such a thing, at least you were prepared for it. No, the sports convertible is the *Sunbeam* Alpine, not the Talbot. The Sunbeam Alpine looked a lot like the Fiat Spyder, but was a pretty poor car by any dispassionate assessment, even if it did score high on style.

As Luke sounded his horn – which was one of those deep, bass-honks, like you get on old Citroëns – he shouted, *Hey, blood!* from the window to Gelling, who was just arriving at my shoulder.

I'd been standing by myself in the playing fields, thinking forward to the weekend, wondering what Saturday might hold. I remember the moment because I was in the middle of talking to myself, which was something I did a lot, particularly at that time. I was asking myself a question, which was this: But where do people go for, like, *proper* shopping?

Because there was an item I urgently required, to help me out in my new bedroom.

Gelling flicked his head sideways – to indicate that we were to respond to the shouting and the peeping of the horn – while answering my question.

Proper shopping? he said. You don't get to where I've got to in life without some knowledge of *that* subject, Lover Boy.

He seemed supremely confident on the matter, as though he knew exactly what was what. It was a good sign, so I followed him over towards Luke and the Alpine.

Sally and I had arrived out there in the middle of nowhere about three weeks earlier. She'd got removal men in, not do-it-yourself van hire like we'd had in the past, but even with this help – not having to do our own loading and unloading – I was still excused school at first because Sally wanted me with her, to help us settle in properly. So I unpacked boxes, hung around, and every now and then I'd be sent out for the things we needed: bread and milk, screws and string, bin-bags, biscuits, batteries, and so on. This gave me the opportunity to explore the area and its facilities.

The shops, such as they were, were as follows: a twenty-four-hour store that only opened until nine at night (this, I found impossible to believe), an estate agent's, a bookshop that also sold artists' materials, a derelict butcher's, a beauty parlour called Solar Lab which for some inexplicable reason was painted to look like soap bubbles, and finally, at the end of the parade, Vallori's Chip & Kebab, Eat-in/Takeaway. The shops were on one side of a village green with a duck pond in the middle. On the other side of the green stood a pink-painted pub called the Nelson with a picture board of Admiral Lord Nelson swinging high from a post at the front. Outside the pub there were slatted timber tables and benches. Even though it was late winter, it was one of those winters that wasn't cold and I would often see people sitting on the benches drinking, workmen in heavy coats, overalls, and tan boots with elasticated sides that went halfway up their calves. They would pause in their drinking and look at me as I passed. They couldn't help it, I suppose. I was a curiosity in a village of just three thousand residents (I had checked this fact on the net, anxious to establish exactly how small the place was – it was three thousand times smaller than London when you worked it out – three-thousand-three-hundred-and-thirty-three times smaller to be precise, I did the calculation). I was certain not to make eye-contact with any of the workmen, because I knew from another search I'd done that statistically some of them would be paedophiles. So I walked round the far side of the pond, in order that I would have a head start should any of them try anything on.

There was a petrol station a little further up the coast road which sold sandwiches and flowers and hardware. The petrol station put up the Closed sign even earlier than the twenty-four-hour shop. This was the sum total of retail outlets. To me, it was wrong. You couldn't get screws or string from any of these places, only bin-liners and the basic foodstuffs, and even then quite often all you could find in the way of bread was bake-it-yourself subs and ciabatta rolls. You might have thought you could at least find string in the artists' materials part of the bookshop, but the lady serving said they were out of stock.

Sally had taken a trip up here on the train, visited the estate agent, and put an offer in on a place without fully consulting with me, only telling me we were moving when she caught me cold one night as we sat on the sofa watching an old film. It goes without saying I was totally underwhelmed by this, but her head was in a mess and I had to make allowances. And anyway, even if I stamped my feet and made a fuss, what was the point? I recognised the situation for what it was, a fait accompli. That's what my dad would say: Fait accompli, son, nothing to be done about it now – it's out of our hands.

In the case of Fait accompli, son, the path of least resistance is best.

Our new home was a cottage. If cottage is not quite as dreary a word as conduit, it's not far behind. Nor was I keen on the place itself when I first saw it. The outside was painted pink, like the Nelson, the roof was made out of straw, and the inside had a smell I found upsetting. It was the stale odour of the people who had lived there before; I think they must have been old people because they had left behind a furry cover on a toilet seat. The ceilings were so low you could touch them just by standing on your toes and jumping. You'd think a teenage boy would like that, but I didn't, it seemed wrong to me too, same as the shops. We'd lived in a flat in a mansion block back home – Streatham Mansions, it was called – where the rooms were tall with long windows and ornate cornices in the repeat pattern of bunches of grapes. Some of the prints we had on our walls back there – the old advertising posters from Belle Vue – well, I'm not exaggerating when I say they were too long to fit floor-to-ceiling in the main room of this cottage, you had to lean them at an angle to get them in, as if you were building a house of cards. Imagine that, a room that's shorter than a poster. There were two of these low downstairs rooms, then beyond them a kitchen, and beyond the kitchen, a bathroom with condensation running down the window, and the furry seat cover. What a set-up. The three thousand or so people I was living amongst were of the sort that would design a bathroom that you had to get to by going through a kitchen.

A door off the kitchen opened on to the garden. We'd never had a garden before, so that was something, at least. The door to the garden was split horizontally like a barn door so you could limbo under it or, alternatively, you could open the top, close the bottom, and somersault. That was something too. The previous people had left a rope swing behind with a branch tied through a knot for a seat. They must have had grandchildren: I couldn't imagine old people using a rope swing themselves. Upstairs there were three bedrooms with small window panes and another bathroom, this one with a black plastic toilet seat. Sally was planning to renovate the cottage with the money she was making from the sale of our flat. It was going to be her 'project'.

Ray, who I had only recently overheard Sally describing as a stupid fuck, had left us behind a few months earlier, the stupid fuck, and don't imagine I didn't resent him for it, because I did. One of the removal men commented on his name when he'd been shifting one of those advertising posters that were too tall to fit in the cottage, shifting it back into the van, to return to London, to put into storage.

Ray Radford, he said, the speedway rider; I remember him.

My dad, I said.

I was conflicted in my new circumstances. On the one hand I missed my friends and my normal life, obviously: moving is a chore, particularly for the young, who are not as adaptable about such things as daytime shrinks and magazine columnists like to make out. I especially missed Milo, my oldest and closest friend and confidant; somehow, though both our families moved flats in London a few times, we only actually changed school once, and even then we ended up in the same new school. He was a year older than me, and he was superb. A boy who could get you into trouble in the simplest way of all, just by looking at you. He could call a teacher an utter, utter twonk with only a very minor twitch of his eyebrow. Not that he *was* in school all that often, because at a tender age he became a professional skateboarder, which gave him something of a dispensation. *Ollie* magazine had used a photo of Milo verting an escalator in the Cathedral Park Shopping Centre in Tooting Bec for a cover shot when he was only in Year 7. It was his gateway to a new life, that image; in no time at all he found he was in demand for adverts and videos and soon he was well-minted. Never mind upgrades to his phone, Pod, or even his wheels – all this suddenly became loose change to Milo: by the age of fifteen he had bought his mum a place in Paris. Only in the 10$^e$ arrondissement, but apparently that was a very up-and-coming district, a proper investment. Prague, Warsaw, Budapest – they all have their advocates, but if you stick with *established* Europe your money's guaranteed safe. This was the advice Milo's accountant gave him, he told me that.

Why not buy her a flat in London? I said.

Wa-ay too fucking expensive, he replied, And anyway, she has a little soft spot for that area, for being quarter-Cameroon on my grandma's side.

Milo had several other professionals looking after him. There was a lawyer who was always in a meeting or else on the phone tearing someone off, a fitness coach who had worked with the Olympic skiing team, and a part-time personal tutor for normal lessons, who Milo evaded as much as possible by saying he had a meeting with his lawyer or his accountant, or else a fitness session with his coach. The beauty of him was that somehow he remained grounded; the money and stuff never went to his head, he totally kept his shape. I knew Milo as well as anyone before he became famous, so I can guarantee this is true. Whatever came his way he remained his own man, the eyebrow-twitching teacher-twonk-caller of old. It's a good trick, being yourself, I reckon.

I informed Milo as soon as I touched down in Norfolk – or East Anglia as some called it – a combination of words so awful it produces a sound that's even more dreary than conduit and cottage combined. For a while I refused to recognise East Anglia, instead I lived in my own independent state of Exile. Actually, there's nothing wrong with East, it's the Anglia that does the damage. It reminded me of the old saloon that might be considered the prototype for any mid-range family car you care to think of. The Ford Anglia had its revival too, if you remember, when it was used on the first Harry Potter book cover. You used to get people driving round in them in a copy-cat homage, and then the actual car that was used in one of the films was kidnapped and taken hostage. We live in a world where a rusting motor can reinvent itself, and then be held to ransom. Best not forget that.

I texted Milo the basics, the things that struck me.

Pigs ☹, I'd go.

And he'd tb: Sillycones x2 ☺

In this way he'd understand that I'd landed in the swamp and I'd understand that he was in a studio doing a job for Pepsi or Nike, kick-flipping over nubiles with gypped-up tits, and probably pulling off some neat body variables while he was at it. I envied him, of course, who wouldn't, not for the tits but for the freedom. But I never envied him as much as you might think. He was a gifted ripper, and that was that; I was just a reg-ular amateur myself – on a deck I was on the road to nowhere. I might find my vocation one day, if I was lucky, but I could already eliminate skateboarding from my career map. Anyway, the important thing was that I was proud to count Milo as my friend: I hammered my board in the slam with the all the rest, to show my regard at the exhibitions and events where he was performing. Except for this one time when they were making a film and this MC was irritating the hell out of me by trying to hype us up for a cutaway crowd shot. Giving respect is a natural activity, not something you do on command for an editor. I shoved my hand in the camera, as I always did if anybody tried it on.

What troubled me was that I knew that over time our texting would diminish – our email and msn life was never better than sporadic anyway, we weren't really the type – and that in the end we'd drift apart. It was inevitable. But as much as I could I suppressed this thought. Instead I concentrated on keeping my pecker up, for Sally's sake. Looking after Sally was a matter of priority to me now because, while we were driving up the M2 on our way back from Dover once, when it was dark and my mum was asleep in the back, my dad said could he ask me a favour. He'd never asked me a favour before, except to hold a spanner or pass him a wrench or a file, stuff like that. So of course I said yes. The favour was to look out for Sally, if anything should ever happen to him. He checked me sideways. Could he trust me to do that?

Happen? I said. Like what?

Anything, Tom. You look out for her, take care of her, yes?

I didn't like this talk, or want it to go on, so I nodded.

And I never expected to have to fulfil the favour, of course. But now it had come to pass. Now I did have to look out for her, because now I had become the man of the house.

If there was an upside to all the upheaval of moving, it was that at least Sally was no longer surrounded by mementoes of Ray, and the same went for me too. Streatham Mansions had also been full of trophies, plates, cups, vases, all sorts. All that regalia had been put into storage, in a lockup. We left it behind us, as it were, so we could move on. The Belle Vue posters had only travelled to East Anglia in the first place because of a mistake by the removal men.

For another short-lived upside, I was finally out of the way of Sally's Clapham Buddhist gang who had been constantly coming round to do my head in. If I tell you that both the male Buddhists and the female Buddhists alike wore trousers with sunflower prints and drawstring waists, and that they had alternative names to their real names, names like Manavendra and Akuti, I expect you'll know the type. They'd been driving me up the wall by asking, every time I made the mistake of showing up in the kitchen, whether I was *grieving* properly. They went on and on, saying it was *only natural* to feel very, very sad and that I should not be ashamed to cry. They thought that by saying this they'd get to see real tears, and then they could feel totally together and at one with themselves. I never gave them the satisfaction. It got so that I stopped even going into the kitchen at all (and that was *my own* kitchen too, now I was man of the house). Instead I went down the high street, picked up a McDonald's and abandoned the wrappings in the hall, just to piss them off: nothing in the world is less Buddhist than a Big Mac, and that is a fact.

So, moving to East Anglia at least meant I could leave all that behind. And I'd never lived anywhere else, either. Like I said, when we'd hired do-it-yourself vans in the past – which was regular, because Sally had itchy feet (like Milo's mum) and was always wanting a new place to do up – it was only to relocate from one London street to another. So this change was an adventure, you couldn't say it wasn't, and even if at first sight it didn't look too promising, I *was* having new experiences. To give you a for instance, when it went dark it was like wading through oil. The only darkness I'd ever known before was capital city darkness, which was, I now came to realise, for practical purposes, lightness. When night fell in Norfolk, you really could not see. I found it exciting, scary. Sally had been so unnerved by it that she sent me out with instructions to buy the biggest torch I could find. It was the petrol station that had it. It was called the Strobe, took eight C-batteries, had six different settings with various flashing sequences, and was the size of a biscuit barrel. As I walked back, testing it out, an old boy in a cap asked me what was up, weren't the stars good enough for me? After a lifetime spent with only the moon and the planets for illumination, I guessed his eyes must have adapted for night vision, the same as these Aborigines I'd seen on television whose soles had become like leather so they didn't need shoes. But for incomers like Sally and me, normal people without rabbit eyes, things were different, and at least with the Strobe we felt confident enough to cross from our front door to our pick-up without jumping out of our skins because we'd been brushed by a fern or bombed by a massive insect that could have been a vampire bat for all we knew.

The reason for all the darkness could easily be seen in the daytime. If you stood there in the school playing field, where I was standing at the moment Luke called out, all you could see were other fields for ever and ever, and off in the distance the propeller blades of ten wind turbines. It was those fields, which were brown because they were made of soil, that were responsible for soaking up any available illumination, such as it was, at night. There were six street lights in the whole place, I counted them, and I never saw them all working at the same time. This was because the supply of local power was produced by the wind farm, of course, one tenth of which was always broke, though which tenth differed from day to day. It should have been obvious, even to the clowns who were responsible for installing the system, that electricity would be an unstable commodity under generating conditions such as that. The only way I could make sense of this utility was to imagine I was on holiday in Corfu, or Paxos, or Lefkada, or Kefalonia. You could ride a moped on those islands at any age – on the road, down the pavement, across the market square, along the back of the beach, anywhere you liked – and with no helmet or any other protective gear either. And you could expect a power cut at any time too. It was the same in our new village, power cut-wise, and not so different vehicle-wise either; there were any number of quads and scramblers being put through their paces in woods and fields, I'd clocked them. So in a way, in our early days in the cottage, in my own mind I was on holiday in Greece. And if you're on holiday, it's not quite the real-life deal, is it? I must have been giving myself that one, now I think back.

I was watching the nine working propellers, or rather focussing on the stilled one, when I asked myself the question about where to go for proper shopping, when Gelling turned up.

Gelling was about a stone overweight, lightly freckled, with pudgy, dimpled cheeks that looked as though they belonged to someone else, as though he might be breaking them in for a fatter, older man. In short, he was cut like a stand-up. He was a little taller than me with a blond mullet, razored at the sides, with tramlines zipped through.

Luke repeated his shout from the gates:

'*Hey* blood!'

(Was this supposed to be a joke? In the three weeks or so I'd already been there I had yet to see a single black person.)

Gelling flicked his head sideways once more at Luke's second shout and broke into a trot.

C'mon, he said, stick with me kid, you won't go far wrong.

Fancy a break from the dismal routine of daily life? Luke said, out of the car window. His fingers flicked the inner edge of the steering wheel.

Gelling leaned his elbow on the roof of the Alpine, and with the other hand pulled an inhaler out of his pocket and twirled it like it was a Colt 45 while he considered the offer. It was easy to see that in his own estimation he had what it took to become a legend.

Gelling had been the very first boy I'd spoken to on my second day. On the first Monday they just gave me orientation, showing me around like a specimen, and I didn't much speak to anyone. Gelling introduced himself at break with a complicated handshake. Other than him, I'd been shoved in the corridors a bit. I expected it, it was bound to happen, what with me being an incomer, and it was nothing, really, it was tame. Worse things went on in Balham before first bell, that was for sure, because that was about the time we had a metal detector fitted on our school doors, the time when knives started coming in

STEPHEN FOSTER

big. I didn't let it be known that in my latter days I would sometimes carry a blade myself, in the pocket where I keep things, because that could get you into even more trouble than not carrying one, if you're with me, because people hear about it if you carry, and then they come your way, looking for trouble. You can stay safe in Balham, but only if you know the scene and you have a few faces pulling for you. I wouldn't have wanted to be an incomer in SW12, let's put it that way.

It was around the time when knives started coming in big, or maybe just after, that I'd begun to shiver sometimes, especially if I felt a bit freaked out. I tried to hide it, but Sally noticed, and she made her own diagnosis, which was that my blood sugar level was giddy. She did most of her own diagnosing, because she had something against conventional medicine (we never went to the doctor's, not if we could help it). To counter my shivering she invented the shivery bite. Shivery bites were dried fruit, nut and honey confections that she cooked herself in a pan and rolled into balls like the truffles we treated ourselves to from Fortnum and Mason every Christmas. She said that these little babies would totally help regulate my body balances, and that I should eat one whenever I felt a shivery coming on, and that that would completely help. Unusually, for one of her miracle cures (because, inevitably, we did go to the doctor's, in the end), the shivery bites actually worked. If I was standing in the corridor waiting to change classes and I started to feel freaked, I'd take my cure – which after all only looked like ordinary sweets, so no one could get on my case about it – and sometimes I'd hand a few out to others too, as if they really *were* ordinary sweets. That was how I had responded to Gelling's

32

complex handshake. I offered him a shivery bite. He well-rated it, so I gave him a couple more.

Get your weight off my wheels, man, Luke said to Gelling as he went into his leaning-on-the-roof inhaler-twirling routine. Are you in, or what? he said. C'mon, I hent got all day.

*Your* wheels? Gelling said. He gestured at me and said, Can Lover Boy come too?

Is he safe?

Safe as, Gelling replied.

Get him on board then, Luke said.

I wasn't so sure about speccing an unauthorised absence with it being such early days, but I understood that declining the invitation wouldn't get me very far. So I climbed into the back alongside Gelling. There was a girl in the front passenger seat.

Hey-up G-Minor, she said. Long time no see.

Likewise, said Gelling.

Luke mirror-signal-manoeuvred and eased away from the gates like a model citizen.

# 3.

We turned onto the main road and headed north as Luke shifted up the gears.

How's Tiffany doing? the girl said to Gelling.

Six stone flat, Gelling replied.

Is that up or down?

Gelling shook his head. About the same, he said, She's having size four Moschinos specially run up for her now. She won't be happy till she's an American nought. A pox upon them all, he said, I lost count of how many times I told her not to do it.

But Gelling, don't you think she'd be dieting anyway cos anorexia is an inherent con*dition* darling, you can't just pick it up just by being on television.

Saff, she went on *Celebrity Slimmer*, you could catch *any*thing from being on that.

I guess, Saff said.

She could sue them? Luke said. Surely?

Gelling wound the window down and spat. Apart from the Greek jeep, I couldn't ever remember being in a car without electric windows.

Who's this Tiffany? I said.

Check that accent, Saff said.

I'd had that a few times, kids going, Awright mate, and stuff. What they thought they were on calling *me* on this subject was anybody's guess considering that they pronounced Tuesday 'Toosdey', and that I'd heard more than one boy call a computer a compootor.

What's your real name, Lover Boy? Saff said.

Tom.

Tom what?

Radford.

He's from Balham, Gelling said.

Balham in London? asked Luke.

Is there another one? I said.

Bound to be, Luke replied. He eyed Gelling through the rear-view mirror. I prefer to remember Tiffany from the good old days, he said, she was sound.

Saff looked at him: Oh was she?

Yes, he said. What was that kids' programme she were in well back. What was it called? I can't remember.

I settled down and made myself comfortable while between them Gelling and Saff and Luke pieced together the story of Tiffany Gelling, Gelling's older sister, who began her small-screen career in a programme called *Gnarlers*, which I had seen once or twice. It was a secret-passage-to-a-secret-world kind of thing on the Kids Channel. Tiffany didn't handle the associated fame too clever, going off on a bender and finding herself the subject of little pieces in *Fate* magazine – nipple-slip and up-skirt shots of her tumbling out of limousines and nightclubs. The usual. The snappers hosed her down, and for a while they made her into the wild-child-off-the-rails daily soap before her moment was over and it was somebody else's go. After her first rehab she made a few no-hope comebacks on daytime trash before showing up out-of-it while presenting a prize on Yarmouth pier, a story which transferred from local to national news bulletins one quiet day in August. She did her second rehab on reality and was back in business. A gig as a castaway island presenter was enough to guide her career back on track. Her agent pulled off the *coup de grace* by booking her onto *Celebrity Slimmer UK*. She was such a natural that she went on to become the European Celebrity Slimmer Champion of Champions, beating off stick insects from all over the Continent. Good going, especially when you consider the unfair advantage that French and Italian women set out with. The consequence of all this was that she might *go down the same tragic path as Karen Carpenter*. This was Saff.

Who's Karen Carpenter? Luke said, as he tested the suspension on a left-hand bend with another big pink-painted pub on the offside called the Nelson. The ride was better than you might imagine, though the interior upholstery was rank, the shade of a Caramac bar. To make it worse, the upholstery was colour-coded to complement the body work. To think someone must have sat in an office with a drawing board and fabric swatches, like Sally had all laid out on the table in the cottage. Someone must have been paid to design it. Luke steered with his right hand holding the bottom of the wheel, his elbow pivoting on his thigh, a dead giveaway: it was the exact same grip they use on Maine Carnage IV.

Saff told Luke that Karen Carpenter was this in-a-weird-kind-of-way-beautiful singer who was in a brother-and-sister pop act called The Carpenters who were a bit like . . . she couldn't remember the name of who they were a bit like. They could be quite depressing, she said, but then they could also be quite uplifting too, and she started into a part of a song, *We've only just begun, to live* . . . click fingers . . . *White lace and promises, a kiss for luck and we're on our way* . . . click fingers. She did the click fingers slowly. She reminded me of a dancer I'd seen in Dmitri's bar way back in Kefalonia, the way she did it. They had dancing every night there, and after dinner Mrs Dmitri would give me extra doughnut balls in syrup and press my face into her bosom and pinch my cheek. It's amazing how someone who is so dist*ressed* can have such a beautiful voice, Saff said, meaning Karen Carpenter, not herself, though she wasn't so shady – I'd heard worse on the talent shows many a time, and well after the prelims too.

I *know* that song, I've heard Tiffany playing it, said Gelling, She has it loaded on her cPod.

What's she driving now? said Luke. Still got that Chrysler?

Nope, said Gelling, She traded it for a 3-Series coupé.

New? said Luke.

Brand spanking.

Cherished plate?

STIK 1, said Gelling. Calf-kid leather, mirrored alloys, you name it.

Done alright out of *Celebrity Slimmer*, then, Luke said. In a way.

That hadn't needed an answer. Private plates were as rare as talent shows, but you still paid top dollar for a proper one like that. Not to mention hitching it to the new Beemer, as good an engine as you'll find anywhere in mass production. You have to hand it to the Hun, as my dad used to say, When it comes to winning wars they don't perform, but they turn out the best straight-six in the world.

Is it the best, though, Dad? What about the Honda four-pot? I'd say.

You have to hand it to the Japs, he'd reply, When it comes to winning wars not only do they not perform, they cheat. But they turn out tidy enough motors, you can't say otherwise.

But which nation, that under-performs at winning wars, actually makes the best car?

You really *do* have to factor in image, son, he'd say, I don't think you need me to tell you that. Game, set and match to Helmut.

Sally used to pull him for this stuff, telling for him not to be such a dinosaur and asking him did he really want to turn into his old man? He would just draw on his Bensons, wink at me through the rear view, and pat her on the thigh to complete the effect.

Gelling had a sudden bad thought. Shit, he said, Maybe Karen Carpenter is a kind of *heroine* to Tiffany?

No! said Saff.

She could be, you know, he said. That'd be just like her. I mean, it's not as if it's the sort of music she used to listen to.

I watched Saff curl her hair round her finger as she absorbed the implication of this. In an effort to lift the atmosphere she said to Gelling, Your new friend is cute. Meaning me.

Got an older brother, Tom Radford? she said.

I hadn't given my number out to anyone so far, but I'd already had a note passed to me at school asking me for a date, and two verbal offers of sex on top of that. The skirt was forthcoming, as my dad would've said. Not like back home where the streets were full of Princesses who were saving themselves for a big phat Superstar with a big phat crib in LA. These invitations were nothing to do with my wealth, looks, or charisma, they were to do with my novelty, that was all. I was the most novelty-like boy around by a mile. Living life surrounded by fields and pigs and wind farms, the amount of new blood they got to see was strictly rations.

Even though her question about an older brother made it plain that she considered herself in a different division to me, out of my league, what she said made me blush all the same. Luke gave me the once-over in the rear view. It seemed clear enough that his co-driver was also his sweetheart. The happy couple were about seventeen or eighteen, but I didn't see them as the student type. They were sharing a two-litre of Razor. Only alkies would be seen outdoors with that stuff back in SW12, but here it was on permanent three-for-two at the twenty-four-hour store that wasn't.

I'm an only child, I said.

Lucky for you, said Gelling. He leaned forward and helped himself to a long pull on the Razor. I could tell by the way this went down that Gelling was regarded as a sort of entertainment: Look at him, he don't half hold it for his age.

Where are we going? he said.

California, Luke replied.

Gelling handed the bottle to me while saying to Saff, You don't get to where I've got to in life without having cute friends.

I regarded the Razor as I took it from him – the opaque black plastic bottle, the gold label with the image of a sweating half-apple superimposed over an orchard. I sniffed it. There was no way that the liquid inside that bottle had been anywhere near a tree. I imagined the germs from their three sets of lips mixing it round the rim, dancing like bubbles. I wanted to clean it with my cuff, but I didn't want to give offence, so I just closed my eyes and took a swig and it didn't taste as bad as I was anticipating. It wasn't all that different to Vimto Lite, which I had a craze on at the time, just sweeter.

Saff started singing again, changing her tune. *All the leaves are brown and the sky is grey, I went for a walk on a winter's day*. She had still blue eyes and smooth pale skin. Her earrings dangled crosses. She was wearing a look that was popular then, and which has come back round: a see-through blouse over a t-shirt vest, leather calf boots with socks pulled up higher than the tops, and some, but not too much, make-up. Hippy-chic with possible political undertones. I can say that now. I don't think the thought crossed my mind then, about the undertones.

Gelling started rapping over Saff, who had lost the words to her song and had dropped into humming, *California, knows how to party, California knows how to party*, and made his voice sound like it was being put through a vocoder. It wasn't a lot like 2Pac, but all the same you could tell who it was supposed to be.

Luke laughed at him, Two-culture clash in de grandstand, he said, in a put-on dread voice.

Did your mum just move into Keeper's Cottage, Saff asked me.

Yes, I replied.

What, de haunted Keeper's Cottage?

Leave him alone, Luke, she said.

Everybody knows it's haunted, sister; I is only saying.

Don't worry about him, she said, He's got a febrile imagination.

I handed the Razor back and she tilted it to Luke's lips
just as he hit a pothole. It splashed over his jacket and he
went, Fuck's sake Sapphire. It was the first time I heard her
full name, it'd been Saff all the way until then. I'd never
known a Sapphire before. There had been a Saffron back in
Balham, a girl who lived on the ground floor of our mansion
block, who always left her bike in the hall in exactly the best
place for people to fall over it. A sapphire was a sort of jewel,
I knew that, but I couldn't think what colour it was. I liked
the name, though, and combined with her easy way with a
song, the rose tattoo on her slight forearm which I'd been
studying through the sheer layer of blouse, and the protective
attitude she was displaying towards me, well, I reckoned she
was neat.

Luke hadn't been too thrilled by his partner jiving me up
about my virtual brother, and then having Razor spilt on him.
To demonstrate his annoyance he put the car through its paces.
In the back we fell attentive and silent as he began to ask
questions of the braking and suspension systems while he over-
took tractors on blind summits and played chicken at Stop
signs. My dad had taught me about body-English, and Luke's
was pretty good, so I wasn't that worried. I wouldn't say I
was used to these sort of stunts, but I wouldn't say my dad used
to drive more slowly than was absolutely necessary, either. I'd
caught him doing 135mph down the M1 one night. He thought
I was asleep, but I was awake enough to have one eye on the
speedo.

Luke's blood is nitro-injected, Gelling said. Fasten yourself in, it's gonna be a . . .

Bumpy ride?

Stick with me kid, said Gelling, grinning, as though he had provided me with a total treat.

This clutch is fucking choice, Luke said, as he missed a gear.

Silently and simultaneously we buckled up. The real owner of the Alpine must've had children, because cars of that vintage didn't come equipped with restraints in the back as standard. In fact, when the car was new, even fastening the front belts would have been optional. The law making it compulsory for front passengers to wear seatbelts was passed the day before Lady Di's wedding. My dad told me that, on our way to the airport in Kefalonia, when we were returning the Suzuki to the hire place and my mum was having a go at him about not wearing his. It was the thing he remembered most about the Royal Wedding, the stupid new law, he said. Not that he'd bothered with it. Nor had he watched the ceremony on television or anything, he said, because he couldn't care less about it.

If they'd have been wearing seatbelts in that car, they might not be all be dead now, my mum had told him.

Ray looked at me. Don't copy your dad, son, he said, You always wear yours, right?

There really is a place up there called California. I didn't believe in it when Luke said where we were going, I thought he was noising me up, like about Keeper's being haunted, but then I saw the name on a road sign.

We arrived in the middle of the afternoon, but it *was* more-or-less a winter's day, like in Sapphire's song, so it was already going dusk. Luke slung the Alpine off the main road and spun down a dirt track towards the beach, swerving side to side, just missing the ditches that ran along each edge. As a rough car park at the end of the track came into view he floored it. He ratcheted the handbrake as he hit into the open space, and to be fair he turned a few nice donuts – he was no beginner. The dirt kicked up putting us at the centre of a dust-storm. Of course it reminded me of shale, of the track. As the cloud thinned he pulled square to the beach and revved until the tappets rattled like teeth in a clockwork skull before flirting the clutch. He really got some thrust. I was surprised, because I didn't think the surface of the car park would be sound enough to give him traction. I guess it must have been because of the time of year. Earth stood hard as iron, like it says in the carol. Luke used the low scrub as a take-off ramp, but he hit it wrong and we went into a flip. We sailed through the air, rolling twice on the beach before sliding to a halt against a pebble-bank that stretched parallel to the horizon. We came to rest on the roof. When you witness an accident, the sound of crashing seems thunderous and full of death, but somehow, when it's you who's inside, you don't hear nothing. Everything comes to a stop, before time starts up again and you look around you and the sea appears to be the sky and the sky appears to be the sea and there are birds flying next to the ground.

Gelling turned to check me, to see if I was man enough for all this. In his inverted state he was a cartoon, he put me in mind of Buzz Lightyear from *Toy Story*.

Radford? he said.

There aren't any shops here, Gelling, I replied, Are you sure this is the right place?

I'd been working on the line as the journey unfolded and it became clear that there was even less in the way of retail out towards California than there was back in the village, and that in point of fact, and in contrast to California USA, California Norfolk appeared to be a one-horse town plus two bungalows. I'd been working on the line not least because I was competing with Gelling's you-don't-get-to-where-I've-got-to-in-life routine. It was a routine that impressed me, not only because it worked, but also because it was persuasive and cool, and I was big into a pose called *sang froid* at the time, which is persuasive French coolness, which is about as cool as coolness can get. Milo's girlfriend had explained sang froid to me. Milo's girl-friend was a French model called Nico who had picked him up on a half-pipe while he was casing out the 10$^e$ for apartments. With sang froid you just act as if everything is normal whatever the situation, as if that sort of thing happens to you every day, whatever sort of a thing the thing is. It's unbeatable as a guid-ing principle in life, because you never have to betray any real feelings, and you can always remain aloof from subjects and events even as they go on around you. With sang froid you can remain aloof from things that are mind-numbingly mundane, like Buddhists, or you can remain aloof from things that are not so mind-numbingly mundane, like a near-death experience involving rolling onto a beach in a '70s saloon with a bad, bad tappet-rattle and pistons that were by now blown out of the block. If sang froid was a sweet, I guess it would be a good hit of shivery bite.

The truth of the matter was, in fact, that I was scared shit-less by landing like we did. I actually felt my skeleton shift within me, and I heard my heart rebound off the inside of my ribs. Also, quite apart from the debt that Gelling and I owed to whoever those rear seatbelts were fitted for, I happened to know exactly what can happen to a full tank if it touches down wrong and catches, because I'd seen it before with my own eyes at stock cars. I'd noted the fuel gauge as soon as I got in. Kids of Luke's age never run a full tank unless they've recently done one off a forecourt, and I could tell that he hadn't because there's a smell you get from a boy after a drive-off and it was a smell that Luke didn't have. So I knew from the very beginning that the car was hot, that it was someone else's petrol we were burning.

I had a couple of other stresses in the back of my mind while I was working on my line:

One: it was too soon for me to be getting up to stuff like this – even taking into account my time off school for helping out at Keeper's Cottage, we hadn't actually settled in yet, our life was in Limbo, things were still in boxes, we were unsettled, nomadic. So:

Two: I would need to be inventing a cover story to tell Sally, which had better be a plausible cover story that wouldn't upset her because she'd been through a lot lately and I didn't want to be adding any unnecessary extras.

Plus which – or *en plus*, as Nico would say while shouting and waving a finger at Milo (she was a natural at that) – *en plus*, I wasn't sure what was going to happen next, out there in California, but whatever it was, it was hardly likely to get me a row of starred As on my report card.

So, all in all, taking my stresses into account, I could reckon I hadn't done so bad; what I said about the shops spread a smile right across Gelling's huge cheeks. He began laughing, and that set me off, and soon we were out of control. Gelling laughed so much that tears ran down his forehead, which can only happen if you laugh while hanging upside down. And then the other two started up as well, though not before Sapphire had called Luke a prick and asked him if he thought that was supposed to be fucking funny or something. Now I think about it, my line would have been only the trigger, the catalyst for the release. Our laughter let us know we were still alive. It was the sound of hysteria, that's all it was.

As the waves of our relief finally passed we unhooked our harnesses, loosed ourselves to the ground, and started to shove at the doors with our feet and knees.

That picture I heard they've been using in the papers – the school photo – was taken on the morning of this same day. It must have been the only image they could find. And I know where they got it, too. Sally kept the smallest of the set stuck to the dash of her pick-up in a little frame. It must be that. The big one's long gone. I slung it when I was in a bad mood one time.

When I brought the pictures home, Sally set the big one on the mantelpiece, up against the chimney breast. I remember watching her do it because I remember she used a starfish paperweight to stop it from slipping, a paperweight she made herself, with resin and a starfish that I found out on California beach that afternoon. It was a great discovery, like treasure, and it totally took me aback by moving slightly. I was astonished, I thought starfish were the same as shells, I didn't know they were living creatures, I'd only ever seen them before in books and on tea towels. Saff said that if I put it in my pocket it would soon petrify.

It will what?

Get all scared, said Gelling.

Become hard, said Saff.

One of Sally's New Norfolk Buddhists brought the resin round and showed her how to set it in a mould. So that element of moving away, no Buddhists, was short-lived. At least the New Norfolks didn't ask me anything about grieving (Sally had probably briefed them not to). But I still didn't like them. They had the same clothes, the same made-up names, and this lot also thought they were morally wonderful because everything they ate was organic which they'd grown themselves from Fair Trade seeds that they'd imported from Uzbekistan, the bastards. What I loathed about them most was their tea. They couldn't just use a bag in a cup like any normal civilian, it had to be herbal, it had to be made in a pot, it had to be loose leaves, so you had to find a strainer, and then it had to be served with *soya* milk, which, unbelievably, you could buy in both the twenty-four-hour shop *and* the petrol station. If only there had been a McDonald's in the village: they'd have got plenty of business out of me. Any number of these New Norfolk Buddhists showed up, offering to help us with decorating and so on. They had all the time in the world, none of them ever had a job. They made ends meet by painting patterns on eggs and penny whistles and selling them at these craft fayres and dance camps that they were always having up there. I tried to think exactly what form of words my dad would've come up with to comment on all this, but I couldn't get them dead right. There was one particular couple who were frequent visitors, almost from day one, a woman called Alice who, to her credit, had no other name, and a man called Brian with a ponytail, alternatively known as Girish. Of course, I thought of him as Girlish. While Girlish made himself useful by stripping wallpaper and rubbing down the woodwork with wet and dry sandpaper he droned on about planting trees and stuff.

I've got this friend who builds boats, Tom, he said. Would you like to come along and see?

I shrugged. I couldn't care less about boats, they meant nothing to me.

He carried on talking anyway, about his friend's plans to sail to Kathmandu, and about how he and Alice would go along too. When he'd finished with that he gave a speech about the wide variety of fauna and flora to be found in the Norfolk broads, which were these rivers that ran about through the fields. Alice said very little; instead, she smiled and offered me chewing gum. She was quite un-Buddhist, for a Buddhist.

I texted Milo:

Im bn bord 2 deth by a gay peznt called Girlish tb

Milo tb:

Girlish fcuk me. New york london paris norflok? i dont think ☺ Nico sez retorn a ici mez ami

It was in my mind all right, that, to retorn a ici, but it was a non-starter. Because of my promise. I could hardly look after Sally if I was a hundred and fifty miles away from her, could I? After finishing all their preparation and crack-filling and sizing and drinking of yet more herbal tea, Girlish degenerated the conversation into a lesson about local architecture. As if it wasn't bad enough that the cottage had a straw roof, he seemed to think that the rest of it was built out of horsehair and shit, 'wattle and daub' he called it, the utter groyle.

At last they left, thank God, and so Sally and I were finally alone. We stayed up late painting the walls together, using three shades of yellow, colour washing, as it was called. I remember I quite liked that. Before the painting of the walls we had stayed up late on other nights too, fixing the floorboards before sanding them down. Sally was going for the natural modern feel (the very first thing she'd done was replace the repulsive toilet seats with wooden ones, she'd actually brought them with her, from Balham). The floorboard sander was one of those drum types, fun to use, in a way. I remember I liked that too. I guess all the work of doing the place up was good for us, keeping our minds occupied.

When the living room was shipshape, I found a framed *Sidewalk* cover of Milo, and another smaller picture of him and Nico sitting on a wall in the Tuileries Gardens from the previous summer. They had their arms round each other's shoulders, and the Palace stood in the background. There was some very good skating to be had round the Tuileries Gardens, if you could get it. Milo ripped a night-time stunt on the Louvre pyramid, for one of his videos. He had to be lightning sharp – security are serious about patrolling against that sort of thing – so Nico, me, and a gang of her comrades caused a distraction by grinding the nearby verges, to draw the heat, while Milo got on with the job in hand. Then we legged it down into the metro and rode back up to the Louis Blanc metro in the 10$^e$ where we met up with Milo's mum and some of her friends. Milo's mum was our official chaperone, but she's one of those chilled-type mums who doesn't care a fart about what you do.

She ordered us crêpes and Stella from a café beside the Canal St Martin while we skated near a bandstand where an Algerian group played drums.

I hung the pictures one above the other in an inglenook. Sally tried other paintings and prints on the other walls (the artists' materials bookshop had at least stocked picture hooks). I stood back saying if they were in the centre, whether they were straight or not, and if they suited. Actually there *was* another picture of me, sitting on my dad's shoulders, with my mum leaning against him. The three of us were standing in a field down at Tyler Hamilton's, my dad's mate (his best mate, actually). I'm only about five or six in that.

And then there were finishing touches: pebbles and shells from our beachcombing filled the fireplace, a vase with wild flowers from the bottom of the garden stood on the hearth. Alice bought potpourri in a bowl she'd made herself from papier-mâché, and later the school picture went on the mantelpiece, in the same cardboard frame in which it arrived. Some people frame them properly, but that was never us. They're temporary, those photos, there'll be another one next year when you've grown and changed. That's the idea. I remember Sally had something to say about them, when I bought the set home.

*Sally*

They were a sight for sore eyes those photos, especially round that time too. I said to him when I saw them, Hey, you're smiling for the camera Tom Radford. Were you on a dinglydangly? That was one of our sayings. Dingly-danglys are heats where you get double points.

It was the last time he ever brought school photos home. They were more than mementoes, they were collector's items. And he was at an awkward age, what with the move and everything else. It was an awkward time all round. So it was nice to be able to see something resembling a smile on his face, if only in a picture. You couldn't count on it in real life. I kept the passport-size one on the dash of the pick-up, and the full portrait went on the mantelpiece. I can remember precisely when he brought them home: it was the day after we'd spread gravel out in the front, I could *hear* him arrive, crunching to the door, which was half the point. Apart from making a surface for parking, I wanted to know when people were approaching. I'd moved us out there for a bit of peace and quiet, as well as a fresh start, but I tell you, the peace and quiet actually unnerved me, especially at night. I wanted a little early warning of footsteps. I had a couple of tons delivered, and Tom arriving home was the first time I'd heard an unexpected sound. Well, I'd *expect* him home, of course, but as to when . . . he was always up to something, he had a lot of extra-curricular activity going on, you might say.

He helped spread that gravel, but then he never needed encouragement to become involved with anything you might think of as a vehicle, and the job called for a wheelbarrow, which counted. I borrowed it from Girish – we'd had no use for a wheelbarrow in Balham. I sat Tom on top of the final few loads and tipped him out, which had him roaring. And that set me off. It was the first time he'd really forgotten himself since his dad.

He was always a driver. Once we were all done, he backed the new pick-up in through the gates for me. He insisted on doing it. He worried about my reversing, which was never the best. Ray's old riding mate, Tyler Hamilton – became a promoter? – well, he bought this farm down in Dorset, nice place, lovely spot with a river at the bottom of the garden and cows in the field beyond. We stayed there one Easter and that was where Tom learned properly, in an ancient Renault 4 that Tyler kept as a runabout. Tom's feet couldn't quite touch the pedals so Ray strapped wooden blocks onto them, and Tyler found him a cushion. After learning in that old thing, driving ordinary cars came easy. My new pick-up was a Nissan Cabstar, which was much bigger than anything he'd driven before, though. I bought it for this business I was setting up, interior design. I'd always been keen, dabbled, you know, for friends, and on our own places. It was a bit of a gamble but I thought the potential out there must be enormous, with all the second homes. So I needed a proper vehicle for that, to look the part, and to move furniture and material around. Not to mention for all the work I had in mind to do on Keeper's. I was planning an extension on the back. I heard Ray's voice in my head while I was at the dealers putting a deposit down: Dirty cheating bastards the old Nips, especially when it comes to wars, but one thing you can be sure of – their trucks never break down. He wasn't big on PC. I used to hear his voice in my head quite a bit.

Tom reversed it absolutely confidently, he was a natural, it's in his blood, I suppose.

I could spend a good while looking at that picture, when I was stopped at lights and when the traffic was bad. He looks full of intent, don't you think? That was just before his hair turned darker; it's sort of dirty blond here, short but untidy. It's a rare talent to have untidy *short* hair, I used to say to him. His skin is so clean it looks bathed. That's youth. It's his eyes that really get me, though; they're Ray's hazel, trying to be cool, and failing, probably because he was so angry, underneath everything. It's a killer combination, isn't it, cool anger.

## The School Photographer

I'd been at it thirty years or more. Family portraits, weddings, pets, a bit of freelance for the local rag, but nothing national. Add in the school work and that was my bread and butter.

So, what you looking for? A bit of local colour? I wouldn't say that dealing with the public had turned me completely mis-anthropic, but I'd certainly had enough of *people* and their ways: their squit, as it's called locally, which means, well, you can tell what it means by the sound of it. I'd *seen* enough of the human race, that was the thing. I'd have cashed my chips in by now, retired, if I could have afforded to, but this game, it doesn't really allow it. You're always investing in new equipment, it goes with the territory, you have to keep up, keep your hand in.

As far as the schools were concerned, well, it was one of those contracts that became less and less of a bright prospect as time went by; kids got worse in their behaviour year after year, not to mention their language. And then there was what you had in the news all the time. It was so widespread it became so that any adult, particularly if you were male, of course, could arouse suspicion just by casting a glance. And with my job, you know, simply focussing a child through the viewfinder could make you feel like you were doing something wrong and dirty. Terrible thing, when you think about it, and ironic too because photography is a line of work that rewards fastidiousness: *Cleanliness is next to Godliness*, that's the motto, at least it used to be before digital. Still, in spite of it all, the school photo remained an annual event, it hadn't fallen prey to the do-gooders, not yet, it wasn't on a government list of banned activity. No, I could budget for it in my annual accounts, though I did find it difficult to keep motivated. Seen one snot-nosed kid, you've seen 'em all, as I used to say when you could still joke like that. The lads in the Nelson might smile but you had to be careful. You never knew who else was listening, waiting to put you out of work – you get no end of pettiness in a small community. You could have your licence revoked for practically anything, even though you'd already been through a police check. I became so wary – you could think of it as *cataloguing* children, if you let your mind start roaming, and paedophiles were public enemy number one, equal first with Muslims and asylum seekers – that I took a policy decision: to abolish talking shop altogether. It's a shame, but there you have it. You still do the job to the best of your ability, whether you discuss it or not. Professional pride, I suppose you call it.

I'd seen him already, actually. I was sitting here in this window having my after-work pint. You notice new people, of course you do. His mother – a bit of here and there, she'd make a good subject – had just moved into the village and evidently she'd been sending him out on errands to the parade. He was a moody-looking lad, solemn, but then we didn't know he hadn't long since lost his father, did we? They'd be told at the school, I expect, but they wouldn't pass on that sort of information to a freelancer like me.

Oh yes, I remember him well enough. I've seen them all down the years, the jokers, the clowns, the gurners, the butter-wouldn't-melts, the can-you-believe-how-gorgeous-I-ams. I suppose I must have photographed thousands if you counted them, but there are one or two that stick out, and I like to think I have a flair for faces. What you had with him was the sullen non-co-operant; with all the resentment he must have been bottling up he looked older than his years, even inside that baby-face. He stood out. When his turn came, I gave him one of my little softeners:

Climb aboard, chief, I said. I meant onto the stool, of course. That's what I'm saying about how careful you had to be.

Climb aboard, chief.

A little phrase, a word or two outside of what they normally hear. It usually does the trick.

# 4.

The photographer had one of those pull-down canvas back-drops painted with blue sky and clouds which were unconvincing, too dense and thick. Clouds are a trick of the light, they don't need laying on with a trowel. Art that didn't look realistic used to upset me. I could have done a better job of them myself. I was in a bad mood that morning already, there was a smell of manure wafting about in the air, and those clouds didn't help. In Balham, the air smelled normal and school photos were taken against a computer-generated background with actual projections of real clouds from the cloudwatch website. But all those old photos from London got lost, they were in a box that went missing in the move.

The photographer thought he was funny. I walked to the stool as slowly as I could, I hated the rigmarole of the activity anyway, it's a liberty, it's not like they ask your permission, is it? First I had to stand in a queue (another one of the words the East Anglians tortured, pronouncing it 'coo'). 'Everybody's cooing up,' they'd say. 'Quick, get in the coo.' So I coo-ed with them, and when my turn came the bloke gave me all his patter: Climb aboard chief. Confound me if you're not the most dashing chap I've seen all day.

He was crouching behind the Nikon as he said it, under the black curtain. He had the big umbrella up too, for the flash. He fiddled with a tripod nut and then he stood up and said, Yup, that's a face that could launch an Ocean Cruiser.

He must have been a movie buff, that's where you pick up lines like that.

So I climbed aboard, imagining the sea.

We'd already been out to the coast a couple of times, Sally and I, beachcombing for the pebbles and the shells. Sally talked about getting a dog, saying that we could walk it out there, that a dog would love all that freedom. She wanted a Dalmatian, but I was more for a spaniel. She said spaniels were a nice breed, but difficult to train because they were mad. There were no Ocean Cruisers but there were more wind turbines planted out in the black water, in a line running square to the beach. I wondered how they were secured, and tried to picture the size of bolt that would be required to anchor such a thing to the seabed so it didn't just float off and get washed away. I was walking in the tide edge, getting my feet deliberately wet, imagining the sharpness and depth of thread on such a bolt, when I saw a seal. It just bobbed up in the shallows, from nowhere. I stopped dead. It dived down. Then it appeared again a second later, fifty metres from the first spot. I never knew they were so fast. And then it came back towards me, close into shore, and stuck its head up high and stared like it was looking at me. It was one of the best things I'd ever seen, live. I took my phone and got a shot and I photo-messaged Milo.

Milo tb:

Wtf's that?

I tb:

A seal! In the c ≈≈≈

He tb:

Zt alors ok. neater thn pigs ☺


## The School Photographer

Make it Natural. That's the other motto. It comes with experience. You just go all out to destabilise the mood you perceive in your subject. You keep alert for a change in expression, from the one that's been *prepared* to something spontaneous. Capture that and Bingo: there's your magic moment. Of course, you often have to *manufacture* the magic moment, but you can guess that. So I had a routine whereby I'd follow the softener with a perplexer.

*Yup, that's a face that could launch an Ocean Cruiser.*

What I find is that if you bring in just a single word from their world, as a pay-off, you're in business. So I straightened up and bowled him a googly:

Exactly how many hearts have you had to break today, *dude*?

It's all in the timing. I squeezed the trigger just as I saw the twinkle rise in his eyes. Very green, weren't they? Though there's no twinkle, actually, I must've imagined it. It's not the first time I've seen my work in the paper, but not on such a wide scale as this.

Mind you, incidentally, Radford himself isn't the reason I remember that particular day. No, not at all. That was the afternoon my car was stolen. I'd have minded enough if it was just an ordinary replaceable saloon, a Vectra or whatnot. But that vehicle had belonged to my father. It was his pride and joy. He didn't leave much behind. I did all the servicing myself, it's best that way; we all know what mechanics and their bills are like.

# 5.

Luke forced open the driver's door and slid himself out onto the sand. Sapphire followed him through, but in the back both exits had buckled and were un-openable. Seeing that we were trapped, Sapphire called to us to keep over to one side while she popped a window with a rock. Gelling and I crawled out and stood up shaking off the tiny lozenges of glass. Outside there was a bitter smell in the air. Luke examined his handiwork, then turned to us.

Sorry about that lads, he said, No fucking power steering, that's the problem. He booted a wing, as if the flip was entirely the fault of the Alpine and its antique engineering. Gelling stood back before offering his opinion:

The residual value is absolutely hammered now, eh?

I'd say, Luke said.

Aside from other aspects, like his overtaking technique and his car theft, I had known all along that there was something wrong about Luke, but it was only now that I could put my finger on it. He was wearing a suit, a white shirt, and a loosely knotted striped tie; he was in school uniform. In fact he cut the schoolboy figure more than we did, he could have passed for upper sixth, except that the upper sixth at the village school didn't wear a uniform, and on closer inspection the clothes weren't school uniform either, they just looked that way. The only jewellery he wore was a signet ring with a Gemini crest on his right middle finger. I noticed him assessing me now, to see what sort of a case I was. What he had in front of him was a boy wearing a green school sweatshirt with a badge who was rubbing his elbow because he'd cracked his funny bone, who was stretching his legs to make sure they were in working order, but who was otherwise feeling reasonably chuffed to be in one piece. I looked him in the eye, totally neutral. My dad would have flipped if he'd found me involved in this. Don't get me wrong, he was no saint, obviously, you don't get saints in his line of work – some riders hate each other so much they deliberately run an opponent off the track, into the fence – but he was *professional* when it came to wheels, even if he didn't always fasten his seatbelt, and this scene wasn't professional; this scene was totally *un*-professional. That's what would've flipped him.

What d'you reckon, Radford? Luke said. Just a little accident, he said, as if this would convince me that nothing much had happened.

But something had happened, of course, and like most things that happen it wasn't all that accidental. Decisions had been made in order to get us here, that much was obvious to a blind man riding a charging horse. But it was not the moment for a debate.

Y'alright, then? he said.

Nothing broken, I replied, dusting myself off.

Choice, Luke said. Stick with Gelling, he said, you won't go far wrong.

Gelling was already moving off to join Sapphire who had

retrieved the remains of the Razor from the wreck. She beckoned me over to sit beside them on this low concrete wall that kept the dunes at bay. The coast stretched out straight in both directions as far as the eye could see. There was another wrecked car much further along to the right, which was east, towards Yarmouth.

I'd already been to that resort. Alice took Sally and me out there after the decorating. Alice told Sally it was worth seeing, at least once, and that I might like it. We shared fish and chips sitting on a bench in a shelter on the promenade, then Alice bought me candyfloss for dessert. I got the feeling that Alice was even less of a Buddhist when Girlish wasn't around, which made her hardly a Buddhist at all. In fact, I wondered what the hell she was doing with Girlish and the Buddhist crew in the first place. We visited the funfair, but most of it was shut, with it being out of season. Alice knew of a go-kart track off the main drag, and when we got there she persuaded the man to let me do eighteen laps for the price of twelve. She and Sally had beers in a bar on a gantry while I raced. I was disappointed that the karts were speed-governed so low, but it was the same for everyone, and I used my weight to my advantage. Some boy had a go at me after, for 'cutting him right up', which was a joke: if he had a clue what he was on about he'd have known that I'd held a line, and that was all there was to it. He'd been beaten by a better driver, simple as, but then you do get all sorts of amateurs on go-kart tracks.

Saff passed me the Razor. I wetted my lips while I watched Luke circle the Alpine, making phone calls as if he were quoting for salvage. He gave every impression of being a man in a hurry, as if he really might have a spot of nitro in his blood. I knew all about nitro, my dad told me that speedway riders were always after it in the old days, they used to tour round model shops where it was sold as fuel for remote-controlled aeroplanes. Once they'd visited every model shop in sight and bought up every drop they could get their hands on, they mixed it with the methane, the normal fuel. Nitro was good for an extra rip, except that often they'd get the proportions all wrong then the motor ran so hot that it melted a hole in a piston and wrote off the engine. You have to be careful with that stuff.

Gelling jutted his chin towards Luke. What's the situation? he said to Saff.

He's calling Scanes, she said, They're going to film it.

Scanes from *Red Star Grenade*?

Yes.

Film it? For what?

For a visual, for their gigs. It's a kind of . . . she tailed off, and began pulling at her fingers, cracking her joints. I wished she didn't, it goes right through me, that.

. . . it's a kind of – have you ever heard of a Happening? she said.

Yeah, said Gelling, sure I have, that's what you have when things happen.

You don't know what one is, do you? she said.

C'mon then, said Gelling, give me the know.

He was scratching at his leg. I bashed my freaking knee, he said, It's giving me right gyp. He looked at me. I raised my elbow at him, to show him he wasn't the only one injured. Sapphire pulled Gelling in and rubbed round his kneecap in a circular motion, while she gave the know.

Twocing – taking cars without consent – and torching – making bonfires of them – had become so routine, so mundane, so *obvious* and so *provincial* a pastime that for practical purposes it could be considered normalised, no, worse than normalised, it could be considered *passé*. There had been a period, a golden age, when it was a cutting-edge activity, she said, but the law was so slack now that a significant part of the thrill had been taken out of it. If you were underage, such as Gelling and I were, you'd barely get a slapped wrist even if you *were* caught, which was unlikely enough in any case given that the Dibble spent most of their time on a media-training course being taught how to deny things. On top of this, and exacerbating the situation, scrapyards had become so over-subscribed – there was so much *defunctness* in the world – that a situation had developed whereby you couldn't persuade a scrap merchant to take a write-off off your hands without *you* paying *him* for the privilege. And so, almost by default, trashing a banger in a lay-by had become a usual method of waste disposal for the poor, the less well-off, and other small-time criminals. Play it right, report it stolen, you might even pick up some insurance. In short, as far as old-skool torchers were concerned, the fun and the glamour had gone out of the game. However, in any given activity there are always the aficionados, the specialists, the *obsessives* who are more than usually dedicated and who *will not* quit: These are the people who *transcend the norm*, she said.

*You* transcend the norm, Saff, Gelling said. You're very beautiful, he said, Have you ever thought about modelling?

Modelling? You are a one, aren't you G-Minor. D'you know Helena Christensen by any chance?

Yes, he said.

Well I share her views on modelling, Saff told him.

Oh, how's that?

Helena Christensen said that if you're a model there's no point in trying to prove you have a brain, so why even bother? She said she'd sooner save the energy for something more meaningful.

So how do you share her view?

I take her starting point, and I extend it to its logical conclusion, Saff said: I don't bother with the modelling.

You save your energy for something more meaningful? I said.

That's right, Tom.

Gelling began coughing and feeling about in his pockets. Fuck it, my inhaler must have fallen out, he said. He headed down to the wreck.

Sapphire carried on talking as if she were making a speech. Creative people have to conduct their lives in a way that is unique, she said, They need to *push at the bounds of experience*. It's very important to turn the ordinary destruction of daily life into something alive and *compelling*.

Gelling returned with his medication. What a load of cock, he said. He threw his arm out behind him. This is all just *nfn*, Saff. Torching one doesn't make you anything but a petty little petty, and everybody knows it. Why do you make this stuff up?

What's nfn? I said.

Normal for Norfolk, Gelling replied. By the way, he said, my knee still hurts, Saff. In fact, I think it's getting worse.

She resumed her massaging as Gelling drew on his Intal. She looked over at me. Are you shivering, Radford?

No, I'm fine.

I blame the authorities, said Gelling. If only sentencing was tougher. One day, when I'm in charge, things'll be different, we'll bring some discipline back to this country, restore moral fibre, you mark my words . . .

It was clear that Saff had experience of ignoring Gelling. She looked to the car. Luke is just trying to keep something alive, she said, He's diversifying, he's trying to be more . . .

Happening? I said.

Yes, Radford.

In London it tends to be profit-orientated, I said.

What?

Well, you know, prestige motors get lifted to order and chopped and exported.

Gelling chipped in: I saw a programme about that, with this gang who were after 911s and Z4s for people in east Europe and wotsit, the new immigrants.

That's it, I said. I'd seen that programme too.

A couple of them actually did do some time for it, Gelling said. It said at the end they got two years each.

Oh yeah, you can get a stretch alright if you're caught because there's corporate image rights as well as auto-crime involved. Porsche are even lumping big into prevention now, aren't they, because the last thing they want is their status getting messed up by seeing gangs of Latvian mafia cruising round Clapham Common in Carreras.

Oh, said Gelling, is that what happens?

Sure, I said. I've seen it loads.

Social engineering, said Saff, shaking her head. That's multinational capitalism for you. So, you're quite an expert, Radford? she said.

I wouldn't exactly . . .

What would you exactly? she said. She gave me a curious look which made me turn away.

It's alright, she said, I don't bite.

I could ignore people too if I wanted, she didn't have the monopoly. If I learned nothing else from having the London Buddhists meditating in my kitchen, and Alice and Girlish at it too in our new back garden, I at least picked up on that technique. So while Saff ignored Gelling, I ignored her.

I looked towards the horizon which was bleeding into itself; dusk had come down in a blink, the sea and the sky had become indistinguishable from each other. Saff continued to massage Gelling's knee in a silence which she herself broke. Red Star Grenade, she said, didn't just want a *ciné verité* of a flaming Astra or a Sierra because you could have that any day of the week. Red Star Grenade were after something more exclusive. They had brought Luke on board because of his reputation as a virtuoso, a cultural creative, a modern thinker, an *artist*.

We might shy away from organised religion, but that doesn't mean that we don't believe there isn't something greater than ourselves, she said, something spiritual, a life with a meaning outside of the rational.

I have to confess that though this kind of talk was new to me, it appealed. Even if I eschewed Mark Twain because of what I'd heard about his fence descriptions, I was nonetheless a fan of words. I read quite a lot, in private. I used to read the race programme cover to cover, and then over again, while shooting down the M1 at 135mph when my dad thought I was asleep. That was what started me off.

Luke had been thinking that an old Ford would be the thing – a Capri, a Cortina, or a Granada. He knew where such vehicles were parked and garaged. And there was a Scimitar he had his eye on too, the type that was modelled on the old Volvo P60; its owner pulled up outside the twenty-four-hour shop once in a while. But the opportunity had not arisen, and, culturally creative virtuoso of modern thought or not, twocing is an opportunist's game. When Luke spotted the Talbot driving through the gates of the school, he saw his moment. He'd been photographed by the bloke himself, once upon a time. He watched him as he went to and fro from his hatchback to the main entrance, carrying his equipment. When he was satisfied that the man had settled down to his work, Luke slipped round the back of the school canteen, safe in the knowledge that he had all the time in the world in which to work. Not that he needed it. In the era of the Alpine, door locks were so crude that a baby could fiddle one with a cable tie, and you could hot-wire the steering column just by using a fold of foil from a slip of gum. In a way, it was down to all that redundant engineering that we had come to be sitting out there in California.

So the way I see it, said Gelling, now I'm in the know, is that the difference between a regular twoc-torch-and-burn and a Happening is that some gang of neds films it, and an old banger is used. Would this be correct?

Sapphire continued working at Gelling's knee. Don't you listen to a thing I say, Gelling? she said. The car is a *classic*, not a banger. And who says they're neds?

I've seen them play live, Gelling said.

Where?

At Caister Pavilion last New Year. Their stuff totally sucks my fat one.

Their sound has changed a lot since then, said Sapphire. She kneaded away at him more determinedly.

I bet it still totally sucks my fat one.

Shut up, Saff said. This is a shiatsu technique, she said, it requires silence. She kneaded at him for a while longer before she broke the silence herself, again.

Is it feeling any better?

Well, you're giving me a stiffy, Gelling replied. You're re-focussing my pain at least, so I reckon it works, yeah, in a way.

Sapphire stopped the shiatsu and flicked Gelling's ear. She shuffled herself a width away from him. He leaned back and looked at me around her as if to say, Stick with me kid, I'll show you how to charm the ladies. I shook my head as if I disapproved, but inside I was smiling. Gelling showed promise. A part of me agreed with his general line too – even though I found Saff and her talk seductive, I wasn't sure it wasn't total bullshit all the same, and that all we had here was vandalism, pure and simple. I returned to staring at the horizon, which had become seamless and wasn't there any more

From behind us came the sound of wheels, followed by an engine cutting out. Down on the beach Luke put two fingers in his mouth and whistled as if to call a dog, while pointing at Gelling to case it. Gelling moved up through the scrub and played look-out over the top, checking it was Red Star Grenade and not the Dibble.

What with one thing and another, the way events turned out, I never did get to see Luke's Director's Cut back then, but a few years later, by absolute chance, I caught a screening of *The Happening, California, February 2004* (as a little white card on the wall titled it) down at Tate Modern. I had planned a meet-up there with Milo. It was the same morning that I saw this Gerhard Richter's painting sequence called *October 18, 1977*. This was how Luke's film found its way into the show: the whole thing was themed round artworks that had dates in their titles. If you ever get the chance to check those Richter canvases, I recommend it. They're usually on display in the Museum of Modern Art in New York City, the MOMA, as it's known, which paid fifteen million dollars for them back in 1990. I read this on one of the little white cards too. What a fat roll, I thought, for pictures by someone you've never heard of. The sequence is of fifteen black and white paintings ($1m each – nice work, if you can get it). Executed in oil-on-canvas, they look just like photographs because they're in the 'photo-realist style'. Each one is a copy of a newspaper print, a blank reproduction of a mass-produced image. Here is the big post-modern joke, the self-referential comment on the 'death of originality'. The only thing, it seems, that artists have been able to hope to achieve for fifty years or more, is to ape something that already exists, and re-represent it in 'the gallery context'. It was Andy Warhol who started it all, with his soup tin and his 'famous for fifteen minutes' routine, of course, but this Gerhard Richter, he was so in on the joke, so *over* it, that he'd come right out the other side. He was beyond post-modern. He was back in the realm of the deadly fucking serious. I read all this in the accompanying pamphlet, as I sat on the floor in the middle of the room.

Then I stood and looked round again. You didn't need the

pamphlet to tell you that this work had intent, and was very likely devoid of jokes, post-modern or otherwise. You could tell it by the craftsmanship, and you could tell it by the subject matter too – still lives, even stiller portraits, and mass funerals. Or funerals surrounded by mass crowds anyway, which I reckon must be the same thing. I spent some more time looking at the pictures, very closely. You can't even see a brush mark. They made an impression on me and no mistake. Gerhard Richter is a man I'd trust to paint clouds on a backdrop, and to make more than a decent job of it too.

After looking at the paintings I suddenly came over shivery, so I walked outside and waited for Milo. I sat on the wall and looked back down the ramp into the mouth of the turbine hall. The angle and perspective reminded me of something, but I couldn't think what. Milo buzzed me to say he was running late, as usual. The shiver passed and I walked slowly back for one more look at *October 18, 1977* and after that I went up to the top floor where I knew you could get a decent espresso in an area where good coffee is hard to find. This was where I saw *The Happening, California, February 2004*, playing on continuous loop on the cafeteria wall. I slid a couple of tubes of sugar into the espresso and stirred it with the little wooden paddle, and then I slid another one in. It was about half a minute before I even noticed the film, and another half minute before I recognised it for what it was. The thought that I'd been sitting on the coast at the time, that I'd taken my part, and that these frames were a document of a kind of initiation, well, it certainly made me think back. I'm no fan of nostalgia, it's strictly for the birds, you must always look to the future, but all the same – *tout de même*, as Nico repeatedly put it each and every time she told me how things were *fin* between her and Milo (she sometimes texted me just to say Hi and stuff, but she *always* texted me when they were on one of their separations) – *tout de même*, the film bought a smile to my face. It was almost a felicitous (how I loathe that word, and the people that use it) moment, the kind that lets you know things are progressing as destiny dictates. I'm even less of a fan of destiny than I am of nostalgia. Destiny implies that you have no control over what happens to you; the very best you can say for destiny is that the idea of it helps make things manageable for those who remain behind, like the victims of events such as a family member getting knocked over and killed. Maybe the family member should've looked before he stepped off the kerb, the stupid fuck, then destiny need never have been mentioned, and Buddhists might not have turned up with their runes and their painted eggs and their tin whistles.

But then on the other hand, to be a rational person these days you have to accept that very often you don't have much control over what happens to you. Hence I am willing to give destiny (and, I suppose, its little playmate, fate) the benefit of the doubt. As if I have any choice in the matter.

I slid another tube of sugar into my espresso and then another as I kept my eye on the projection. I was fascinated; it seemed like another world, as if it, too, were in black and white, like Richter and *October 18, 1977*, whereas in fact it was shot in an entirely appropriate and wholly effective super-saturated grainy 8mm format. I watched as the bodywork of the Alpine cracked and the flames began to oxidise the steel below. There was a sea fret rolling in. I watched the damp air, and I could taste the salt again. The fret would have precipitated rusting before the car was even cold. Rusting is the most common example of oxidisation, incidentally, the process whereby a subject undergoes a reaction which causes its electrons to be lost to another species. I read that information on a little white card in the turbine hall itself, where there was a display of iron sculptures falling to pieces. Maybe I am more the *oxidant* than the live catalyst. It definitely sounds better. Maybe I have lost some of my electrons.

The fire burnt blue at its heart as the copper genie escaped from under the blistering paint, the licks of orange at the tip of the flame lighting up the scene. The sand below fizzed and spat beads of glass. The whole thing was a real composition. And it looked so warm.

Though in truth, before the show sparked up, and even though I took a shivery bite from the pocket where I kept things, I could disguise my shaking no longer because my teeth actually began to chatter. Sapphire handed me a jacket. She thought I was feeling the cold, and I played along. But it wasn't that. I was thinking about my dad, that's what it was. It must have been a delayed reaction to landing onto the beach like we did. It was too close to home.

*Sally*

Ray and I met at a club near Wilmslow in Cheshire.

I'd handed in my notice at Claridge's and gone travelling in Europe with some of the other girls. We'd all had enough of split shifts. I'd come back stony broke, and found work to pay the bills while I wondered what to do next. I was demonstrating products for a firm called Worldex, promotions on trade stands. So I was out on the town most nights. We did the big halls in London and we went all over the north too. At the end of the day I was up for action, same as any other rep. So, one of these nights, at this club in Wilmslow, we were all a bit tired and emotional. It was a few years before the term ladettes was bandied about, but that was what we were like.

I was having a moment on my own, sitting at the bar when some old letch started pestering me. Ray came along, stepped in, and ordered a couple of Ricard & Blacks 'on the rocks'. He never bothered to introduce himself or ask what I'd like, and he didn't even look at the letch, he just blocked him off with his body-English. In speedway, body-English is everything. You have to move around the bike to win, move forward to keep the front wheel on the ground and move backwards towards the rear to get weight over the back wheel, to get more drive. There are no brakes, you can only throttle back and use your boot to slow down. Ray taught me all that; body-English was his forté.

No one drank Ricard. We moved into a side bar where they were playing chill music. It was Fleetwood Mac, the *Rumours* album, which was retro then. 'Dreams' became an 'our tune'. It was about the time of the second Summer of Love, and that's what it became like for us.

At first he lied about what he did for a living; he made out he was a roofer. His hands supported the story, at least; he'd got this scar on his left which ran from the base of his thumb diagonally across to the root of his ring finger. Though he'd cleaned his nails you could still see the remnants of some sort of dark stuff. On our third date he told me he was going to give me a surprise, which turned out to be a visit to the Belle Vue track in Manchester. It was all surrounded by funfairs and so on then, a bit like Yarmouth. How bizarre, when you think back. When we arrived, I thought we'd be spectators, and I did wonder what he took me for: it wouldn't exactly have been my idea of a night out. He walked me into the grandstand, introduced Tyler and disappeared to the paddock to get changed. I didn't know what to think. I had no interest in motorbikes, but, well, he looked fabulous in his leathers. Then there was the racing itself: flying round an oval on two wheels is charismatic work. Straight away I loved it, the excitement and romance, and the scent was intoxicating, burning rubber and fuel; it's really quite special, you should try it sometime. And Ray was a winner, at the top of his game. There was that too. People think it a funny sport, a bit downmarket, Hackney dogs to Ascot, but it attracts a bigger crowd than you'd think, and very loyal too. I started following him about, and, well, the rest, as they say, is history.

We'd only been together a couple of months when Ray was tapped-up from the Aces – that was his team in Manchester – by the Lambeth Lions, who were big shots in the Elite League at the time and offered him a great contract. It was ideal for me, being as I was still semi-based in London anyway. It wasn't long before I gave up my flat-share in Putney and we moved in together in our first place in Wandsworth. Tom was born only about a year after we'd got together, 30 September '88. He came as a bit of a surprise, but we were never in any doubt.

We lived a normal life, we did normal things. Ray wasn't on a star-trip even though speedway was bigger back then and people did sometimes recognise him. And we weren't loaded

75

either, though we did alright because his terms were good, and the wins and the bonus points kept on coming.

But my nerve for watching him dissolved as soon as Tom arrived. They put their lives at risk every time they ride, you know, with all the maniacs there are about, the suicide divers and the fencers and all the rest. Ray lost two friends while I was carrying, good friends too, Troy Redmond and Tommy Taplinka. I was there the night Troy came off. I can't tell you how much it upset me, and Ray went off on an absolute bender.

But then he sobered up, cleaned up, calmed down, rode one for Troy, and carried on.

You can't let it get into you. That was what he said. It's a big boy's game, not the fucking ballet. You could just as likely get knocked over by a bus.

Tom went along to the track as soon as he was old enough, well, sooner than that, really. He knew his dad did something unusual – he could tell because of the posters, and the programmes with Ray's pictures in them, and probably because there were engines stripped down on the kitchen table half the time. Tom loved the track, he thought it was thrilling. His first ever visit was at a time when Ray's form was on a bit of a dip, but that night he picked right up, won all the bonus points going, and from then on it became important to him that his son was there. Tom became his talisman. So we were generally in attendance, despite my feelings. The club made Tom some Lion Cub leathers, with his dad's name and number on the back: Radford 3. Ray would sit him on his knee when they did their lap of honour at the end of each meet, lifting him to the crowd as they passed the grandstand.

I tried not to think about the worst-case scenarios. He'd got through most of his career practically in one piece; I mean he was full of nuts and bolts, his collar bones were corrugated like handle-bar grips and he had a plate in his skull too, but, 'nothing serious', as he put it. He usually managed to contrive a minor injury early in August each year – that's how we got our couple of weeks away in the Greek islands even though the season was on.

Recharge the old batteries, he'd say.

Given all the chances he had to bow out – clipping a fellow rider going into the first bend any night of the week could do it, that was how it happened with Troy – it was an irony to get knocked over in the street. At least it wasn't by a bus. He was 'in collision', allegedly, with a red Corvette, as he stepped off the kerb in Denmark Hill. He'd pulled in for a packet of Bensons. The idea of giving up smoking never once crossed his mind. He'd left his car on a double yellow, as usual, which someone at the insurance made into an issue (it still isn't settled, actually). This alleged red Corvette tipped him into the path of a Transit, which was practically on top of him. He never stood a chance. The Transit driver said he knew you shouldn't do it, but he couldn't help himself; he turned Ray over onto his back. Trevor – that was the driver's name – said that there wasn't a mark on him. He didn't look dead. But appearances can be deceptive. Around the world more than a million people a year are taken by the roads. I looked it up.

'They should watch where they're going.' That would have been Ray, if you gave him the stats. 'Goodnight Vienna, farewell cruel world, and learn how to walk straight while you're at it.' That would've been him too.

I'd think about it, his general attitude, his *laissez-faire*, how he might have handled it. I clung onto that, and it did help, a bit. Of course, telling Tom killed me. I'll never forget the look on his face.

We had a cortège of bikes, one last burn-off. Fans joined in with co-riders, there were air-horns blowing, it was nice, fitting. It was a public event, the funeral. I thought that was right. His career was just about at an end, as I've said, but people remembered when he rode for England in the Nationals, and there were notices in the papers, and fans sent letters; some of them even attached old ticket stubs and pictures torn from programmes, from way back. It was sweet. And later they had a minute's silence too, at the Lions. They arranged a testimonial.

There was a type of mourner round the fringes, a woman of a certain age, absolutely at home in black. I should have minded more than I did. Oh, I know what goes on, at Belle Vue, Rye House, Monmore, where-have-you, on any given Wednesday far from home. I'd been there myself don't forget. The track attracts a dedicated cult of groupie, and there are plenty of riders about with Jagger-syndrome. Ray wasn't one of those, but there's always temptation. I'm no fool. If he strayed, I didn't want to know about it. I'd started to visit a therapist not long before, that's true, but it was to do with myself, not my relationship. I used to do a spot of backing vocals while I was chambermaiding, for a band called *De-funkt*. I don't know if you remember them? They made a small noise in the '80s. We played the Limelight in Shaftesbury Avenue, and Coconut Grove too, off Oxford Street. There was one top twenty single called 'Fanta-tastica'. I did *Top of the Pops* with them for that. They were just about split up when I met Ray.

I kept dreaming about that night at the *Pops*, singing and dancing on a podium. It was a recurring dream in which the floor melted away and I was left all alone in a silver hoopla skirt with people shouting at me. That's when I started the therapy. It helped, to talk to someone neutral, about anything, anything at all, trivial or important. It still does. And after the accident it helped me even more. My mentor, Pam, said to me, Sally, it's *so* important to celebrate the life that's been *lived*, that's the way it is in other more tuned-in cultures – it's only the English who are so *hung up on death*.

I held onto that, arranged the celebratory burn-off, and afterwards Tom and I went over to the stadium and scattered his ashes on the track, just the two of us. After it was all over, I concentrated on staying as positive as I could, though I did go a bit mental and crack up a couple of times: I'd sit in the bathroom running the taps to drown me out. But in my rational moments I'd manage to feel peaceful and to think, clearly and logically: we'd had over fifteen years together, a good stretch, with more ups than downs. How many couples can say that these days?

Of course, you couldn't expect Tom to see it in that light. And the police, well, in his mind they never did anything like enough to find the driver of the red Corvette, the murderer, as he saw it. Trevor, the van driver, said he thought the Corvette took the next turn left, though he couldn't be absolutely certain about that, or even, in fact, that it was definitely a Corvette. No one blamed him. In fact, he had to go on sick-leave, the poor guy. We invited him to the funeral to show we harboured no ill feeling, absolutely the opposite – he had stayed beside Ray until the ambulance arrived, which was very good of him. I reassured him there was *nothing* he could have done; the post–mortem said it was instant. In the cold light of day, it was a hit and run.

It wasn't just Trevor that saw nothing. Eye-witnesses were unbelievably thin on the ground, and there wasn't one that could do better than *think*, but not be sure, that half the registration was MEX. It was just one of those things: wrong time wrong place. The file stayed open, but nothing happened.

We'd visited East Anglia a few times because the Lions were in a league that included teams from Kings Lynn and Ipswich. I was always taken by the place, not for the flatness, which I didn't much care for, but for the light. The sky is so vast and if there's a mist rolling in . . . well, you'd imagine that would be the scene approaching the gates of heaven. And then there's the peace and quiet, the pace. And the sea too. All in all I decided that a move would be for the best. Tom didn't just lose his dad, he lost his best mate. Streatham Mansions was too full of memories. London was too full of memories.

Yes, a fresh start. It was more than beneficial, it was essential.

# 6.

It wasn't the Dibble pulling up behind the dunes. I could have told Gelling that without looking: you don't often hear a squad car die down on pre-ignition, they keep their motors in better nick than that because they have a whole crew of mechanics on call twenty-four/seven. I bet they have more mechanics in the Dibble than detectives. Not that it enables them to keep up with boy racers in their Mitsubishi Lancer FQs (0–60 in 3.5 seconds) mind you (that's *one* second slower than a track bike, incidentally). But then that's the Dibble for you, they just don't try hard enough. Because what, essentially, is a copper? A pen-pushing mouse-clicking form-filler is what. A civil servant. You can't expect people like that to show initiative. Sit in a lay-by catching honest citizens doing 35mph in a 30 zone? No problem.

But seek out the robber who lifted the front end and helped himself to your mobile while he was at it? Or apprehend a hit and run?

More chance of winning the lottery.

The spluttering, dying cough was the endnote of the Red Star Grenade tour bus, a Commer 'Walk Thru' hand-painted in green Hammerite with *Red Star Grenade* sprayed along both sides in the style of a tag. Red Star Grenade appeared over the dunes. There were three of them: the main man, Scanes himself (this was how Luke greeted him, *Well, well, if it isn't Scanes himself*), followed by the drummer and the bass player. They were the classic three-piece, and they were from Pluto. How they fitted together as a band was anybody's guess. The drummer, in a do-it-yourself Mohawk quiff and mauve paramilitary combats, was a one-man people's army. The bass player wasn't even from Pluto, he was from a moon of Pluto, lost inside curtains of hair and testing out a pashmina over a vintage Puma zip-up top in combination with Buddhist drawstring trousers and pink All Stars. Scanes fronted a leather jacket with massive lapels, and ripped leather jeans over denims. When he turned his back it was to reveal an image of a naked woman rising out of a volcano on the rear of the jacket. The whole ensemble was just totally unrealistic, though at least it was accessorised properly with cowboy boots with silver tips, and hair that was frizzed out like Robert Plant's.

My dad had a picture of himself with Robert Plant, taken at Monmore, the Wolves track. Plant was big into speedway. Led Zeppelin and Plant were heroes for my dad, and I think it was a two-way thing; they seemed to have something in common anyway, though I wasn't sure what, except that they could both wear leather exceptionally well, which, like being yourself when you're famous, is a difficult trick to pull off, and one that this Scanes wasn't managing. Dad often had 'Stairway to Heaven' playing at full blast in the car on the way to the track. It was played at the funeral too. First there was the Fleetwood Mac tune, then there was 'I'll Be Missing You' by Puff Daddy, which was my choice, and finally Led Zep.

Red Star Grenade made their way over to Luke and engaged in a routine of bear hugs and brother handshakes, all the frat, before stepping back to assess the next move. Saff made her way over to them, leaving Gelling and me behind on the wall. Each of the band kissed her on each cheek like she was a proper lady, and they were proper gents. They entered into conference for a few seconds, and then they started trying to bump the car back onto its wheels. Luke called us down – extra hands were required. Body panels were heavier in the old days. It took some doing, but we were seven altogether, and though it fell back twice and we had to jump away to avoid being crushed, we up-ended it third time lucky.

Scanes himself kicked the wing with the tip of his cowboy boot to celebrate the moment, then he asked Luke why he hadn't gone over to the beach up by Yarmouth as per Plan A.

Conservation, Luke said.

Scanes snorted at this.

Little terns breed there, I don't like disturbing their beds, Luke said.

Right, good thinking, dude.

What? Luke said, rising at something in Scanes' tone.

Nothing, Scanes replied, I mean great work, man, for sorting it out, but what's with this exactly – he gestured at the Talbot – I thought we were going for like something a bit more stretch limo?

I considered it, Luke said, but then I had a think about the laws of physics: you'd never get it beached – the chassis is just too long. And this baby is a vintage 'seventies classic, if you follow.

Follow? How d'ya mean?

Isn't your music retro glam? Luke said.

Whoa, Scanes said. Don't try to categorise us.

Is it, or not? said Luke.

Yeah, it is, said the drummer.

Okay dude, said Scanes, So this is like . . . a theme?

It's better than that, said Luke.

How?

It's a concept, he said.

A concept, said the drummer. Far fucking out.

And it's better than that too, said Luke.

Red Star Grenade stood, looking expectant, waiting to hear what could be better than a plain concept.

It's conceptually intact, said Luke.

Scanes whistled. You are the *man*, he said.

The bass player had remained silently soulful, like they do, but now the moment had arrived for him to pronounce a small issue of his tiny complement of bass-player-words of bass-player-wisdom. *Con-ceptually in-tact,* he repeated, as if he'd just invented the phrase, and as if the phrase he'd just invented was pregnant with magic symbolism. He nodded a big, slow nod.

I looked over to Saff. At least she wasn't glazing all over and falling under the spell of his pashmina and his nodding technique. Scanes looked at me looking at the bass player, and spoke to Luke.

What these kids doing here anyway, dude? he said.

They're along for the ride, said Luke. They're safe.

Don't call me a kid, Scanes, Gelling said.

Awright, kid? Scanes addressed this to me. You shivering, kid? he said.

And don't call Radford a kid, either.

Fee-awl the cold do you, Radford? Don't worry, we'll soon warm you up.

He must've heard me say something to Gelling to be doing my accent with the first thing he said to me. You know what it's like when you're young – you take an instant view that someone's a tool, and you tend to stick to it.

I sat stirring the sugars into the espresso with the wooden paddle as I watched the film one more time.

Luke would have appreciated the fact that it had made it to the mainstream, the irony would not have been lost – in fact, it was well within the bounds of possibility that the irony might even be conceptually intact in its nature. It wasn't just the veneer of respectability conferred by his work playing on repeat loop in the café bar of one of our principal art galleries, there was the location too: the video was on show within range of the Houses of Parliament itself, the seat of Her Majesty's Government of Wasters. He'd have noted that. I was only sorry he wasn't here to see it for himself.

My estimation of him began to shift as he started running the show on California beach that day. At first I'd taken the uncontroversial view that he was a dangerous chancer, one that I'd steer clear of in future, once I was home. I'd never heard the two words conceptually and intact put together before; I even looked up 'conceptually' later, to check its precise definition.

Having established authority, he took complete control. He sent the drummer to the van to pick up this heavy old black camera, and he had us all stand back while he guided the drummer, whose name was Tucker, on a practice lap circuit round the Alpine. He took him by the elbow to achieve an improvised steadi-cam effect – Tucker was to be the camera-holder on the grounds that drummers have safe hands. In his mind's eye Luke knew precisely what he wanted: a 360° of the whole happening, a panoramic.

As I sat there sipping my coffee, which was syrupy now, which was how I took it, it suddenly occurred to me to imagine that Luke had taken his inspiration for this film from the end scene of *The Wicker Man*, the cult movie famous from Top 50 Film-ending shows, when the copper gets burnt alive in the big straw effigy. But maybe that's a bit fanciful. Maybe he was working from his own vision.

As a director he shaped up like a pro, anyway; I could tell that because I'd seen directors in action before, when I'd been in studios with Milo. Luke blocked out one more run-through, and in so doing he scraped a groove into the sand with the heel of his boot, so that on the first take proper they had a track to follow, a primitive dolly. Then he removed the lens entirely and checked the gate in the big old camera, to make sure there was no hair in it.

We all stood well back while Luke let a rag into the filler cap and sparked it with a disposable. You'll have seen cars burst into flames many times on the news, and more particularly in films. What you don't get on the screen is the awful noxious smell, the more so with a classic like the Alpine because of the vinyl upholstery, which I doubt would have passed any kite-mark test for flame retardancy. Luke waited until the blaze died down a bit – there was just too much fire when it was licking at its height. Once the shape of the car was discernible he led Tucker on a repeat of their orbit but this time they were rolling for a take. The finished result is a lazy carousel. The background shifts from the black North sea, to the trace image of the faraway wind farm, to the swell of the dunes, to the long coastal stretch north-west, and back to the black sea, again and again. The only sounds are the spit and splinter of burning. The rest of us moved in a crocodile behind, in order that we were never caught in shot because the presence of any of us in the frame (it became absolutely clear to me now) would have corrupted the conceptual intactness. Towards the end, as the fire settles, the camera comes to rest and pulls away for a long wide-angle to the sea (we all backed off to the dunes). If you look closely at this sequence you'll notice a solitary figure by the edge of the incoming tide. If you listen very carefully you'll hear a faint sound, like the calling of the last post. The figure is a man blowing an instrument that looks like a trumpet, but is in fact a flugelhorn. If you look even more carefully you'll see he's trailed by an animal, a greyhound.

Watching *The Happening* practically put me into a trance which Milo broke by texting me he couldn't make it at all now; he'd been waylaid in a meeting. So I left the Tate Modern and walked down to the Thames, and waited for the Tate Boat to take me back up to where I'd left the car. I listened to the water lapping at the platform as I waited, recalling how we sat in a line on the scrub watching the fire die, passing cigarettes like kids on Bonfire night; Saff offered me the bottle of Razor one last time. The remains had become warm, sticky, sickly and disgusting so I handed it to Scanes for him to finish.

# 7

We were to make our return journey back to the village in the Red Star Grenade van, which was pretty handy now that we'd trashed and torched our own wheels, wasn't it, because I didn't fancy walking miles home down country lanes with no street lights. Not only was it dark by then, time was pressing too. I should have called Sally, but I waited. Like anyone on pay-as-you-go, I was saving my credit for something important.

Gelling, Saff, the bass player and I climbed in the back of the Commer Walk-Thru, while the three seats up front were taken by Tucker, Luke and Scanes. It wouldn't start, of course. Scanes sat there turning it over, sapping the battery, flooding the engine and saying fuck. The diagnosis was obvious – the plugs were soaked. The pre-ignition I'd heard earlier told me that. The back of the Commer was a mess of flight cases, drum risers and other boxes, which we were using as seats. It was possible that there could have been a tool box amongst all this, but I doubted it: neither Scanes nor Tucker bore any resemblance to a grease monkey, and there wasn't a chance that a bass player from a moon of Pluto would know a thing.

How you fixed for tools, then, Luke asked.

Er, maybe something, like, somewhere, dude, Scanes said.

There often is something like somewhere, if you know where to look. I searched around in the back and I found what I was after, a D-ring on the floor. Both the D-ring and the flap were stuck with grease and spills of beer and Coke, but it opened more easily than I expected and in the rotting well below I found a wrap of perishing vinyl containing two combi-spanners, a screwdriver and a plug-wrench. Under that there was a jack but no jack-handle. I pulled out the plug-wrench and called to Luke who was on the middle front seat, leaning backwards over the bulkhead with his arms outstretched, shaking his head. He turned, and I held the plug-wrench up.

Choice, Radford, he said, At least someone here knows what day of the week it is. D'you know how to use that, bor?

Yeah, I said.

Yeah, said Scanes, mocking my accent again.

Luke instructed Scanes to pull the hood release, called him a dim twat for not knowing whether he had a tool kit or not, and beckoned me out. There was no torch in the van but I had one on my phone which gave out just enough light for us to work by. The plugs wouldn't budge: they had recently been hot of course, so they were still expanded. I went back into the van and picked up the screwdriver, in order to use it as a lever through the plug-wrench handle. There's a hole at the top for that purpose, if you know what you're doing. Fucking bastard, Luke said, as he struggled. Finally the first plug gave way. Luke unscrewed it and handed it to me by the insulator. Can you take that to the fire and dry off the electrode? he said, You know how to do that?

Yeah, I said.

Back at the wreck, the flames had died down enough for

me to crouch and dip the plug into the embers. The tip flared blue for a second as the note of petrol burnt away. My hand was too near the fire for comfort, it scorched, but I felt certain I wouldn't be finding any mole grips or the like back there to enable me to do the job at arm's length, so I just had to keep dunking it back and forth like juggling a hot bun. I repeated my task four times, once for each cylinder. As I stood and turned after drying the final plug, the man who you just see in the film, the man at the water's edge with the greyhound, approached me from behind. He didn't frighten me, he didn't take me by surprise, because I'd already spotted him. I smelled him first – he had been sitting in the dunes smoking a small cigar, the greyhound lying beside him on its belly in the sand. He was about fifty, with wild corkscrew grey hair, wearing a long, dark overcoat. He had come over to take a light out of the fire for his next small cigar. In his other hand he had the flugelhorn held down by his side.

Vot are you doink, son? he said (this was how he spoke).

Drying out these plugs, I said. Their van wouldn't start, it was flooded.

Ah, he said. He stood for a while and then he said, Improvisation, very good. But how about all zis . . . mayhem? He gestured at the remains of the Alpine, then looked at me, as though he expected me to give him an explanation.

It's not really my business, I said, I'm new round here, I'm just . . . caught up in the middle of it.

Ah, right, the man said, I see, so you are new; so this is your new home, this beautiful place, and this is how you treat it?

I gestured over the dunes towards the van. They're only kids, I said, as if I was somehow more adult than they were, aloof from the activity in which I was taking my part. They've lived here all their lives, I said, so I guess they're just showing me the ropes.

It was a weak explanation, and I knew it. It sounded like a lame excuse, even as I said it. The man had succeeded in making me feel guilty, that was the thing. He'd somehow put it on me that all this debris was my own personal fault.

My dad died, I said.

I felt a bit shitty using such a transparent device to get myself off the hook. This is supposed to be a fresh start for us, me and my mum, I said.

I'm sorry, the man said, and his face, which was naturally sad, turned sadder. Vos this recently?

Not long back.

Very sorry, he said. To take his mind off it, I asked him what he was doing out there alone by himself anyway, smoking a small cigar and holding a brass horn.

Thinking, he replied, I often come here to think: it's always been one of my favourite spots for that. Also, he said, I've had a recent loss of my own, though nothing compared to yours.

I asked him what his loss was.

Ze pink slip, he said.

Pink slip? What's that, I asked.

The boot, I think you say here. The P45 form, the heave-ho, the sack. So I find myself in a situation that promotes thinking.

I asked him what the job had been.

I was manager of a football club, he said. Bayer Leverkusen – have you heard of it?

I nodded. Of course I had. Were you losing, then? I asked.

One way or another you're always losing, he said. Winning only postpones it.

Actually, it's only the fear and hatred of losing that makes you win in the first place, I said.

Correct, young man, he replied, and he looked at me very closely. How d'you know that?

I just do, I said.

Listen, he said, shaking himself out of it, listen, you don't want to hear about the problems of an old man. He offered his hand saying Klaus, Klaus Toppmöller. I took it saying, Tom, Tom Radford. I knew he was familiar from somewhere, and now I remembered him; he was the manager who took Leverkusen to the Champion's League Final a couple of years back. He was the gaffer of the team who beat Manchester United in the semis. My dad had been a big fan of his because my dad was originally from Manchester himself, so of course he supported City. Seeing old Helmut put one over on the Stretford scum seemed only to enhance the pleasure he took from *any* United defeat. Also, Klaus Toppmöller had a remarkable jig in which he jumped about crazily in the technical area, and on top of that he was a great touchline smoker. My dad admired this, saying that Herr Toppmöller was one of the last of a dying breed, that the dugouts were full of robots these days, drinking mineral water while practising breathing exercises from the *Little Book of Calm*.

Where are you going with your life, though, Tom Radford? Klaus Toppmöller said. What is zis hooliganism all about? Where vill it lead you?

I don't honestly know, I said. I paused. I liked Klaus Toppmöller, so I searched my mind, trying for a better reply: If anybody asked me, right, I'd say I was just helping them get back on the road, I said.

Like a pits man? he said.

Yes, like a pits man.

He was happier with this. That's not such a bad answer, he said, You're only the crew, a hand for hire. I'll give you that. And the other face of destruction *is* construction; the world divides between attackers and defenders, there's truth there. And you're young as well, so I'll give you that also. But listen to me: stay on the right side of the line, eh, the side of the good guys: be a force for the constructive, yah?

He put his hand on my shoulder. I liked the whiff of it, it stank of cigar which somehow reminded me of the track. He looked me in the eye.

Concentrate on good energy, ze creative, don't fall into the old traps, the old ways, like we had, when I was young, with the Red Army and all that. You won't have heard of them, will you?

The Nazis? I said.

No, not them, he said, and once more he looked sad.

Man United?

Klaus Toppmöller took a nip from a silver hip flask and laughed. No not them either; Sir Alex – fuck him anyway. No, the Baader-Meinhof gang, as they were better known.

This meant nothing to me.

You start by throwing a custard pie at a politician, fair enough, he deserves no better, but then, that's done, you get your face in the papers, feel yourself important, but it's not enough. So you escalate, you expand, and soon enough you're out of control, blowing up departmental stores and ze people in them too – collateral damage, accidental, you say, because explosives are not your expertise, are they, and you didn't think anyone was still inside, did you? And so now you're a killer, on the wanted list, on the run, and what's more you don't even know why you did it. And then, one day, the authorities, they catch you. They come with their big boots and they kick your door down while you doze in your bed-sitting room with the television on in the corner. Or you go to the café, order your tea, take your seat, make yourself comfortable, glance up from your newspaper, and there they are, the men in overcoats and suits and ties, one on each and every table, and all exits covered. You're trapped. And now how do you end your days? By hanging yourself from the bars of a prison cell, that's how. It's no way to live.

Is this a true story?

Yes, he said.

Was it someone you knew, who hanged themselves from the bars of the cell?

A little bit, yes, friend of the family, he said. Be careful, Tom, that's all I'm saying. To give the old cliché: channel your energy. You're a practical boy, that much is clear; put your talents into proper use, be a force for *ze constructive*, yah? Concentrate on good energy, *ze creative*.

I didn't know why he was giving me all this spiel, but he had me hooked. I suppose he was just doing a team talk, a habit he couldn't drop. His small cigar had gone out. He re-lit it by holding the tip against the bonnet of the Alpine, which was still glowing.

Luke appeared at the top of the dune to see what was with the delay. He whistled. The greyhound turned its head, but it didn't move.

Is that your dog? I said.

No, Klaus Toppmöller replied. It's a friendly sort of animal though; it's been following me all day. It fell in beside me down the beach. I threw a stick but it soon tired of that, and I fed him some cheese from my sandwich, which he seems to like. And we've talked. But I think it is a stray – look, he wears no collar.

Are you going back to Germany? I said.

Herr Toppmöller drew on the small cigar and blew out a smoke-ring. I have no intention to keep the animal, if that's what you mean.

So would you mind if I found it a home, then?

He seemed happy, even delighted at this. He performed his remarkable jig. Constructive, Radford, he said, That's the angle. Go ahead: beckon him, see if he'll follow.

I went to stroke the dog's head; he backed off.

Luke called out from the prow of the dunes: Under the chin, he shouted.

What? I said.

Toppmöller narrowed his eyes, taking Luke in.

Go in under the chin, he shouted again, They don't like things coming in over the top of them.

I went in under the chin, tickling his jaw. The dog was happier. Its fur was warm and soft. You couldn't tell exactly what colour he was in the light, but you could see the coat was lighter than black. C'mon boy, I said. He made no move.

C'mon, come with me, I said.

The greyhound looked at Klaus Toppmöller, a bit confused. Klaus helped the situation by walking round the back of him and chivvying him away.

C'mon boy, c'mon. D'you want a bone? I said. The dog got up and licked my hand. Good boy, I said.

Slowly and with plenty of glancing back, but with Klaus helping out by making more exaggerated shooing gestures and saying, *Verscheuchen!* the dog followed me up towards Luke. Goodbye, Radford, *Choos*, Toppmöller said. He stared long and hard at Luke, then he put his horn to his lips and sounded a few notes. I turned round and asked him the question I'd had in my mind all the way through our conversation: Herr Toppmöller, why are you carrying that trumpet with you?

I played with the town band, when I was young, he said, but the truth is I'm terrible. He sounded a couple of deliberate bum flats to demonstrate and exaggerate the fact. Then he laid out his arm to indicate the darkness and the beach. Out here nobody else has to put up with it. By the way, he said, to the untrained eye it looks similar to a trumpet, fair play to you, but in actual fact it's a *flugelhorn*. It makes a sound more mournful, more dark.

# 8.

I rejoined Luke with the final spark plug.

Who was that maniac? he said.

Klaus Toppmöller, I said, the ex-manager of Bayer Leverkusen.

Is that so? he said, and he narrowed his eyes at me, the same as Toppmöller had done to him.

Back under the hood, Luke tightened the final spark plug, connected the lead, and gave Scanes the O with his thumb and forefinger. After several long coughs the engine fired. Luke slammed the bonnet down with the air of a man who had done his job and done it well. I stepped into the back of the van, shooing the greyhound ahead of me.

Radford, Gelling said, what's the meaning of this? Don't you know that dogs affect my asthma?

He's a stray, I said. Well, he *was* a stray, he's my responsibility now. I've taken him off the hands of Klaus Toppmöller.

Klaus whater?

Don't tell me you don't know him. He was the manager of Bayer Leverkusen, remember – when they beat Man U in the Champions League semi?

Radford, what planet are you on? Gelling said.

It's weird, I know, I said, but that's who he was, the man down there on the beach.

What man?

The man with the flugelhorn.

Was it your first drink, the Razor? Gelling said. Don't worry, Radford, it happens to us all; to this day I still remember my first half-shandy.

Hand-shandy more like, said Luke as the van bumped down the track.

Sapphire scratched the dog's neck and then she called me in close to look inside its right ear.

See that?

There was a number tattooed on the pink flesh, in green ink.

D'you know what that means?

What? I said.

That means he's an ex-racer, said Gelling.

She, Luke said, lighting a cigarette. The roof of the Commer scraped the branches of a tree as we swung back onto the main road.

What? I said.

She . . . it's a bitch, he said.

Gelling lifted the dog's tail. He's right, he said.

How did you know that, Luke?

Size, he said. Bitches are smaller than dogs.

A bitch, said Gelling. You got yourself a ho', Radford.

Sapphire gave him another flicky and then pushed him away with her feet while she stroked the dog. She'll have to have a name, Radford, she said.

I thought about it. She was neither Sally's Dalmatian nor

the spaniel I had in my own mind, but she was mine now, because I'd found her, and I knew the only home I'd be taking her to was with us back at Keeper's Cottage. I needed a name Sally would like, because that would help her get over the surprise. I looked at the dog. Wolf? I said.

Wolf?

They all turned to look at me.

That's not that bad, said Luke.

I don't know, said Saff, she seems a bit sweet to me, for Wolf.

Why Wolf? said Gelling.

After one of my dad's teammates, I said, it was his nickname.

Where is your dad? said Gelling. Divorced are they?

No, I said. He's dead.

Oh, said Gelling.

I tickled the dog behind her ears. I could feel the silence develop, but Gelling soon snapped it.

How come? he said.

Car knocked him over.

Oh, that's so sad, said Saff. She darted a glance at Luke, as though flipping the Alpine onto California beach had been totally thoughtless of him, in the light of this news.

An accident? said Gelling.

We don't really know what happened, I replied.

A hit and run, then?

They never found the driver, I said, So yeah, it'd have to be.

That's the Dibble for you, said Luke from up front. They're excellent at pointing speed guns and stopping people enjoying a little spliff. But give them a job to do, a matter that calls for *detective* work, *investigation*, stuff like that, and it's a different fucking story.

He may have nearly killed us, but he knew his way round an engine, and now here he was holding the Dibble in contempt with an exact and correct analysis. I was beginning to like him.

What sort of teammates did your dad have, Radford, he asked.

Riders, Lambeth Lions, I said. Speedway.

Oh, right, said Luke.

Speedway? said Scanes. That's rare.

I noticed Saff looking at me with pity. I didn't want her sympathy. I kept my eyes down, and joined in with stroking Wolf along her back and tickling behind her ears. She had especially soft ears. Her coat was grey, you could tell that now, it shifted through tones of soft steel, depending which way you stroked it, like iron filings moving with a magnet. She settled her head on my knee. She could certainly take a change of ownership in her stride. I guess she had a natural talent for it; it must go with the territory, when you're a stray.

Wolf isn't really a girl's name, said Saff.

What would you call her?

Blue, she said, without even pausing to think.

I asked her why. She said it was because Blue was a word people sometimes used to describe the tone of the dog's coat, but that it had other meanings too, like it was the name of a butterfly, and of a precious stone, and a word for when you feel sad.

Blue. I said it out loud.

Bloooo, went Gelling, like the sound of a wolf.

Hello Blue, I said. Hey Blue, come here girl, I said. C'mon Blue, fetch.

Though Blue made no response to any of this, the name sounded good, better than Wolf, more appropriate for her, I had to agree.

Stick with me Blue, you won't go far wrong, said Gelling.

Blue. I was satisfied that Sally would fall for a dog called Blue.

I looked out of the back window. We were on the main road now, winding along the coast. Radio One was on, that DJ Chris Moyles was whinnying away. Luke asked why we were listening to the dull flid and his pathetic band of mediocre media whores. Scanes switched it to a CD of Red Star's music. It sounded more neo-grunge than retro glam, and it was a rough demo too. I was into grime at the time, Roll Deep were my favourites, so it didn't do a thing for me. It was totally, *totally merde*, as Nico always said about anything that she utterly loathed, or that was going wrong in her life.

She'd txt: Tommy, Milo is treeting me totally *totall-y* merde, spk 2 him 4 me.

I'd send her a sad smiley (and then, since I was up in Norfolk, a picture of a cow or a flower or something, to cheer her up). Then I'd txt Milo:

Whats up?

He'd tb: All cool. How r tings der?

It was always 'all cool' with Milo. Whatever total merdeness was going on between him and his girlfriend, it never seemed to affect his life. I guess Nico just didn't understand skater psychology.

★

Saff tapped her foot in time with the Red Star CD, and when it had finished she leaned over the bulkhead, took Luke's phone from him, and – it became clear from her end of the conversation – called the Fly-tipping Tip-off Line to report a burnt-out car on the beach at California.

I looked at her.

We get them picked up, Radford, she said. We don't like litter.

It's a job creation scheme, said Luke. Local councils are one of the last reliable employers remaining in the shires and counties of rural England.

Stick with me, said Gelling, I'll show you the natural cycle of nature.

Some way down the coast road we drove into a small resort. In the centre of the place Scanes pulled the van in, scraping the tyre walls and the wheel rims against the kerb. I stepped out. There was a short stretch of amusement arcades running down one side, and across the road there were takeaways and ticky-tack shops which were mostly shut. A holiday-home caravan park occupied the field beyond. The arcades were lit in yellow and purple sodium; a soundtrack of sirens, gunfire, and manic laughter cracked out onto the street. A Vauxhall crammed with teenagers passed by with worn-out St George flags flapping above the back doors.

The nearest arcade was called Caesar's Palace. Gelling beckoned me inside. He changed a pound for twos, and we went to hustle a penny falls machine. Meanwhile Scanes negotiated about setting up a gig on the campsite across the road with the guy in the change booth. Scanes seemed to know him already – from what I overheard it sounded like the change booth guy owned the campsite as well as the arcade, or was something to do with it anyway. Saff crossed the road to buy some juice and gum. Luke remained outside on the pavement pacing about and making calls on his mobile. I looked at my own phone. It was really getting on now. After we'd blown all the twos I walked over to the van, took Blue out using a guitar strap for a lead, and wandered about trying to get a signal. It wasn't until I crossed the road and moved along the fence by the campsite that I could find a spot with at least a bar of reception. It was suddenly peaceful there, at a distance from the racket of the arcades. I chose my words carefully. I said I was with Gelling and could I stay round his house for tea? That his mum had said it'd be okay, that I'd be back in a couple of hours. Sally was fine with that, said to take care.

I stood for a while, looking at the caravans on the site. My dad's friend Tyler, the one who taught me to drive in his old Renault 4, had a chromed, custom-finished, US Airstream down on his farm in Devon. He'd converted it into a private cinema with a screen at one end, plush velvet seats set out in three rows, and a fridge at the back with ice-cream and beer. It was quality. These caravans opposite Caesar's Palace were nothing like that, not at all. They were made of corrugated metal, all painted identical, green at the bottom and cream at the top, and were laid out in little plots on the field, like counters in a game. They were the kind of caravans you see at the edge of tracks sometimes, pressed into use as changing rooms or snack bars. Most of them were in total darkness, but one or two had chinks of light glittering through the cracks in the curtains. I wondered who would want to be on holiday in a dank field at that time of the year. A boy walked out of the darkness, leaned over the fence and put his hand down to stroke Blue. She flinched away, so I showed him how to do it by putting my hand under her chin. He followed suit and smiled.

Zdravo, he said, holding his hand out to me.

I didn't know what language it was, but I could tell it meant Hello.

Hi, I said back, and we shook.

Dog, he said.

Yes, I replied.

He offered me a stick of Juicy Fruit.

Cheers, I said.

Tcheers, he said back, trying out the sound. Tcheers.

Across the road there was a sudden commotion. Luke and Saff were squaring up to a gang of boys on the pavement. I'd noticed this gang in the arcade. They were the only other people in the place, they'd been hunched round a poker machine, muttering, and setting world records for chain-smoking.

Don't you dare, I heard Saff shout. I moved off towards them, turning to say goodbye to the boy, but he was already gone.

I ran back. Luke was holding his arms out wide, shielding Saff. It was a defensive gesture, he wasn't beckoning them on; good idea, because there were four of them to one of him and four-to-one is a fight you can never win. The tallest of the four jutted himself forward and prodded Luke in the chest with his big finger.

Do that again, Luke said. He might've been outnumbered, but there was no mistaking his invitation as a threat.

The members of Red Star Grenade had caught on to events

and were spilling out of the arcade. Tucker and Scanes stepped forward, flanking Luke either side, while the bass player hid behind Saff, and Gelling hid behind the bass player. It turned out that Tucker was the born diplomat.

What's the fucking problem, cuntbags? he said.

They were *hiss*-ing at me, said Saff.

Hissing? Like snakes?

Yes, she said, like snakes.

Haven't you ever had that before?

No, she said.

That's their wolf whistle, Tucker said. He flicked his Mohican at them dismissively. Look at the state of 'em, he said, Fucking clapped-out Bosnian Units.

Tucker! said Saff.

Never mind *Tucker!* Tucker said. They'll roast you as soon as look at you. Try and picture that.

The gang said nothing. The atmosphere of aggression they'd been fronting when it was four of them versus one of Luke had melted right off. They looked suddenly defeated now it was evens, four-v-four, maybe even seven-v-four if you counted in Gelling, Saff and me, and we had a dog with us. I guessed they'd understood the words fucking and cuntbags alright, the swear words are quickest to learn in a new language – *va te faire* and *merde* were the first things I picked up from Nico. But I wondered if they'd understood how they'd been insulted too, on the grounds of their appearance and status, having someone who was rigged-up like Tucker saying, *Look at the state of 'em*. They were an easy target, so far as their style went, because they cut a shambolic line-up. There was the tall one, a pair of non-descripts and a short one, all wearing the same expression of gloom.

It was gloom that united them, it was stamped into their faces like a brand and ran through everything about them. Their hair was gloomy, their shoes were gloomy, their clothes were gloomy; they wore the worst kind of sportswear, chosen for its low-rent utility, not for its retro-fashionability, nor for the conceptual-intactness of being so totally '70s, like Scanes' recycled leather jacket, or the bass player's vintage Puma zip-up.

Tucker hissed at *them*, to see how *they* liked it. They took a collective surly step back.

Is that where you're from? said Saff. Bosnia?

Why you driving a car covered in St George flags, then? said Tucker.

Cover, said Luke, For their illegal activities.

The shortest unit suddenly started singing 'Eng-er-land' and clapping. His friends joined in, in a way that was impossible to interpret as anything other than sarcastic.

Tucker hissed again, louder and longer.

But that didn't shut them up, no, they only stopped their singing when Luke said that he supported Serbia, and that he was a big fan of Slobodan Milošević.

The tallest, the finger prodder, said to Luke that he was 'a fucking *omosexual* cuntbag'.

Tucker was built along the lines of a whippet, but he didn't take kindly to seeing his mate called gay, and to demonstrate the fact he jumped forward in a Kung-fu posture.

The man from the kiosk had already deserted his post and was watching the situation from just behind us. I'd noticed him. He had his foot jammed against the automatic door, holding it open. He was a lot bigger than he'd seemed when he was inside his box. He had one of those necks that ran straight into his head.

Gelling moved out from behind Tucker. You need to sort yourselves out here, he said, 'cos there's no way Luke's queer, you fucking peasants.

The gang said nothing, but the short one moved as if to make towards Gelling. Tucker intervened, stepping between Gelling and the short one and aiming a kick at his chest. Watch it, Tiny, I'm a Black Dan, I'm fucking lethal, I'm warning you, Tucker shouted, dancing about like he was Zhang Ziyi. A split second later he was kicking into plain air and flying like Zhang Ziyi too, as the kiosk man ploughed in, lifted him by his shirt, and held him out to one side.

Black Dan? Desperate Dan more like, the kiosk man said. Leave it out, he said, No need, is there? Why don't you lot try using your noodles for a change? he said, swinging round, addressing us all: Don't you think you could live without the unwanted publicity, eh?

Put him down, said Luke, Or—

*Or what?* said the kiosk man. What you gonna do? Sue me? I see you were happy enough to let *him* (he shook Tucker about, as if he was a Bingo prize), and the little lad fight your battles for you.

Luke stood rigid, but said nothing. You could see how the kiosk man might have seen things that way, but the alternative, and to my mind more accurate, view of the situation was that Tucker was trigger-happy and had gated too soon. The way I would have reported it was that Luke hadn't been backing off at all – with the attendant cowardice that would imply – rather more that his blood was pumping full of nitro-adrenalin, but he was controlling it, waiting for the moment to strike.

Listen, take your attitude – your Milošević cracks, your

petty *racism* – you take it somewhere else, because it's not welcome here, the kiosk man said.

*They* started it, Luke said through his teeth, with their fucking fronting and their fucking hissing.

The kiosk man eyeballed Luke. The Bosnian Units stepped back and hissed a few more times.

Oh, is that right, they started it did they? I saw you, son, I was watching you, the way you were looking at them, while you were on your phone.

Luke shook his head. What you talking about? he said.

You were looking at them like they were the shit on your shoes, he said. You don't have to *say* anything, to make an insult.

Oh, so you can see what my looks mean? You a mind reader, are you?

No need to be, the kiosk man said. It's obvious.

Obvious, eh? A NASA team of psychologists would struggle to make sense of what goes on up here, Luke said, tapping his head like a psycho. Why you so biased, anyway? he said. What's it to you? Why are you on their side? he said, sparking a cigarette.

Oh, you'd rather I was on your side, would you? the kiosk man said, What side *is* that, exactly? The side of Albion? Defending Queen and Country, are we?

I noticed him clock Luke's lighter as he said it. It was a Union Jack design but it was just a Clipper disposable, it wasn't a Zippo or something you'd keep. It meant nothing, surely. And anyway, the Union Jack was everywhere up there, fluttering outside the ticky-tack shops and stamped through sticks of rock and on lollipops.

And as for this 'Cover for their illegal activities' stuff, said the kiosk man, You're a fine one to comment.

You what? said Luke.

You're not exactly on the right side of the law yourself are you, son, with your portfolio?

The kiosk man felt in his pocket with his free hand and pulled out a couple of Chewy Louee bars.

I've seen things you boys could never dream of, he said to me as he handed us the chews. D'you know what I used to do, hmm, when I was at my peak, who I was with, where I've been?

Gelling and I shook our heads. All of us stood waiting for him to tell us what he used to do when he was at his peak.

I walked with the man, he said.

Walked with what man? said Tucker. And put me fucking down.

The kiosk man dropped Tucker. Mandela, he said.

Scanes spoke for the first time. Mandela? *Nelson* Mandela?

That's right, I walked with the man, walked with him through the bush and the prairie, down in the dust, down in Jo'burg. I provided security, for *Nelson Mandela*. Imagine. Security – for a man like that.

We continued to stand, waiting, and wondering if there could possibly be a point to any of this.

D'you know what blessed words he uttered when he was released, after all them years of incarceration?

We continued to stand and wait. He had our attention now, you could at least say that.

What? What words? said Scanes.

'Extremists on all sides thrive, fed by the blood lust of centuries gone by.' He boomed it out. Think about it, he said.

Think about *what*? said Luke.

I know about you, said the kiosk man, leaning forward. There was foam spittle bubbling out of the corners of his mouth now. He was working himself into a frenzy. I've *seen* you, he shouted, There are eighty-six thousand four-hundred seconds in a day—

Ain't you a proper statto, said Scanes.

The kiosk man didn't even hear this, he pressed on directing it all at Luke. *Eighty-six thousand four-hundred seconds,* each and every day, and what do you do with them, how do you *waste* your life exactly, hmm? By crapping in your own backyard, that's how.

He said this last with a huge sneer in his voice.

'*We will drive them onto the beaches, and set fire to them*' he bellowed, I don't think that was Winston Churchill's *precise* call to arms, was it, laddie? What a gallant contribution to the war effort you really are making, aren't you?

Luke stood rigid, saying nothing. What could he say, to this stuff? He was under attack alright, but from what? None of it made any sense. One thing though: the kiosk man had info on Luke; he could finger him, if he wanted. How did he know about the torching, anyway?

There isn't a war on, said Saff, and I don't believe you.

Oh, the little lady speaks does she? Don't believe me what? I *don't-believe-that-you-walked-with-Nelson-Mandela-what*.

It don't matter what you believe girl; I was there, on Mandela Watch, *I* know the truth, and that's all that matters. And there's *always* a war on, by the way. Don't you ever take your head out of a magazine long enough to read the paper? That lot (he gestured after the disappearing Bosnian Units, who had used his rambling incoherent defence of them to make their retreat, muttering incomprehensible oaths and curses as they walked off in the direction of the campsite), those poor bastards, do you know what they are?

What? said Luke, What the fuck are they (you demented twat)?

The kiosk man folded his arms, accentuating the big Maori tattoos that encircled his biceps. Casualties, he said, That's what. D'you think they want to be bombed out of their homes, watch their mothers weeping in the dirt, see their sisters raped and sold into prostitution? Do you really think they want to find themselves out here hoiking carrots from the fields and dragging the gizzards out of turkeys?

*Illegally* hoiking carrots and dragging gizzards, for well under the minimum wage, said Scanes, Stealing the bread out of the mouths of local people.

That wasn't the question, the kiosk man said. He was calmer now, but he was still speaking too loud. I asked you: d'you think they want to *be here* – he stamped his foot on the ground – so they can be treated like kaffirs by the likes of *you*?

They can clear off and sort their own country out if they don't like it, said Tucker.

Yes, that's right, that's what you're doing isn't it, sorting your own country out. All you have to worry about is which trainers to wear in the morning, which car to nick in the afternoon, and how much spliff to smoke at night. Easy street. Don't know you're born. Learn some history, the kiosk man said.

*Easy street?* Just because you can't see our persecution, doesn't mean it doesn't exist, said Saff. For your information, Luke wasn't being *racist*, he was defending me from *their imported sexism*, that's what; as if there isn't *enough* of that here already as it is. That's an issue for me, whether you like it or not, Mr Fat Sexist Pig Kiosk Man, and yes, the *little lady* does speak.

They must tip a lot of dough into your fucking poker machines, said Luke, the way you kiss their ringpieces.

Sling it, he said, all of you. Fuck off. Now.

What about our gig? said Scanes.

Call me on it later, he said. He gestured at Luke and Saff: But you two – Bonnie and Clyde – consider yourselves barred.

Barred from Caesar's Palace, said Luke. Shit me Bonnie, we've really hit pay dirt now.

No, said the kiosk man, you're barred from this whole area. Let me see your faces round here again and you'll know it.

Luke took one step forward to Mr Fat Sexist Pig Kiosk Man and in the same movement smashed his forehead into his nose. I heard it crack.

# 9

Even as the kiosk man was picking himself up off the pavement, we were all already piled into the Commer and out of there. It was our good luck that it started first time, because to be honest, I wouldn't have liked to see the kiosk man getting stuck in to Luke. For me the head-butt was a bad move, the sort of stunt that would come home to roost.

As Scanes sped off, burning rubber as much as he could in that crate, Tucker started going on that there was absolutely no chance that the kiosk man had ever bounced for Nelson Mandela, it couldn't be possible, not the way in which he dropped like a stone as he had done.

I caught the mouthy tool off balance, said Luke, that's all. It doesn't prove anything.

Maybe, said Tucker. But what would someone with *that* on his CV be doing stacking up coins in a tin-pot amusement arcade?

Maybe he's looking for a quieter life? I said.

And maybe he's a king-size bullshitter, said Tucker.

So you believe him then, Radford? Scanes said.

I had a starfish petrifying in the pocket where I kept things. I was stroking Blue, a greyhound who I'd taken from the ex-manager of Bayer Leverkusen, a man I'd only recently seen lighting a small cigar from the smouldering bonnet of a burnt-out Alpine and playing flugelhorn on California beach. Plus which, I was still alive. To me, suddenly, this was what it was like out there; from the boring brown fields of the morning – which I now knew to be full of Bosnian Units illegally hoiking carrots – to where I was sitting right then, things had picked up. Anything was likely.

Why shouldn't I believe him? I said, Why would he make it up?

Because he's a big fat sexist fuckpig of course, said Gelling.

With no life, said Scanes. People invent these things to try to give themselves a name, to make themselves out to be something they're not.

But ordinary people do meet famous people don't they? My mum knew King Hussein of Jordan, I said, she used to drink Dom Perignon with him.

Everyone looked at me and started laughing.

Oh yeah, said Scanes, my mum's a personal friend of the Pope. She used to do all his blessings and stuff when he was feeling a bit off colour.

Fuck you, Scanes, I thought. I reckoned it best not to mention Bob Geldof, though, or Robert Plant either.

That word 'kaffir', though, said Luke, that's a word from down there, isn't it? You don't hear that one too often. You know what it means, Tucker?

No.

You should, with your training in Oriental fighting disciplines. That's Chinese, bor, Luke said, layering on his Norfolk. That means 'bitterly hard use of strength'. It's what them Yanks used to call them slaves down from China.

No, they called them coolies, said Tucker.

Oh, you might be right, said Luke. What's a kaffir, then?

Before anyone could answer, his phone rang. I heard him saying Yeah, yeah, and arranging a detour, we'd be there in fifteen minutes, yeah, no problem, yeah of course, pockets full of it, no problem. I looked at the time on my own phone.

Do we *have* to detour, I said, I should be getting home.

Will your mum be worried, kid? We can drop you off and you can walk if you like, give your mutt some exercise, Scanes said.

Hey, said Luke, shut it.

Yeah shut it, said Tucker.

Yeah shut it Scanes, said Gelling.

Hey shut it yourselves, I was only joking, said Scanes.

He wasn't joking though, he'd have kicked me out and let me walk all right. I don't know what it was, but our animosity was two-way. It was right there from the beginning.

No need to hang me by the balls from a Christmas tree, Scanes said, to get himself off the hook.

What balls? said Luke. Listen Radford, he said, this won't take long, we'll have you back before midnight.

Yeah, nobody wants to see you turn into a pumpkin, kid, Scanes said.

Shut it, said Saff.

A few miles inland, we took a right into a lane and crunched down a driveway coated with gravel. At the end of the drive I could see what looked to be a huge house, with lights dotting all the windows. Luke got out and walked round the side of the pile. The rest of us sat in silence. Blue began to circle and Gelling said, I reckon that dog needs the toilet, Radford.

I think he's right, said Saff.

So I used the guitar strap again and walked her out. She stooped and took a huge leak, one she must really have been holding onto, it went on forever. I surveyed the scene while I stood waiting. There was a long lawn running up to the front of the house. It was a mansion with pillars either side of the door. I saw Luke come out from round the back, and move over to a greenhouse, which was partly hidden behind a line of trees, in company with a woman. Blue started pulling at her lead. Maybe she needed to stretch her legs as well as to piss, I thought, so I took her over the lawn towards the greenhouse. The lawn was beautiful to walk on, with a spring in it like you get on a running track. I stopped short by the trees and watched as Luke stood in the greenhouse rubbing leaves between his fingers. He sniffed the leaves, then dropped them into a carrier bag. The woman touched Luke's forehead inquisitively − I guessed there was a bruise coming up, from his head-butt. He held the hand that touched him and pulled it behind his back, bringing her close. He kissed her quickly but fiercely. Then they parted, and then they kissed again, more slowly. I edged Blue away and ducked into the shadow of the line of bushes that fringed the lawn. I wanted to get us back to the van without being spotted, without anyone knowing what I might have seen.

Did she need to go? said Saff.

Yeah, I said, she was desperate.

I tell you something, said Gelling, I'm desperate too, I'm desperate for grub. I'm absolutely famished.

Likewise, said Tucker. Stop at Vallori's on the way back in? he said to Scanes.

Hmm? Scanes replied.

Tucker repeated it. I looked up. Scanes was squinting intently through the windscreen. What? he said.

Stop at Vallori's on the way back in, Tucker said, louder, right into his ear.

Okay, no need to shout, I'm not deaf, fuck's sake, said Scanes.

Luke jumped back into the van.

Got it? This was the first time the bass player had spoken a word since the filming on the beach. And he'd asked a question too, which might imply he'd need to speak again quite soon. Believe me, if there's one thing that bass players love, it's dope.

Show me the money, Rickenbacker, Luke said to the bass player. The way he said it was like he was doing Tom Cruise in *Jerry Maguire*.

Rickenbacker. It was a while until I discovered that that was his nickname and that his real name was James Edwards-Moss, totally typical of a bass player. The double-barrel introduces an extra word into their monosyllabic lives, doesn't it, that must be the divine purpose of it. The bass player in Led Zep had a three word name too, which was John Paul Jones. He used to be plain John Baldwin. My dad told me that. He came round to our flat with Robert Plant and a monitors man once, when I was little. They were stopping off for some coffee and cigars on their way to a studio to record a charity song. The reason bass players have so little to say, of course, is because they are seldom, if ever, not stoned, and the type of stonedness in which they specialise is the introspective guru-type of stonedness. They like to pass off silence as deepness, that's their big thing, and the beauty of their big thing is that they often get girls to go along with the conceit: watch any crowd at a gig, notice the number of devotees mooning away at the bass player. Not a single one is thinking: he's chosen to play the bass guitar because it only has four strings, which is less notes to remember than lead or rhythm, he's probably quite idle and none too bright. No, not a single one is thinking that. They're some of the greatest confidence tricksters going, bass players. You have to hand it to them.

James 'Rickenbacker' Edwards-Moss showed Luke the money and built his joint as we drove away. Luke sub-divided a portion of the remainder of the grass into weights. He sold a quarter each to Tucker and Scanes, and he palmed Gelling a little twist 'for Sister Tiffany'.

The joint was passed. I asked Gelling if it didn't affect his asthma. No, he said, It helps my karma.

It's exactly the oral pacifier that a colicky adolescent like Gelling needs, Saff said as she took a delicate, disdainful ladylike toke.

I declined. I only do Class As, I said, which was another line I'd been working on: it wouldn't be long before I was back home, and I didn't want it to be obvious what I'd been up to, I didn't want my eyeballs all vibrating and the giggles coming on. I didn't want to look a shambles, not as well as bringing Blue home.

By the time we pulled up outside Vallori's and piled in, everyone was in high spirits, what with everyone having the munchies, everyone except me, that is. But even though I hadn't touched the stuff I was a little high off the passive which had been ripe in the back of the Commer. I felt dizzy and slightly sick. Inside the takeaway, Gelling tipped a couple of sugar sachets from the counter-top down his throat while he and the band placed their orders – doners with taramasalata and extra chilli sauce all round. Scanes picked up a copy of the *Sun* and found a pertinent question from their Millionaire Lotto quiz: how many tons of doner kebab are eaten every day in *Germany*?

Is it: a) one ton b) two tons c) ten tons or d) one hundred tons.

It's a million tons of dead Jews, said Gelling as he and Tucker got a fencing match going using chip forks.

Hey, minda language please boysh, said Mr Vallori.

Rickenbacker Edwards-Moss leaned on the counter, watching a small television which was fixed high on a bracket in the corner. On a football pitch somewhere in Spain, David Beckham was shaping up to take a free kick.

I expect your mum's rather a good friend of Beckham is she? said Scanes. Often shares a bottle of Dom Perignon with him, hmm?

I ignored Scanes and moved up to the rear of the café, which was set out for the benefit of the eat-in crowd with white plastic chairs and tables with ketchup bottles shaped like tomatoes. Saff sat on Luke's knee with her back upright against the wall, as though she were stretching it, as though it was sore, but I don't think it was that; I think she was more likely doing her shiatsu posture. The food was served up. I'd ordered double Saveloy and chips. I'd left Blue tied up by the guitar strap outside because Mr Vallori had shaken his finger at me and said, No dog inna restaurant, please.

I pulled one saveloy out of the wrapping paper for Blue and I tucked the rest of the takeaway under my arm. I went outside and fed her the sausage and then I realised that I wanted to stay out there and be on my own, so I popped my head back in to say my goodbyes.

Bye-bye Lover Boy, said Saff.

Take it easy, said Tucker.

Stick with me, kid, said Gelling.

Rickenbacker nearly but not quite looked away from the telly.

Scanes held up the copy of the *Sun* and shouted, Hey! Radford, kid — what's the correct answer?

Never believe what you read in the papers, I replied. And I made a wanker gesture with my own saveloy, specifically at Scanes, specifically for his benefit, and he knew it.

Luke gave me the O sign.


On my way back I found a suitable low wall where I sat and ate. I didn't want to be carrying it home, not after I was supposed to have had my dinner round Gelling's. The old man with the cap, the one who'd asked me if starlight wasn't good enough for me to see by when I bought the torch, lumbered towards me. I thought he might have something to say, since I was sitting under a streetlamp, one that was actually working too.

Sitting down, bor, he said. Are your hips alright?

My hips?

Mine are replacements, he said. Got two new uns. Made out of Teflon, like a frying pan.

Right, I said. They work, then?

Good as new, he said. I don't lollop about no more.

Great, I replied.

Do she ketch rabbits? he said, indicating Blue.

Yeah, I said, I reckon.

That's the way, bor, he said.

I offered him a chip.

No, you eat 'em all up, I've had my tea, he said. He tickled Blue's ears and went off on his way, without making any comment whatsoever about my eyesight. To me, he rolled along right bandy, but to him I expect he'd got a proper spring in his step, with his excellent Teflon hips.

As I was finishing up, and feeding the last crispy bits to Blue, I received a text from Gelling:

Save truble if any1 ask – we wnt to Lion wood – thats where u found Bloo, yeh.

I tb: oK

## Sally

With Tom eating over at Gelling's, I called Alice round for a girls' night in. We were drinking wine, and she was reading my runes. The Odin kept coming up, symbolising the transition of death, a step into the unknown, and personal development. Also, on a general reading, I was encountering a turning point, a period characterised by changes, growth and consciousness.

Tom bumped in under the top of the split back door with Blue. I never heard them arriving at all, they must have floated over the gravel. He treated me to 'the look' when he saw the runes. He was always hostile and suspicious towards anything spiritual. He must've caught it from his father.

But this time I could return 'the look' with interest, because, hello? What did we have here, young man?

You'll have seen that picture from the Sky-grab in the paper by now, with Blue in it. So you'll understand she wasn't exactly what I had in mind. I was taken with the idea that we'd be keeping a gundog, now we lived in the country. Not a working animal – I had no plans to go hunting – but a pet that would look decorative as well as being company for the daytime, a Dalmatian, the type of happy animal who could go to work with me, sit in the cab of the van, and that I could take out for a walk at lunch for some fresh air. I needed the work first of course. Things were a bit slack at the beginning.

So, Blue didn't fit the image I was going for, and I have to confess that I was a touch reluctant to take her in. So I suggested we put 'Found, Greyhound' signs around the village. Which we did. We made posters, scanned her picture, and used Tom's mobile for a contact number. He said it was best that way because he didn't want nutters pestering me on mine or the landline. He'd noticed a couple of men from the Nelson look me up and down, he said. He was very protective like that. So he used his own number and he went out and fixed the posters to lamp-posts and in one or two shop windows. I even took her to the vets to see if she was micro-chipped, but she wasn't. Nobody ever claimed her, but then they wouldn't, would they, because if you looked closely it wasn't actually Tom's number on the poster, though it was close – he'd simply reversed two of the figures. I had to admire him for that; he'd decided from the outset she was ours for keeps. He adored her, not least because she was very fast – speed is in his blood – and in no time I grew to adore her too. Blue was easy. She saved the whole of her energy for two concentrated bursts of running a day, the rest of her time she devoted to lying asleep in a basket. I must say, it was an approach to life that I appreciated.

Where on earth did you find *that*, I asked, as he came in.

He said he'd come across her in some woods that he'd been knocking about in with 'poor Gelling'.

Why is he 'poor Gelling'? I said.

He has a sad life, he replied, His sister's very ill.

But then I met Gelling. Well, you've never come across a more chipper lad. He was the life-and-soul, with his dimples and his catch-phrases. That was a signal there, a sign, of how Tom started to change in that period while he was finding his feet. He began dealing in these slight versions of the truth. They were quite subtle, not really lies, and not always so easy to spot. And, of course, I made allowances for him. Gelling was always round, a sweet little nuisance; he could smell a baking cake from a mile off. And that Tucker from the band, he was a maniac, though impossible to dislike. He was a cake-lover too. He tried to put his hand up my skirt the very first time he set foot in our kitchen, but I soon put him right on that. And Luke, well, obviously a bad boy, but not without a certain something. One or two of the other hangers-on I wasn't so keen on. They were a bit above him, in age, but that can cut both ways. And anyway, what was I to do, bar him from seeing people when he'd only just started making friends? Turn him into a stranger in his new surroundings? That would have been a bit strong, and I don't believe in those sort of interdictions anyway: they don't work. Worse than that, they're actively counter-productive. I was always anxious to avoid creating a bad atmosphere between us; I know where that leads from my own teenage years – one of the reasons I took the job at Claridge's was because of the accommodation that went with it – I was desperate to get away from home, into a place of my own, to escape the rows I was having with my parents about rules and behaviour.

I *did* have boyfriends before Ray, of course I did. That was what the rows were about, though I wasn't loose. In fact the first time I ever went to bed with a boy was actually in Claridge's. He was one of the valets. We'd been flirting for weeks. After our shifts were finished one night we let ourselves into an unoccupied double. He brought along a good bottle of stolen wine and a corkscrew. Afterwards, we opened the windows and stood on the edge of the balcony. We watched the taxis pulling in and out of the main entrance. In that moment we were no longer staff, we were guests. It didn't last, it was never meant to; he was Cypriot and had hundreds of girl-friends, and I knew that.

So I let Tom have his head. He was a pretty straightforward boy, albeit with the London edge, obviously, but there's nothing wrong with a bit of streetwise. I reckoned he'd come through in one piece. It's funny, but in a big city, kids tend to stay on their own block, where they know the score, where it's safe. Their orbit is actually quite limited if you pace it out. Being out there, well, I suppose seeing all that space, he began to lose the idea of boundaries.

The morning after Blue arrived I heard crunching on the gravel. It was the police. Did Tom know anything about this stolen car?

No, he said, he didn't.

Where'd he been, the afternoon before? There'd been no record of him attending classes.

He came clean, said he'd bobbed off and gone to mess about in Lion Wood with Gelling.

What, all afternoon?

Yes, he said. He said there was a big old rope swing tied up in there and they'd been playing on it, for ages.

The policeman looked at him hard, as if he didn't believe him. And then Blue wandered in. Tom glanced at me, warning me not to say anything. He pulled her to him and nuzzled her, as though he was afraid that the police would take her away.

So you were in Lion Wood all afternoon?

Yes.

And you know nothing about a stolen car, crashed and burnt out on the beach at California?

No, already told you.

How did you come about those scratches on your face?

Fell. From the rope swing.

And then he showed him a bruise on his elbow too, saying he'd done that at the same time.

Do yourself a favour, Mrs Radford, the policeman said, watch the company he keeps.

Once the coppers had left, Tom went into the garden, trying to interest Blue in chasing a ball. I checked his shoes. I turned one upside down. A fine stream of sand trickled out of it.

# 10

Sally wasn't too thrilled about Dibble turning up, I could tell. There was no smoke without fire, whatever I said. But she played it down. Once the law had left, to help lift our spirits, she drove us into the big city to look for the item I was after, the thing I had in mind when I was asking about shopping right at the start.

The big city was this town called Norwich. At some point Gelling advised me that that was where you had to go, for the proper shopping. *Yew hav tew gew to that big ol Ci-ey of Norridge, bor,* was how he actually said it: East Anglia split into those that spoke in the East Anglian dialect and those that didn't. It was a habit of those that didn't to mock those that did, a habit I never heard work the other way round.

My dad had left me a thousand pounds in a building society account. The item I wanted was a Galaxy Radio, which was a digital receiver with a built-in projector lamp, the kind that turns images through a disc, of planets and spaceships and UFOs. In my new bedroom the ceiling sloped at an angle above my bed, and I knew the projections would look radical up there at night. You could buy these radios online, of course, but me, I like to touch before I make a purchase, because it's all too easy to con a picture up of a thing that's badly finished and knocked up on the cheap and make it look decent on a website. Or to use a picture of a different thing altogether. Never mind the quality son, feel the width, my dad used to say. That's why I needed to get into a proper shop. The only radios you could find in the village, of course, were the type they gave away with petrol, shaped like footballs, on key-rings.

Sally parked in the car park of this department store, and though they didn't stock the Galaxy there, the lady who served us pointed the way to a shop that did. The assistant in that shop took a set out of the box for me. It was neat, and it had weight too, which is a good sign in Hi-Fi. I'd already taken my money from a hole in the wall so I bought it cash. Then we looked in some clothes, interiors, and music shops, and then we had pizza in this glass-fronted restaurant. I sat outside on a wall while Sally went in some more clothes shops. I'd had enough of clothes by then. Up a side street I saw a red Corvette. I looked around. I waited for a couple of people to pass by and then I sauntered alongside it and with the penknife that I kept in the pocket where I kept things I scored the paintwork on the offside.

Back home I set up the radio and lay on my bed watching the planets and the spaceships and the UFOs rotate across the ceiling while I listened to 1Xtra and Kiss. Why I desperately needed digital was so I could pick up London stations. They had something called All Hit Radio Windmill FM out there in East Anglia. Believe me, it's the worst thing you've ever heard, *Next on the line we have Norman from Wroxham, who's here to talk about cyclists on the pavements.* Now I would never have to hear anything from Norman from Wroxham ever again, or listen to any more music by Abba or the Wings or the Bee Gees.

I loved that radio, it was perfect, it was my single most successful purchase ever. When I woke up early, or in the middle of the night, which I often did, because I was in a strange room and the wrong bed, I would switch on and set it to random tune, so as I watched the planets moving I'd pick up a souk station from Mozambique, or hip-hop from Romania; music which reminded me of skating on the Quai beside the St Martin Canal that time, or sometimes I might get BBC World. I remember once listening to this Garry Kasparov on that. He had a great voice, like a baddie in a Bond film. He was explaining how he became world chess champion by dominating the board in a physical way.

Really, is chess actually a physical game? the interviewer questioned him.

Oh, for sure, he replied.

I reckon most sport is like that, and a lot of life too. In speedway, for instance, you have to win the gate, which means get away first. Win the gate, then own the space.

Sometimes in the middle of the night when I heard these male voices in the air talking about things an image of a red car crashing into a man would flash through my mind and I wouldn't be able to stop myself from crying. They'd start off tears of rage, and eventually they'd dry out the other kind.

I'd hide that face from the daytime, of course. Once more the Buddhists had been helpful to me, in a sense, at least; allowing me to practise at concealing my real feelings from them had given me a certain expertise at something I needed to be good at.

Because, although I settled into the timetable of the school, I felt lonely amongst all these wrong, unfamiliar people. The teachers were more disciplined than in Balham; more old-fashioned, formal and detached, even when they were trying to be nice to me and offering pastoral care. And in turn I found the building itself austere; though modern annexes had been added to the main building, the heart of the school was Victorian, with corridors floored in parquet and tiled to dado height in crazed green ceramics with gloss cream paintwork above. One day, as I was stood queuing for a Citizenship class, I remembered where I'd seen this colour scheme and these tiles before. It was at the hospital, after the accident. I tried to scorch the memory from my mind; I took a shivery bite out of my pocket and sucked on it so hard that it burnt into my tongue.

I was selected for the school rugby team, which was a sport I'd never played before. I had been misinterpreted, I had appeared to show too much willing, that was where I went wrong. The thing I was interested in was the rugby ball itself, not the sport. I'd never kicked one before (we only had football in Balham), and the way it moved fascinated me, the seemingly random element of its flight. After games, and after last bell, I would sometimes stay behind on the sports field, launching the ball as far as I could, and then seeing if I could get to it — run under and catch it — before it had the chance to bounce. I had another motive for this, which was that I was trying to improve my sprint times for the races I was having with Blue when I took her out to the fields beyond Lion Wood. But since pure running on its own is boring as hell, I was using this technique to keep myself motivated. And if I didn't get there soon enough and the ball did bounce, I couldn't tell which direction it would take, so I could put an extra sideways sprint in, trying to beat it before it bounced again, which was good agility training. An agile body leads to an agile mind. I'd heard Alice say this, when she and Sally were doing their Pilates. When I was exhausted, or fed up with sprinting, I experimented with how high I could kick the ball. At my best, with the trick of perspective, I could put it right into the top blade of the stopped propeller at the wind farm. To the games master who stood watching from the window of the changing hut, I must have looked seriously dedicated. That had to be how I got the call-up.

It was Gelling who released the information. He came running down the corridor, clattering the parquet, practically hyperventilating, saying, Radford! Radford! have you seen the team sheet for the match against North Walsham?

No.

You're in, he said. Fuck me, are you ever in trouble now.

I came to understand what this fuck-me-ever-in-trouble-now meant. Rugby in games lessons was one thing, but a competitive match was another thing altogether. In games we were split into two groups, and there was messing about, mud-sliding and play-fighting – it was larks, and I enjoyed it, I got lost in myself. But then came this real match against this North Walsham.

In the first scrum one boy ground his head into mine sideways, swivelling it in my ear and neck. It was a bald head, not shaven; he must have been the first bald fifteen-year-old in history, the freak. And as the freak tried to break my neck, another of them gouged his fingernails into my thigh while a third pervert grabbed my balls and squeezed. Apparently there was some history between us and North Walsham. On top of this, I found that when it came to match play I didn't understand the rules of rugby, not at all. I kept getting blown up for being offside, giving away penalties and line-outs. As there were bodies seemingly everywhere, all conducting battles with each other, the 'pattern of play' seemed less random than entirely non-existent.

In truth, I couldn't even keep up with the score, and for much of the match I didn't know whether we were winning or losing. The weather turned hostile; I was desperate for full time to arrive, desperate for it all to end, and when the final whistle sounded I prayed that my performance had been bad enough that I'd never be selected to play again so long as I lived, please God. North Walsham had beaten us, by two points, as it turned out. And so it was us, the home team, who had to rank up into two files, as a grey sleet lashed in from the brown fields, to form a corridor, to applaud them off while our captain shouted Hip-hip hurrah three times. The whole team joined in on 'hurrah'. To me, the scene was medieval. There was none of this involved in football, the only team sport I had played in the past, and the only team sport I would be playing in the future. As I limped towards the changing rooms, Gelling fell in beside me. Gelling had been a spectator. Gelling was excused games, for his asthma.

You were twatted, he said.

I took the remark personally, not as a comment on the team

display. Yes Gelling, I replied, you really don't have to tell me that, to be honest.

What you got to show for it?

I treated him to the backs of my legs. Apart from the gougings there was a full set of teeth marks on my thigh where some retard had actually bitten me in a tackle – it was livid, the indent of each individual incisor, molar and premolar easily discernible. The following day it melded into one huge bruise the size and shape of a split pomegranate. Next, I lifted the back of my shirt to show him a gash where some other serial killer had attempted to stamp on me, but had slipped while he was at it so that his studs had slid over my kidneys in an arc towards my shoulder blade.

Gelling was delighted with this last. You'll be pissing blood, mate, he said, as he admired it and slapped me on the back.

Cheers Gelling, I said. Glad to help.

Yep, not bad, he said, A decent collection and good timing too, because chicks dig scars.

What?

Listen, he said, I bear shit-hot news.

The shit-hot news was that Gelling had got us set up on a double-date with these two girls, Chelsy and Zoë. They were both a year above, so he'd done us proud, fixing us up with older women.

And now you've got the scars, Radford, you're bound to get laid.

Stick with you, eh Gelling?

You won't go far wrong, he said.

★

In the changing rooms after the match North Walsham's captain, the bald freak, starting calling on Ryan, our captain. He made two remarks about his performance on the pitch and then he called his girlfriend a whore. They were pumped, both of them, the type of conscripts who live in the gym, gobble supplements all day long, and more than likely went home to pull tractors at night with their bare teeth. Ryan, who came with the thousand-yard stare of the natural-born psycho, stepped up and ground his forehead into the bald freak's nose, but that didn't stop the freak from repeating what he'd already said. He wasn't scared, after all, was he, because he was from exactly the same mould as Ryan. I don't know what his problem was, hadn't he already won the fucking match anyway? He had his back to me. Though he was starting to become obscured as members of both teams piled in for the ruck, I threw my boot and caught him square on his back of his dome.

*What the fuck* . . . he shouted, swivelling.

What?! What was that? There'll be none of *that* language in *my* school, understood?

The arrival of the games master came just in time to prevent the full riot getting going.

I didn't think any member of the Walsham team had seen where the boot came from, and I didn't get ambushed afterwards, so I reckoned I was right about that. But as it turned out Ryan *had* seen, as well as one of our prop forwards, and the hooker. Whereas before I was still a new boy, now I wasn't so new. In the following days I noted the little nods I received in the corridors and I found myself included in the backstabbing and jokes that went around. Whereas before I'd only really had

Gelling to call a friend, now, for a probationary period at least, I was in. This turned out to be another fuck up: in the next training session Ryan insisted that I was an asset, that I should keep my place in the side, that they'd bring me on, develop me as a player.

# 11.

I'd seen Chelsy and Zoë around. Chelsy had a part-time job in the twenty-four-hour shop. Her hair was brown with a sharp, geometric centre-parting, and her breasts were enormous. They were the main talking point about her – even though East Anglian girls were generally gifted on the breast front, hers were still remarkable. I imagined the abundance of these plumptious orbs was to do with all the daily cow's milk they drank, as well as everything else they ate that came in off the land. As I limped away from school after the match, Gelling put me right on this, saying that very little that was on sale in the shops in the parade actually originated from the fields where we lived, and that most of the local jobs had been out-sourced to India and South Korea.

The tan in that salon's about as natural as it gets these days, he said, indicating Solar Lab. We stopped to watch a toasted woman emerge out of the soap-bubble-painted doors and step into a lilac Clio. Gelling spread his arms wide to indicate the brown fields beyond.

D'you know what? he said.

What?

Out there it's just one giant factory, Radford, I'll tell you that for nothing. They spread chemicals like there's no tomorrow. They don't give a flying fart what poison's in it provided everything grows bigger and faster and shinier. Just as long as it looks good in the supermarket, that's the thing.

Supermarket? What supermarket? There was never going to be a supermarket out here. There was even a campaign *against* one. I'd seen people standing with banners on the corner at the weekend. I couldn't understand it – if they got a proper shop then they might be able to buy bread that wasn't a bake-it-yourself sub once in a while, and pick up vegetables that weren't either last week's or else covered in shit, like Sally had started to buy from this farm shop she'd discovered in this *other* village.

Chemicals? I said, Maybe that's what's responsible for Chelsy's breasts, maybe that's why they're so . . .

Mahoosive and super-enhanced?

Yeah, I said, mahoosive, super-enhanced and turbocharged, chemically modified by the poisons that get spread on those fields.

It's a theory, Gelling replied, and cheaper than plastic surgery too, but if it was true, why hasn't every chick got them that size?

Like Zoë? I said.

Like Zoë for one, he replied.

Zoë was a different kettle of fish, with a rather fine grasp of body-English. Zoë was also a shopgirl; she worked part-time in the artists' supplies part of the bookshop. Zoë was a slim blonde with a flat chest and pockmarked, slightly bad skin which I found deeply attractive. The blonde hair was long and matted into pre-dreadlocks and her eyes were very blue and a little bit too close together which I also found very attractive. Once or twice I'd been into the bookshop to pick up acrylic paints that I didn't strictly need, just because of Zoë. I would have liked to have gone out with her on a date on my own, with no third parties present, but I was afraid of the knockback; I would never have plucked up the courage to ask. I knew it was Chelsy that Gelling was setting me up with, not Zoë, because Chelsy was always looking at me from under her lashes when she was passing me change for a bake-it-yourself sub roll. Zoë had never looked at me at all, as far as I knew. It was the woman who owned the shop who took my cash for the tubes of burnt umber and raw sienna and ultramarine. She stalked me round the place, keeping an eye on me, because, being a thieving Cockney incomer, I'd likely slip a sable brush up my sleeve as soon as blink. Zoë seemed to idle most of her time away by rearranging sheaves of coloured papers. Other than at her shopwork I'd see her with groups of girls hanging on the corners of the green. Some of them called things out to make me blush, though not Zoë herself.

Our double-date was set for Friday night. Before I left Keeper's Cottage I sat in the garden on the rope swing, imagining conversations and considering my lines. Blue came out and stood by the back door, watching me. It was over a month now since I'd taken her from Klaus Toppmöller, but I still didn't feel safe that she was really mine, because one or two of the posters were still up. Even if they had gone damp and smudged, and I had fixed them in places where I didn't think people would see them – halfway round the backs of lamp-posts and high up telegraph poles – and the phone number was small, difficult to read, faded, and wrong, I still feared someone might recognise the picture, and maybe see me around with her and follow me home and claim her. She was lightning fast in the field behind Lion Wood, I had absolutely no chance in our races. She more than won the gate, she murdered it; I worried that she could still be a great racer, that someone could really be searching for her, to make money.

I left early for the date. I felt an urgent need to pull those remaining posters down. Why I had ever put them up in the first place was a sudden mystery to me. I kissed Blue on her head on my way out, and in turn Sally kissed me on my head. She said to enjoy myself. I guess she knew what I was up to because I had used some of the aftershave that my Nan had given me last Christmas, even though I wasn't shaving yet.

On the way over to Gelling's I dealt with the posters. I'd been worrying about nothing – they really were totally illegible, the image of Blue was practically an abstract. Still, I was determined to take them right out of commission. The last one I retrieved was the one that I'd pinned highest up a telegraph pole. I stood on a wall to get it, and in stretching to pull it down I lost my footing, slipped, and twisted my ankle. I tried walking along to ease it off, but it was wrecked. I stopped on the wall of the twenty-four-hour shop rubbing and kneading at it, like Saff with her shiatsu massage technique, but it didn't help, so I had to hop, skip and jump to Gelling's, in order to make it to his for the time we'd arranged.

Gelling lived at the edge of the village, on an estate. You had to pass through most of the houses to get to his place. At the front of the estate, facing the main road, were the bungalows for the old people with tin sculptures of owls in the gardens, then in the next few streets it was rows of four or six little homes with painted horizontal timber slats between the upper and lower windows. Some of these had matching rows of garages behind them where boys played, jumping from one flat roof to the next. Then came the semis with bay windows with leaded panes and two cars, or car plus a trailer or a caravan, and finally, at the furthest end, were the cul-de-sacs with the bigger detached houses and the double garages. Gelling's was one of these, in a cul-de-sac called Jubilee Close. His drive was laid out in herring-bone paving like the parquet of the school corridors, and the double-garage had Edwardian panelled doors. The front garden was freshly mown in lines, the smell of cut grass sweet in the air. This lawn was protected by a white chain fence that was so low and dinky it looked artificial. Small purple, orange and white flowers peeped out of the beds surrounding the lawn. The 3-Series with the STIK 1 plate was parked in front of the Edwardian garage. The wheels were safe, seventeen-inch parallel spokes. I peered in. Sports alloy pedals, aluminium selector lever, Smartnav, beige hide, it was well fixed up.

This was the first time I'd ever called round on Gelling. I could tell from the exterior that it was not the sort of home I would be invited into. The whole atmosphere around it seemed to say, Go away, get lost, no tradesmen. I rang the bell, which double-chimed, and I stepped back feeling that I'd done something wrong. Gelling's mum answered. She was a thin woman with glamorous make-up on a tired face. She was wearing an apron. She drew the door half-open and looked at me without saying anything. I had to speak first. I nearly said I'd come for Gelling, but in the nick of time I remembered to ask for him by his first name.

Is Aaron in? I said.

She simply nodded and made a sort of murmuring noise before retreating inside. As I stood waiting in the porch I made a mental note that next time I'd text Gelling before I got to Jubilee Close so he could meet me at the end of the road. There was some rare, clinical smell coming out of the house, something beyond disinfectant. Carpet fluid or something. Through the gap where Mrs Gelling had left the door slightly ajar I could see a collection of birds' eggs in a display case fixed to the wall. I stared at it. I found it spooky, like the British Museum. Below the birds' eggs was a telephone table with a built-in seat covered in velvet with stud-buttons. The Yellow and Local directories were stacked neatly in the rack below. As I took in these details I realised that I didn't want to be invited inside anyway. In fact, I hopped out back onto the herring-bone drive, just in case it should happen that Mr Gelling might call me in while I waited – dads can be more relaxed about that sort of thing, in my experience.

I was glad I didn't live there, that was for sure. I looked around me. Every house in Jubilee Close matched. It was so neat and tidy it was like watching high definition, it practically hurt my eyes just to stand there. The scene was totally at odds with Gelling himself and his whole demeanour and personality. I thought about this. He was rebelling against his background, clearly, it's elementary stuff that you learn in Citizenship, when you do opposed personalities. I waited and I thought about the situation some more. I came up with an analysis for Mrs Gelling and her back-off atmosphere: I remembered about Tiffany and her condition. Most likely she was just trying her best to protect her daughter. Too late of course, the horse had long since bolted there, but at least I could see a reason for the way things were. You can imagine the temptation for any old Tom, Dick or Harry, once they were inside, to sneak a shot on their mobile and sell it to the papers for one of the weekly anorexic slots. I looked upstairs and noticed the curtains were all drawn. You couldn't blame her family for seeking to protect her and encasing her in a shroud of cotton wool. I cast my gaze around the trees and bushes to see if any lowlife were staking the place out, but I didn't spot anything.

Gelling emerged suddenly, falling out of his porch like an escapee. He'd trumped my Nan's aftershave big time. He absolutely reeked of unctions and he'd done something radical to the razored mullet, he'd had it gelled and tortured into a sequence of little spikes and knots like that footballer Taribo West, if you remember him (he used to play for Everton, a team for whom I had an inexplicable soft spot, they didn't even have good players). Gelling had two hairstyles going on there, if not three. As we walked away I glanced back and I saw a curtain twitch in the upstairs window. Tiffany, I guessed. I wanted to ask Gelling something about her, but I didn't really know where to start. I wanted to know why people starve themselves like that; how they turn something ordinary and regular like food into an enemy.

Did your sister do that, I asked.

Do what?

Your hair, Gelling.

My hair? he said, with an incredulous squeak, as if struggling to understand such an absurd comment.

It's pretty sharp, I said. Looks mint.

Oh? he said, It's nothing, just a bit of gel.

But is she at home, I asked.

Who?

Tiffany.

Her car's there, he said, by way of reply, as if he didn't know for certain one way or the other. Why, anyway?

No reason, I replied.

You're asking about my sister for no reason. D'you fancy her or something Radford, you pervert?

I've never even *seen* her, Gelling, I said, how could I fancy her?

What, you never saw *Celebrity Slimmer*?

No, Gelling, I never.

How come?

What day was it on? I said.

Wednesdays.

I was normally out on Wednesdays, I said, at a track.

Ah, okay, he said. I wish I'd been out really. But you have to watch, when it's family, and you have to get everybody you know to vote too.

I guess you do, I said. So how is she then?

You haven't got a sister, Radford, have you?

He already knew I hadn't.

Sisters think they own the place, he said, they're a nightmare. They're just about the last thing in the world you'd ever want to talk about, or even think about once they're out of your sight. You'd know that if you had one, it's a pure relief to stop breathing the same air, and that's a fact.

Did you vote to keep her in or to get her out, then? I said.

I never got the chance to vote till the end did I? She kept losing weight every week, didn't she, so she was never up for eviction.

How would you have voted?

I'd have voted to get her out, of course, she looked fucking terrible. Fucking sisters, fuck 'em, he said.

Oh? I said. But what about Chelsy and Zoë?

What about them?

They might be someone's sister.

Jesus, Radford, there's no comparison. Someone *else's* sister is . . . comp*letely* different. What *is* your point anyway, you maniac?

Just . . .

Are you chickening out?

No, no, no, I said, I'm just saying, one person's sister—

—is another person's Chelsy Nobbs, said Gelling: Get with the project, Radford – I've heard she goes like a train.

One or two adults nodded at Gelling as we made our way out of the estate back towards the village centre. They nodded politely. It struck me that Gelling was being treated with an element of civility and respect that his hairstyle did not deserve.

You seem to be a pillar of the community round here, I said.

This shit hole is the kind of place where they judge you by what you've got parked on the drive, he replied.

That may have been the first regular thing I'd heard about East Anglia. There was nobody in Balham, or the rest of London, who didn't take a view on someone according to where they lived and what they drove.

At least your sister's good for that, I said.

Who wants to be judged by their sister's car, Radford? Just shut up about her, for fuck's sake, he said, Don't be a freak.

Stick with me Gelling, I said, and you might learn something about the difference between being a freak and just making polite conversation, you tool.

And then we had a fight, to establish who was a freak and who was a tool, a fight during which I rearranged his stupid hair a bit while he rabbit punched my kidneys. Coming in on top of the stud-mark bruisings, they were punches that brought tears to my eyes.

Woah, Gelling you fucker, I said, I'm already pissing blood as it is, remember.

Sorry Radford, he said, Just leave my sister out of it, okay.

We pressed on in silence. And then I pulled up with a wince because of my twisted ankle.

Did I do that? said Gelling.

No, it came on after the match, I said. I didn't want to tell him how I really did it because then I'd have to bring the posters into it, which would bring Blue into it, which would give him a chance to start bleating about his asthma and then he could get all touchy about dogs again too, as well as about his sister.

As we passed the parade Gelling set his hair straight, using the window of the derelict butcher's shop as a mirror. Tramps live in there, he said, They're probably even watching us. He pressed his face right against the glass. You couldn't see a thing through it, it was all smeared up with window polish. Gelling turned round, dropped his strides, and mooned the cheeks of his arse at the window, for the benefit of the tramps. That seemed to set him up.

C'mon, kid, he said, it's show-time. Let's cop ourselves a taste of punanni.

I could see the future for Gelling. He was going to be a red-carpet jerk with a mic. He had the whole right attitude for it. Maybe Tiffany would make a recovery, co-host the Grammy's with him, complete some sort of showbiz life-cycle.

Chelsy's parents ran the Nelson. We went in round the back gate, navigating a yard full of beer kegs and piled-up crates of empty bottles. There was an Alsatian near the back door, pulling and barking at the end of a length of chain. The barking brought Chelsy's face to a window on a half-landing. You could hear her belt down the stairs where she slid the bolt on the back door. She ushered us in and followed close on our heels as she urged us quickly on ahead up two flights and then finally up a third turnpike staircase into the loft.

Chelsy's loft was a long room, stretching the full length of the pub. It was a half-converted storage space, gothic and grim. There were tiny arched windows at each end but they were so dirty they let in no more light than the panes of the butcher's shop. Chelsy had set fragranced candles on a low table in a corner so the air was scented with cinnamon and lemon, an aroma that failed to disguise the prevailing smell of ancient soot. Items of mess were stacked about the place; rolled- up carpets, garden umbrellas, garden furniture, a grandfather clock, an old cigarette machine, hundreds of stair rods, and a dust-coated table tennis table. A couple of battered sofas faced each other, either side of the low table with the candles.

Where's Zoë? said Gelling.

She's coming, said Chelsy, she won't be long. She was wearing a short denim skirt with a jewel-spangled belt. A retro grey-marl t-shirt advertising her as '100 percent babe' was stretched across the famous chest. It was mountainous in close-up, and packed into the t-shirt it seemed out of context with the rest of her, which was, in all likelihood, a normal size. This time I wondered for real if they *were* real. I avoided eye-contact, or eye-to-orb-contact either, played table tennis with Gelling instead. We found a ball but no bats, so we improvised by using books to knock it about with while Chelsy watched from the side. Eventually we lost the ball under a wardrobe. Gelling agreed to call the game a draw even though he was ahead.

I'll make allowances for you, for your ankle, Radford, kid, he said, as though he was one hell of a swell guy.

We moved over to the sofas. The table was set with cashew nuts in bowls and bottles of hooch, Stella and Razor.

Sit down here next to me Tom, said Chelsy. Don't be shy.

So I did. Gelling made himself comfortable on the sofa opposite. Her breasts hung so low they caught my knees as she stretched back and forth to open a bottle and offer nuts. She'd brought proper glasses up from the bar, and she rubbed her leg against me as she stretched to pour me a Razor (I didn't like hooch, and I'd once got sick on Stella with Milo and Nico in the $10^e$ so I couldn't touch that ever again.) Chelsy smelled of cigarette smoke and wine and her cheeks were flushed. I could see her underarms were slightly damp with sweat.

How did you hurt your ankle, she asked.

At the match against Walsham, Gelling replied, answering for me. He's got scars all over him, he said.

Where? said Chelsy.

I lifted the back of my shirt to show her the stud marks.

Does that hurt? she said, touching them with a clammy hand.

No, I replied, and I tried not to flinch.

They look totally convincing, she said.

That's because they are actually real, Chelsy, said Gelling.

Have you ever been inside, Tom? she said.

What?

In prison?

No.

Oh, she said, I thought all Londoners had done time.

That's Chelsy's fantasy, said Gelling, to cop off with a jail-bird.

Maybe I could get myself banged up, then – rob a bank or something? I said.

Oh, she said, you'd do that for me? So you *do* like me, then, Tom?

I could have kicked myself. I'd walked right into it. I had no idea what to say next. The only first-hand experience I had of boy-girl relationships was what I'd seen of Nico and Milo, but they were a one-off, specialised: Nico's Frenchness made her seem removed and exotic, like a picture in a magazine, and now I lived out here and saw next to nothing of them, their affair seemed to exist in the ether. It was almost as though I'd invented them. They were intense together, that was my main residual impression. It was an intensity based on conflict, in fact their whole relationship seemed to revolve around arguing; I don't think I'd ever seen them kiss, except to make up.

Chelsy persisted. You do like me Tom – you find me *attractive*?

*Mais oui*, I said.

It must have been thinking about Nico that made me drop such an almighty bollock. Zoë arrived at precisely the moment

I said it. She was wearing black boots, a black skirt and a black skinny rib jumper. Like Nico, she seemed alien, actressy.

Oh, you like to speak in French when you're being romantic do you Tom Radford? Zoë said. How compelling.

I had a mental image of what I would like to happen next. I saw myself dropping through the floors below, smashing through the horsehair and shit of the wattle and daub of the Nelson, coming finally to land four-square on a barstool in a shower of splinters and plaster and dust, casually asking the barman to set me up a large one.

Are you blushing? Zoë said, as she sat down next to Gelling and crossed her legs so the black skirt fell away to reveal the outside of her thigh between the boots and the hem. Her flesh was very white. Do we *country* girls embarrass you with our forwardness?

No, I said.

Why don't you kiss Chelsy, said Zoë. She'd let you, you know, she's mad for it. Her radar's been on red alert ever since the moment she set eyes on you.

Zoë! said Chelsy. But she laughed as she said it, as though it was fine with her to see this information slip, as though its release was actively pre-planned.

Go on Tom, put the poor girl out of her misery, Zoë said.

Zoë had messed with my fantasy image of her as a mysterious artist's assistant with a sensitive inner life and a passion for Michelangelo, that was for sure. She had a way about her that I found difficult. Not that this did anything to quell the feelings I'd been nurturing, on the contrary. How had I got myself into this position? Having to kiss this one girl in whom I had no interest in front of an audience of this other girl in whom I certainly did. I'll tell you how, I had followed Gelling again, like with Luke and California. But whereas that outing had ended up no harm done, and I had even come out of it with Blue, I wasn't so sure about this situation. The last thing I wanted to do was to get intimate with Chelsy Nobbs. She might have been okay for some specialist knocker fetishist, but she just wasn't my type. But what could I say? 'I think we'll leave that sort of thing until later, when we've got to know each other a little better?' Who did I think I was, Roger Moore? My dad met Roger Moore once, in a restaurant in Switzerland. He expected him to be a gent but apparently he was a bit of a wanker, and he'd had so many facelifts that you could see through his skin, like tissue paper.

I could go French again, *Non, ce n'est pas, a çe moment*?

I smiled to myself in a sickly way. I couldn't bottle it, not in front of Gelling. So I turned to Chelsy and closed my eyes and pressed my mouth against hers. She forced her tongue through my lips and wriggled it about. She probed me as if she had lost something. It was repulsive. To my shame I had to swallow back a tear. This was all wrong. I would never have admitted as much, but this was my first heavy kiss and it should have been with someone I craved, not with someone who I barely even knew, who was pinning me to a sofa with her enormous chest while meantime opposite sat Zoë whose ear I wanted to nibble, as an hors d'oeuvre to greater things. But now, out of the corner of my eye, which I had dared to open, I could see that it was Gelling who had begun to do that. Not for long though, Zoë pushed him away almost as soon as he'd started, asking him what did he think he was on, trying to get fresh with her? That was my single crumb of comfort in this altogether dismal start to the world of double-dating. Once the oral probe was over, I drank the whole Razor in one, as a palate cleanser. And then I let out a huge belch.

Radford, manners! said Zoë, as Chelsy cuddled up to me and said I'd have to marry her, now we'd done that.

That's right, said Zoë, you might have gotten her in the family way.

Wow, I could be pregnant, we could start a family, said Chelsy. Her eyes twinkled insanely, like the laughing doll in Caesar's Palace. How many children would you like, Tom?

None, I said.

Hey, Chelsy said, no need to take that attitude.

What attitude?

That tone, she said.

She stood up and tugged down at the hem of her skirt, and went to change the music on the CD. Zoë moved to join her. The girls began to dance together, and to ignore us. Gelling gave me the thumbs up, as though everything was going pretty well. He leaned forward, cracked himself a Stella and whispered, What do they feel like?

What?

The mahoosive breasts.

I never touched them, I said.

Yeah, but you've had them bang up against you close and personal, he said, You must have some idea.

They feel hot, Gelling, I said. They feel hot and soft.

Hot and soft? he said. They just need a bit of soap to finish them off, he said.

Soap?

I've got a little dispenser in here, he said, pulling at his flies.

Listen Radford, he said, I know girls, I understand them. What I'm thinking is this: they're probably over there planning a switch right now.

Switch?

Yep, d'you know what?

What?

I reckon Zoë might suit you better than me.

Really? And you'd be happy with Chelsy?

Gelling pulled his face, as if he was seriously considering the matter, and then he nodded, with a slightly pained expression, as if to say it might just be worth a try. For me, neither alternative was exactly favourite, but for the time being I'd rather put up with Zoë's haughty attitude than Chelsy's tongue. So while the girls danced, Gelling and I swapped sofas. I noticed that Zoë had left her phone on the cushion. I saw she had taken a picture of Chelsy and me kissing, which I deleted.

Oh, what's all this? said Chelsy, as they came back from having finished their dance, Musical chairs?

C'mon here Chelsy darlin', Gelling said, extending his hand in invitation. You know I've always loved you, babe. I'd do a ten-stretch for you any day.

Chelsy looked at Zoë, who looked at me. Zoë sat down next to me without a word while Chelsy made a repeat performance with Gelling of the drink-pouring leg-rubbing routine that we'd already been through.

Always loved me? she said.

Ever since Year Three, said Gelling as he put his arm round her.

She pulled the arm away, he put it back, she pulled it away, he put it back. She let it stay. After a while his little fingers headed south to the entry slopes of the breasts. She pulled them away. She ran her hand through Gelling's hairstyles. You need to do something about this, she said.

That comment told its own story; if a girl is considering changing your hair, she's considering taking you on. Even though this was a result as far as I was concerned, letting me right off the hook, I felt a bit disillusioned. If all it took for her crush on me to disappear was for me to have said 'None' to the idea of how many children I wanted, then she was more fickle than a person has a right to be.

Zoë crossed her legs again, displaying the milky thigh once more. Other than that she sat frostily watching the developing dance of passion between Chelsy and Gelling. We spoke not a word to each other.

I took another bottle of Razor and stood up and hobbled across to the table tennis table where I sat and spun a coin. My ankle was really stiff now, I could barely put it down. I began to think I might just as well go home. I was resigning myself to a total disaster of a night out with these fucking inbreds when to my surprise, Zoë came over. She took the spinning coin and flicked it. Heads or tails? she said. I called heads, which it was. She didn't like losing so she made it best of three, which I still won. I shifted my position and flinched. In that sideways manner that some girls have, she asked me what was the matter.

I twisted my ankle over, I replied, it's really swelling.

She made a point of glancing away to Chelsy and Gelling with a look of distaste, and then she said, Come with me, I can help you with that.

We made our way down the turnpike staircase. I hung on

the banister and looked back to see the remnants of Chelsy's resistance disappear as Gelling dived in to handle three or four kilos or more of what he had been after from the start.

Downstairs I waited by the back door as Zoë went into the cellar. She emerged carrying a plastic bag and led me outside. The Alsatian looked up but he remained silent, because he knew her, I guess. Beyond the beer kegs and the stacks of crates a dilapidated metal fire escape ran up a side-wall. Zoë took my hand and led me under it, sat me on a crate, and knelt down and packed the plastic bag, which was full with ice cubes, round my ankle.

She settled on her haunches, her back resting against the brick wall.

Is that better?

Yes, I said. Thanks.

It's okay, she said.

We sat there for about ten minutes, saying nothing. Zoë lit a cigarette, and after a few draws passed it to me. I took a couple of drags and handed it back. She finished it off, ground it under her boot and said, d'you think they're screwing?

Maybe, I said, I've heard that Chelsy Nobbs goes like a train.

She looked at me.

What's the French for 'goes like a train'? she said.

I don't know, I replied.

She touched my cheek with the back of her hand. What's the French for 'I love you'? she said.

*Je t'aime*, I replied.

What?

I repeated it. *Je t'aime*, Zoë.

She raised herself and pulled me up with her. We stood under the fire escape while she guided my hand under her skirt to the front of her pants, which were ribbed, the same as her jumper. She held my palm over her mound.

Have you ever touched a girl there? she said.

I made no reply.

She led my hand up higher and slipped my fingers inside the elastic. Go on, she said.

I touched her hair and felt down into the warm soft flesh and slid my forefinger into the crack below. She let me linger for a second while she pressed against the front of my trousers to see if I was going hard. I started to move my finger in, but she clamped my wrist to stop me and eased my hand back out.

I looked at her.

I'm not easy, she said, if that's what you think.

I made no reply. I shook my head. She moved her lips to mine and brushed them across my own. You wouldn't call it a kiss, it was more than that. I put the back of my hand to *her* cheek, feeling the delicate braille of the slightly bad skin. She stepped away. I could see the nipples of her flat breasts poking through the ribbing of the jumper. Her phone bleeped.

She looked at the screen. I have to be off, she said.

She walked away backwards to the gate, looking at me, nearly smiling, and then she skittered out of the yard. The Alsatian, who had remained lying on the floor, quietly keeping his watch, rose and barked once.

I sat on a rung of the rusty fire escape and squeezed the bag of ice hard around my ankle. There was no call for me to go back up to the loft, I'd only be interrupting. I imagined Gelling with his pecker buried deep, I imagined Chelsy going 'par un loco-motif', or whatever it is in French, hanging onto le top knots of his beaucoup hairstyles, her breasts thwacking together like bells in a church tower. He was welcome to it. The plastic bag was beginning to leak, my socks were getting wet. The dog barked once again. I hobbled out of the yard before he woke the whole neighbourhood.

I made my way around the ill-lit streets of the village in company with all the drunks who were staggering out of the front bar of the Nelson into the fresh air. One or two of them laughed at me, thinking I'd been on the sherbet like they had, whereas in the fact of it my unsteady gait stemmed from more or less different causes. I dragged along as best I could, and then I saw a sight on the village green which pulled me up. Sitting on a bench overlooking the pond, with his back to me, was Ryan, the rugby captain. He had his arm round a blonde girl with long pre-dreadlocked hair, a blonde girl who was wearing exactly the same outfit as Zoë. This was because it *was* Zoë. I pulled in for cover behind a tree. Ryan seemed to have to complete a lengthy trial involving a certain amount of begging and rejection, but finally she allowed him to kiss her, fully, at length. I held onto the tree until the bark branded tramlines into my palms. An owl flew over the green, a real owl, the first time I'd ever seen one. I wouldn't have been surprised if there was a real fucking seal swimming in the pond to go with it, to complete the beautiful, romantic scene.

The following morning when I tried to get out of bed, I failed. I had to flop straight back onto the mattress. I couldn't stand at all. I examined my ankle; it was swollen purple and blue. I lay there staring at the ceiling, remembering the night before. As I reviewed events the only thing I could be happy about was that I'd come out on top at heads or tails. Otherwise it was a wholly winless sequence:

One: I'd lost face with Chelsy Nobbs. Not that I cared, but stuff like that spreads.

Two: Zoë had toyed with my body and my emotions and gotten into me. This, of course, I did care about.

Three: I'd had my fingers on a sacred part of the rugby captain's girlfriend. Here was a real local crime, a time bomb that could only lead to trouble. Though technically no one should find out anything about it, because Zoë herself was the only witness, news was bound to emerge, it's always the way. And just as I was beginning to get my feet under the table with the main men at school too.

I raised my finger to my nose as I had done several times as I made my way back to Keeper's Cottage. The scent of her herbs had been sweeter than the cut grass of Gelling's front lawn. But now it was another day, now the perfume had evaporated completely.

# 12

There were certain things I needed to avoid over the next few weeks: Ryan principally, Chelsy for another, and games lessons and training sessions too, as additional insurance for avoiding Ryan. As I continued to lie on my bed analysing the night before, I had to wonder what in hell Gelling had been doing in the first place, attempting to set *either* of us up with Zoë. Come to that, what was *her* game? Just keeping her friend company? That's the excuse I'd use, if I was in her boots. Believe me, I wouldn't want to get on the wrong side of Ryan, whether I was his girlfriend or not.

The sight of the Nelson started to give me bad memory associations, so I took the scenic route to school to avoid passing it. I pulled out of the next rugby match anyway, because my ankle was a canvas of fading yellows, swollen to about twice the size it should be: no way would I pass any fitness test. I caught sight of Zoë a couple of times, between class changes. The pulse in my wrist grew visible, but I kept my distance, you never knew who might see. And how would I start a conversation anyway? And then our paths crossed directly, in the corridor, me in my group of boys, her in her group of girls. We made full eye-contact, and in that eye-contact it seemed to me that I was being informed that the incident had been erad-icated from history, never to be mentioned ever again, a figment of my imagination. I could neither see nor hear it, but behind me I could sense her girls laughing at me.

At the end of school days, I spent my time in Lion Wood with Blue, trying to get a signal on my phone, texting old friends, most of whom only just about bothered to text back, if that, because, it became clear to me now, texting is an activity based around setting up meetings in your local proj-ect. In fact, Nico texted me more than anyone from London. I found a tree in Lion Wood that had a thick branch growing out perpendicular at just the ideal height for doing pull-ups. I spent hours on that, improving my upper body strength while my ankle was still too sore to run on. Blue chased rabbits while I built up from ten at a time to twenty at a time, then to sets of tens, then to sets of twenties. Lying in bed at night listening to news of the regrouping of the Taliban in Afghanistan on BBC World, I would flex my forearm and feel my biceps. I tried not to, but of course in the end I did what I had to do to get back to sleep. I would not use Zoë, that was my rule. Alice the Buddhist was my favourite fantasy, amongst real people. Alice was a swimmer, we had driven out to this other village called Bungay a few times, where the nearest pool was, so I could use residual images of her in her bathing costume, and imagine her drying herself off and all the rest.

The boy from the Bosnian Units, Zdravo, was at the pool once. Zdravo! he said, high-five-ing me as we held onto the bar at the deep end. He had a big smile and terrible teeth. We had two twenty-five-metre races, one crawl, one backstroke, both dead heats. In the changing rooms I noticed his feet were circled with a dark rim of dirt like speedway riders get on their braking boot.

In time my ankle recovered, though it never entirely returned to its original shape. And in time I forgot that passing the Nelson gave me a bad feeling. That was how I found myself walking outside it one Friday night as Luke burnt into the kerb with his signature 'honk, d'you want a lift?' routine. He was driving a dirty Land Rover, and was wearing his trademark school uniform suit. I was in my preferred Hoax zip-up and an old NYC beanie. It was early evening. There were already some drunks in the window-seats of the pub, laughing and joking as they began to set themselves up for the weekend, until one of them saw Luke, that is; then the joking stopped and the collective hard stare kicked in.

Come on Radford, Luke said. Let's split, we don't want to be curdling their beer.

I made a quick decision, and an easy one too. I'd always loved Land Rovers. I slung my bag over the back of the 4x4, which was the short wheel-base covered-over-by-a-green-tarpaulin type, a cowboy's truck, one of my favourites. I jumped in and sat on the side-box. As we pulled away the comforting smell of diesel fumes overpowered a cloud of muck-stench that was coming in off the fields. It was one of the things I had begun to hate most about living in the middle of nowhere, the smell of farmers spreading. I don't know what Gelling was on about – if they *were* using chemicals they certainly disguised it to smell like normal shit.

I was surprised how pleased I was to see Luke. He'd stopped by our gate a couple of times to watch me wheel-barrowing stuff around and chew for a while. Sally had brought him out some of her cake, but I hadn't seen as much of him since that first time out at California. It was good to catch up with someone I knew. Gelling was on the missing list because him and Chelsy had got it together that night in the loft and now they were a loved-up item who lived in their own private universe, secluded from society.

'There are certain things a man's got to do, Radford. When you get to my age in life you'll know that.' This was how Gelling explained himself, when I mentioned to him that he was a sad loser who never came out anymore. I'd been a catalyst for that liaison, at least, after a fashion (*and* I'd lost some of my electrons too while I was about it).

Luke and I conducted a shouted exchange over the bulkhead – the racket those Land Rovers kick up, shouting is the only way to talk.

What's with that lot, then? I asked him, meaning the drinkers in the Nelson.

Small town mentality, he said. Doesn't take much to earn yourself a reputation in a hole like this.

What reputation?

I don't know Radford, what have you been up to?

It was *you* they were looking at, I said, not me.

Oh? he said, Are you sure? Aren't you the one that broke the heart of the landlord's daughter?

No way, I said, I only went out with her for half an hour. She's tight with Gelling, now. If anything I helped, I was their cupid.

Cupid my fanny, Luke said, She's just on the rebound, it's a textbook case. It'll last five minutes, her and the G-boy.

You reckon? I said.

I've seen it all before, Luke replied, and as if that wasn't bad enough, then you start getting emotional with the rugby captain's chick, giving it the old injured soldier routine, hmm, and picking up more than just a little sympathy.

It was the first time I'd heard talk of this in the public domain. I thought it had passed, I thought I was safe. How could Luke know?

And on top of all that, you're a goddamn *incomer*, he said. Small wonder they're giving you the evil eye, bor.

How d'you know that, Luke? I said.

Know what?

About Zoë.

Who's Zoë's sister, Radford?

I don't know, I said, Who *is* Zoë's sister?

Guess, he said.

I had the blinding flash, and suddenly, in my mind, I could see the resemblance, it was all in their eyes, the same flat blue. Sapphire? I said.

Right first time, Radford, Luke said. She's got a cute little arse, your Zoë, you can't say she hasn't.

She's got a cute little everything except for her fucking boyfriend, I said, But one thing she ain't is my Zoë. D'you know what my problem is out here, Luke?

Yes, he replied.

I lack the local street, I said.

Correct again, Radford, he said, you're on good form.

So why *were* the regulars giving you the look of death, then, I asked.

Changing the subject? Bit of sore spot for you, is she?

She *was* a sore spot all right. But there was no way I was going to give him that, so instead I said, No Luke, I'm just trying to improve my local street. Of you. What's their problem?

Work it out, he said.

Because you torch their cars?

Let them try and prove it, he said. But anyway, it's not that, not really.

What then?

It's resentment for the entrepreneur, is what. Look at the state of them – what are they all, eh, when it comes down to it? I'll tell you what, they're your nine-to-five wage-slaves, chained to the payroll. And what a fucking payroll it is too, sitting on a tractor all day long shaking up a boner you've no use for.

I thought the farming was dead, and the jobs have all been exported to India and South Korea, I said.

Mainly true, you've picked up some village street there Radford. There *is* still some work about, though, but what reward does it bring? A car made in Singapore, bar-b-que briquettes set on the patio, a fortnight in the Costa, a turkey for Christmas, a couple of kids and another on the way. No wonder they fry their brains every night on two gallons of piss. What else is there to live for?

Put like that, I said, nodding.

Zackley, Radford. At least you've lived a bit, shifting round the oval tracks with your dad. He took you along with him, right?

Right, I said. We bumped along. Rough old suspension on these, I said. Luke appeared not to hear. How d'you mean, entrepreneur? I shouted.

I'm a commodity broker, he said.

You mean a dealer, don't you?

Some might say that, Radford, but that would simply illustrate the limitations of their understanding. There are these Spanish fishermen that pull in at California sometimes, I pick up sea bass from them and sell it for a handsome profit at Aylsham barns. I sell mushrooms and all sorts there on a Monday. That's not dealing, that's trading. The way I put it is this: I'm a good middle man – that's the secret to success in the world of commerce.

I bet they *do* know about the torching, I said, even if they can't prove it. I reckon it all stacks up.

Eighty-four other offences to be taken into account, your honour, Luke said.

Yep, that'll be it, I said. They object to your whole lifestyle package. That's what it is.

You might be right again there, he said, cornering on two wheels and laughing.

I held onto the side-bars. Be a bit of a waste to burn this one, I said.

Give me a little credit Radford, please, he said. 'Never trash a Landy, they're way too handy,' that's my motto.

Oh, I said. I was surprised he even had a motto.

Plus which, this one's family, he said.

Whose is it?

My uncle's: he'd kill me if I torched it, even in the name of cinematic art. Though it would look good, like something off MASH.

We drove out in the direction of California. At an intersection beside a big pink-painted pub called the Nelson we turned right. This took us along a road that was new to me, it took us into the country, and it took us directly underneath the wind farm. I leaned out the back of the van, craning my neck. The turbines were much, much bigger than I expected, wider than electricity pylons, taller than the tallest tree. Up close, the blades appeared to turn even more slowly than they did from a distance. I watched their lazy rotation as they receded and disappeared and reappeared as we went through a sequence of bends. A few miles further on we pulled in beside a church opposite a tiny triangle of village green. There was a rowing boat on the green, planted out with flowers. Next to the boat was a sign saying 'Best Kept Village, Silver Medal'. Luke undid a padlock on a strongbox behind the cab and took out a long gun. What was he up to now? What conceptually intact concept were we going to be getting up to by carrying *that* piece with us?

Who we gonna kill, Luke? I said.

It's not 'who', it's 'what', he replied. We're on a mission, he said.

A mission?

A mission. Everyone needs a mission in life, Radford.

He led us across the church yard, along the path between the gravestones, which were covered in moss and leaned at crazy angles. We jumped the back wall, and we made our way through the low grasses and scrub that led up into the dunes beyond. We kept on walking, about a mile, all the way to the lip of the dunes where Luke surveyed the scene before laying himself down in the sand. I followed suit, peering over the top to the sea and the beach. There was nobody there, not a living soul. The tide was going out, a long thin lake had been left behind in a depression in the sand. Next to the thin lake were a couple of upended root sculptures, the remains of ancient trees, gnarled and blackened. I wondered how it was that trees got washed into shore, where they might have come from. As far as I knew, trees didn't grow on beaches. Perhaps they weren't there at all, perhaps they were a mirage, perhaps I was making them up, or maybe they had travelled backwards in time through the seven seas, perhaps they were debris from the forthcoming tsunami, or collateral damage from the hurricane that would sweep America one day. They reminded me of the Statue of Liberty at the end of *Planet of the Apes* (always in the top ten in the Top 50 Film-ending shows), half-dead, half-alive and totally out of place. Further down, to our left, beyond the root sculptures, there was a rectangle fenced off by posts and thin wire. It was to this area that Luke trained his rifle.

What's down there, then? I said.

Look, he said. Look.

He pointed. It took me a while to see that there were many birds skittering about, tip-toeing on the sand. Some were full-grown birds, but most were much cuter. Babies. The babies were so small that they could hide behind some of the larger pebbles; they weaved about like crazy, which should have made them easy to distinguish, but somehow didn't, it just made them blend with the pebbles. Luke handed me the gun so I could get a better view of them through the sight.

See the red dot in the sight? Luke said.

Yes.

Concentrate your focus on that, but keep your other eye open, it's a special trick, the red dot superimposes the image from your free eye into the shooting eye. Makes it a very quick sight.

The birds had white wings with black tips, black heads, and pointed orange beaks.

These are little terns, right? I said.

Affirmative, Radford, he said. Now how's a city slicker like you know that?

I knew it because I'd remembered. I'd remembered him saying to Scanes, about not burning the car out at Yarmouth because that was where the little terns bred, and that he didn't want to disturb their breeding beds. This area was the breeding bed of the little tern. I'd worked it out.

You don't get to where I've got to in life, I said . . .

. . . without knowing a thing or two about the breeding habits of *the little tern*.

We said the last bit in chorus. Will it fire? I said.

The lock's on, he replied. He took the gun back; don't want any little accidents. You see them alright, nice and clear? he said.

Yes.

Of course you did. It's a choice piece of kit, he said, I bought it myself, with my earnings. Spend on the sight, keep your change for the rifle, that's what they used to say, when I was a boy.

Given his concern for the little terns, I wondered why Luke was training a rifle at them at all. Also I wondered why we weren't in Yarmouth, where their breeding beds were supposed to be.

There was a kestrel up there last year, picking them off, Luke explained, so they've moved down here, they've adapted, as nature decrees.

The place the terns had moved to was called Winterton-on-Sea, I'd noted it on an old-fashioned sign with embossed lettering beside the boat with the flowers.

Why do we want to shoot them, Luke? I said.

We don't. It's not them we're after, he said. We're lying in wait, for the predator.

What predator?

The obvious one. Here's the weird thing, Radford – the number of little terns that successfully hatch is well down, year-on-year. But the number of breeding pairs *hasn't* decreased. So what's going on?

Somebody's stealing the eggs?

Good guess, but it's not that. They have rangers and wildlife people patrolling round here on look-out during the hatching season.

What, then?

It's all down to the fox population, that's what, he said. The fox population has increased by *four hundred* per cent recently, he said. Imagine that, they must be all over like a rash.

They *are* all over, I said, I saw one on the roof of a bunga-low on the estate where Gelling lives only the other day, bold as brass he was too, sitting there surveying the scene like he was a track-caller in a gantry. (I'd even texted a picture to Milo, and then I'd got the usual reply saying 'all cool,' so I texted the pic onto Nico to cheer her up.)

The little varmint, Luke said.

I didn't know they could climb like that, I said.

Well, I suppose it was only a bungalow, Luke said, but all the same, foxes, you know, they don't call the bastards cunning for nothing – they get everywhere. They'd find a way to the top of the Empire State Building if there was something in it for 'em. Foxes don't have no rangers or wildlife people looking out for their young, Radford, they absolutely don't need to because they breed like crazy.

Then they're a successful (I searched for the right word) . . . species? I said.

Too successful, Luke replied.

So that's what the gun's for, then? I said. Goodnight Vienna, farewell cruel world for Mr Fox? That's your mission in life?

It's *one* of my missions in life, Radford. That's how I'm lucky, see, I got several missions in life, it's that what keeps me going. This one, it's a mission from God, it surely is, *I'm jest an agent of the Lord, sent down to even up the odds.* He delivered his words in the style of a white trash minister addressing his congregation.

What is it with the little terns, Luke?

I'm on their side, he said.

Why?

Because they're free. You must have thought about what it's like to fly like a bird, surely, Radford. To be your pure self?

Maybe, I said.

Maybe? Have you or not?

Sure, I said.

I hope you have Radford, because a free bird needs others, a flock to fly with.

You mean like me and you?

Perhaps, he said.

But shouldn't foxes have the right to be free too? Where are they, anyway?

Jesus, Radford, he said. Rights? For foxes? And it's not foxes for a start, it's just a single fox – the fox works alone, that's one of his traits, that's one thing that makes God's work tricky and painstaking and worthwhile. You can only pick off the fox one at a time, and you have to wait, because by and large the fox don't clock-on till dusk. The fox ain't no nine-to-fiver. You have to stalk him, you have to be crafty like he is, and patient too, you have to wait, wait, wait – stake him out. You have to know his ways.

Set a thief to catch a thief? I said.

Zackley, he replied.

So we wait, wait, waited. The sky broke up into horizontal ribbons of burnt grey as the light dropped away. We said nothing, and the longer we were silent, the more I listened to the calls of the little terns. The sound they made was an urgent, panicky chirruping that seemed to have no shape or design at first, but after a while I could begin to work out their rhythm, it was like the conversation of bike engines ticking over in the pits, before the race begins, it was the quiet rhythm of quiet work, with little interruptions to the pattern, like when a spanner is dropped. The adult terns flew back and forth to the sea, picking up fish for their babies. We wait, wait, waited some more. To break the monotony I asked Luke one of the questions that had been brewing in my mind: I asked him how long he'd had a gun.

Since my fourteenth birthday, he said.

It was your *birthday present*?

Mmmhmm, he said. Fancy a bit of chag, he said, handing me a stick of gum.

That's pretty young, isn't it, to be given a gun, I said. That's younger than me.

Luke paused, and then he said, Well, how it came about was like this: my dad, he was . . .

He paused again, as if he too was searching for the right word, or as if he was wondering whether to go on with what he was saying.

. . . he was a *chronic* gambler. My mum had already picked him up this rifle – and it's a choice piece, too, incidentally – for *his* birthday. I think she was trying to set him back on the straight and narrow, get him out poaching and hunting, bring a bit of food to the table at least.

Poaching? I said.

Jesus, Radford: shooting rabbits and pheasants and stuff for the big pot.

Okay, I said. (I could picture what he meant, but only because I'd seen it in old films on TCM.) They don't actually have pheasants and stuff in Balham, I said.

Luke made no reply to this, he just kept concentrating on the fenced-off tern's rectangle.

What did he gamble on? I said.

Anything you can think to name, he'd lose on it. Chronic, like I said. He kept it reasonably quiet, he held down work.

What did he do?

He managed a golf course, tended to the greens and so on. Put the flags out. People began cottoning on when he went round collecting for charity, saying my mum was ill with cancer.

And she wasn't?

No way. She was shocked when the neighbours started

asking her how she was feeling, if she was coping all right. My mum worked out what was going on straight off, because she knew, of course. She was already hiding single fivers under each tread of the stair carpet, to protect the family spending. But *I* didn't know, did I? He finally got the sack when they clocked who it was that had been putting his fingers in the clubhouse till.

Was he into the horses?

Horses? Yep, for sure, but I heard it was the dogs that was his big thing. There's greyhound racing over at Yarmouth, did you know that?

No, I said.

That's most likely where your Blue came from. Not that the old man went over there much. He'd have been better off if he had, he'd have got a meal out of it at least – they throw in a chicken-in-a-basket with the admission. No, he spent most of his life cabined-up in the bookies in North Walsham, doing the contents of his wage packet, the collecting box, and the clubhouse till. And after he'd lost all that on the heats and the fixed-odds machines there was the wonder stuff, to try and pull it back – colour of the next car to pass the window, which raindrop would get to the bottom of the pane first, shortest straw. Even the lottery, at odds of fourteen million to one. They never learn, gamblers. Always chasing losses.

Didn't he ever win?

I've heard he did all right at one time, at the beginning; that's when you have beginner's luck, isn't it. I heard he picked up a fair bit on dominoes in the Nelson, I heard it even got so they stopped playing with him. But gamblers don't win

Radford, gamblers only lose, because *brains'll only get you so far, and luck always runs out in the end*.

He said this last as if he was an American cop. Where's that from? I said.

*Thelma and Louise*, he replied. Did you ever see it?

I don't think so, I said. What's it about?

It's choice. It's about these two broads that head off on a road trip because one of them hates her husband on account of him being a boneheaded dip-shit. Brad Pitt's in it, when he was young. One of the broads, the fit one, she takes a liking to him, and he has this neat scene where he teaches her how to stick-up a shop – 'Everyone stay calm and no one gets hurt, y'all have a nice day now,' kind of thing. It's his chat-up line, the way he does it, it's sweet as. The next thing you know, he's got his trigger in her knickers – I think you know what I'm saying, hmm, Radford?

It was nice of him to include me in like that, as if we were all super studs, Luke, Brad Pitt, and myself.

Yeah, girls like that sort of thing, I said, remembering Chelsy and her lust for jailbirds. What happens? I said.

At the end Thelma and Louise, well, they run out of road, they find themselves cornered at the edge of the Grand Canyon by hundreds of cops, a bank of squad cars, a helicopter buzzing them up, the works. They've got two options – either turn themselves in, or launch themselves off.

And? (I was amazed I didn't already know, it sounded a cert for a Top 50 Film-endings show. How had I never seen it?) What happens?

What would you do?

I'd launch, I said. That way you might have a fighting

chance, especially if there's a river in the Grand Canyon. Is there?

I think so, yeah, said Luke.

So do they go for it?

Yep.

What sort of car? I said.

You're a real specialist aren't you, Radford? I almost forgot you were such a pure-bred petrol-head.

Well?

A 1966 Thunderbird convertible.

That's not bad. That's not a bad way to go, I said, if you're faced with the choice like that, that is.

Luke nodded. It has the element of style, he agreed.

Conceptually intact, I said.

Luke smiled.

Does he still live with you now, your dad? I asked.

No.

Why, what happened?

Like I said, my mum had already got him this gun for his birthday (he ran his fingers up and down the barrel), but she hadn't got me *my* present yet – our birthdays are close together, mine's exactly a fortnight after his. So, she's going to go into the city to sort something out for me. She's got herself ready, slipped her finger behind each tread of the stair carpet, but the money's all gone. And she says he knew, too, what it would be for. He knew it wasn't to be touched. So my mum did the only thing she could think of – she gave me what she could: what she'd already got for him.

That's extreme, I said.

It's only a rifle, Radford, not a fucking Uzi. It's normal to keep one of these round here, for ingredients for the big pot. We tend not to use 'em for drive-bys like your homeboys back in Balham.

Luke aimed the rifle around, looking for imaginary crack dealers.

I didn't mean that, I said, I meant your dad stealing from your mum.

Want to know the worst thing? he said. The worst thing is, it was normal. That's why the money was where it was in the first place. I've thought about it. But that particular time, that *was* extreme. He was on a final warning, apparently, and that was his last short straw. My mum would have slung him out anyway, I reckon, if it wasn't for the fact that she never saw him again, after that day.

What? How come?

He bolted of his own accord.

Why? I said. Was he ashamed?

Ashamed? Luke laughed. Gamblers don't have shame, he said, they have blind addiction instead. No, he was in it up to his neck, out of his depth. He was staring out into shit creek, like Thelma and Louise. You remember those Bosnian Units, at the arcade?

Yes, I said.

Well, they're just slaves, that lot, like Mandela's minder said, the fat fucker was right about that. I mean, your regular English nine-to-fiver slurping away in the Nelson, he's a free man in comparison. But think about slaves – what is it that keeps them in slavery?

Fear? I said.

Correct, Radford. Fear is precisely what it is. They're run

by some proper mafia scum, those units, and no mistake, I can tell you that for nothing.

Mafia? You mean the gang-masters?

That's them, he said.

They were often on the local news, the gang-masters. They were supposed to be turning over millions, up to everything, yet when you saw them being collared by some elite squad of MI5 Dibble, they were always being led out of a shanty bungalow in the middle of nowhere in the Fens. The Fens were to the west of East Anglia. I'd never been there and I never wanted to go either; television pictures of the Fens made the village look like Chicago.

So what, your dad got involved with the Bosnian Mafia?

One or two of them started playing golf at the course, trying to integrate with the local community. And he was stupid enough to start playing cards with them (Luke shook his head, like this was totally unbelievable), staking everything he'd got, which was nothing, and everything he hadn't got too, which was even less that that. When I think about it, I don't think the dip-shit even had enough *brains* to *only get him so far*.

And his luck ran out in the end?

You got it, Radford. That's why I stick to entrepreneurial activity, honest graft, supply and demand, market forces. I make my own luck.

I counted on my fingers: You're eighteen now?

Eighteen goin' on fifty, he said. That's what my mum says.

You look after her, then?

Me and my brother, we both turn some over.

Have you seen your dad since all this?

No, he said. Last time was then, four years ago.

D'you think he's still alive?

He twisted from his position, prone in the sand, and looked at me. That is a very serious question, Radford, he said.

Well? I said.

As if I fucking care.

I bet you do care, I said.

He looked at me hard. And I knew what he was thinking: he was thinking that I would know, I would know that somewhere inside a son would obsess about a missing father, whatever sort of loser he was, even if he hated him. It's human nature.

We had to sell up because of him. It was chaos.

I persisted. But d'you think he's still alive?

As far as his debts are concerned and everything, the best answer might be no, in any event, Luke said. He looked at me again. I'm swearing you to secrecy here, Radford. Understand?

I licked my finger. Trust me, I said.

He glanced around, in case anyone should hear; he even checked the sky, as if the terns might be wired for sound. The honest answer is yes, he said. He is still alive. He texts me once in a while. I don't tell no one.

That could just be someone using his phone, though, I said. He might have wagered it, used it as a stake.

Sharp thinking, Luke replied, but I know it's him.

How? I said.

There's a particular word we have, like a code.

Like me and Ray, I thought: Goodnight Vienna, farewell cruel world.

★

Suddenly the pitch of the terns rose. I felt Luke tense up beside me as their singing became ever more urgent and frantic like engines hitting 11,000 revs before tape-up.

And now here he came, deep, dark red, with his tail straight out behind him, slinking along the back of the dune a hundred yards to our north. The breeding terns circled frantically overhead, panic coming off them like steam as they tried to warn their babies who scattered helplessly about below, grounded, exposed, inexperienced, and defenceless. They swarmed up into a flock and, to my amazement, they tried dive-bombing the fox, swooping down on him, aiming their beaks like daggers. But, in his cunning way, the fox disappeared into a hollow. The terns kept up their circling. Then there was silence, just silence, and he broke it by hitting out, flying across the sand like a thoroughbred. Luke put his eye to the sight, pulled the trigger, blew up a storm of sand, and he must have missed because the animal seemed to turn sideways. But it hadn't turned; the bullet had blown it off its feet. It rolled and kicked, tried to rise, then fell back again. It scrabbled madly, attempted to stand once more, but it was no use, its legs just buckled and it lay there twitching and jerking in spasm. Overhead the mother terns were squealing like there was no tomorrow. I looked to them. Had they worked out that the fox had died, that their chicks were safe? Were they celebrating? I couldn't tell; the sound was indistinguishable from the rising terror I heard when they took fright upon first sight of their predator. I asked my dad once if he was ever scared before a race. Every time, he replied, Without the fear, mate, you'd never do it. But you have to put it out of your mind, because you can't allow yourself to think about fear.

I looked at the dead fox, the damp hole in its pelt, the seeping blood, darker than red, like blood is, and I felt sorry for it. I didn't say anything though, because I could hear it already, 'Jesus Radford, law of the jungle, city slicker.'

So instead I said, Nice work, Luke.

One for the money, two for the show, he replied. Not a bad shot, even though I do say so myself. Follow me, he said.

We went over to where the fox lay, about fifty metres from where the shot was fired. Luke knelt down, dipped his finger into the wound and drew a warm cross on my cheek. Then he did the same to himself. I understood without being told; the secret about his dad, my initiation into killing – this mark was the signal that we had become brothers. He took a length of orange nylon twine from his inside pocket and tied the fox's feet together. Then he made a double loop, constructing a strap which he used to sling the animal over his back.

Mission accomplished, he said.

The buildings of Winterton-on-Sea, such as they were, lay at a distance, maybe half a mile away. All the same, we kept to the concealed side of the dunes as we made our way back, as though we were up to something. I wondered why we'd crossed the ground on foot in the first place now, especially since we had a Land Rover available – we could have put the 4x4 to use and driven in much closer. I guessed Luke didn't want to be attracting too much attention to himself by pushing the vehicle into terrain where it would stand out. I didn't know whether it was against the law to shoot a fox, but to me it didn't look too legitimate. He passed me the gun while he stopped to roll a joint. That was probably illegal too, giving a gun to a kid to hold. I aimed it around. The light was going but the sight had night vision; the landscape was spectacular, like film of the moon. I looked at the dead fox hanging like a rucksack from Luke's back. I looked at its dead eye. And then I had a thought.

What about survival of the fittest? I said.

What about *what*?

Well, you know, without you shooting the fox, the terns would have less of a chance to live, wouldn't they?

Nothing gets past you, does it?

But maybe that's how nature means it to be, Luke, maybe it's the destiny of little terns to become extinct, be driven out by foxes and kestrels.

You'd have a point, Luke said, but for the fact that the massive increase in the fox population is *man-made*. *I* may be interfering with nature, perhaps, but everyone interferes with nature, don't they? Like those wasters in Parliament with their hunting ban. If those do-gooders were even remotely politically aware they'd know just how environmentally unsound that fucked-up law actually is. I suppose they think they're being *nice* or something, do they?

He looked at me, as if I might have the answer to this, just because I wasn't long out of Balham, SW12. I shrugged. I had no opinion on the matter.

Being nice, to *foxes*, he said, I ask you. I bet they have a Be Nice to Foxes Day in London, do they, where all the commuters wear little red ribbons and carry banners in support of our furry friends?

I shrugged again. I knew nothing about any of it, except that it certainly wasn't my fault.

D'you know what it tells me, the hunting ban?

No, what?

It tells me that not a single one of those politicians has ever actually met a fox, mano-a-mano. All we're doing here, in actual fact, is providing a check against the imbalance created by government interference in nature.

They *might* have met a fox, I said. You *do* get them in London sometimes, raiding bins in the service bays.

What service bays?

Behind flats. They have service bays, it's where the rubbish goes.

Luke raised an eyebrow at this. Really? he said. Foxes have been sighted scavenging about the bins of central London?

Yes, I said. I'd never seen one myself, but I knew of people who had.

So, even with the situation spreading like that through their own back yard, they *still* put the hunting ban through? Well, well, he said. The problem with them, of course, is that they think that killing animals is *un*natural. Where do they think their fillet-fucking-mignon come from at the Savoy, hmm? That's what I'd like to know. What do they think goes on in an abattoir? Spastics. Come to that, why do you think we have set-aside?

I looked at him blankly. What now? I'd never heard of 'set-aside'.

Overproduction, Radford. The fields *over*-produce, so they have to be laid off, made redundant, *set aside*. That's down to Europe, though, to be fair – Europe is even more backward than London.

Backward? That was a bit much coming from someone

who lived in a village that didn't even have a supermarket. I'd noticed the anti-Europe stickers about, on cars and vans and farm vehicles. There was one on Luke's uncle's Land Rover too. At least there were no anti-London ones; that would have pissed me off, because I still thought of London as my home.

Why is Europe even more backward than London?

The thing about Europe, Radford, is that it's one law for them and another completely different law for us.

Like smoking while serving petrol, I said.

Do they do that?

Sure, I said, I've seen them, in Greece.

Fuck's sake, Luke replied.

All their traffic laws are different to ours, I said. You can ride a 50cc in Europe at any age – on the pavement, or across the market square, or along the back of the beach, anywhere you like – and with no helmet or anything either. They don't even bother with drink-drive.

Hmm, he said, perhaps if they ever bothered with drink-drive that clown might never have mashed Lady Di into the tunnel, eh?

Yeah, I said. What makes you mention that?

Dunno. He pulled on the spliff. Must have been talking about birthdays, he said. It's my mum's birthday, the day she died. I'd got up early to make her breakfast in bed, the full English. But with the news, she got up to eat it. I remember watching it all on telly.

We were on holiday, I said. It was hard to find a newspaper, that's what I remember, the stands were wiped out like they'd been hit by a plague. It was a Mercedes S280.

I somehow thought you might know the model Radford,

Luke said. It was a big deal at the time, wasn't it, the ultimate crash and burn.

It never burnt, I said, it was just an impact smash.

He looked at me. You're right, he said, I could have sworn it burnt. He started counting on his fingers. Two years before my dad left. You know what started him gambling in the first place?

What?

He couldn't meet the repayments on this car he'd bought, to show off to the neighbours.

Wha . . .?

Don't even ask, Radford: it was a fucking Mustang.

We were nearly back. The church yard lay ahead, the brown fields spreading out beyond. I looked at the scene.

Why did the fields overproduce? I said.

Why?

Yes, why?

Because of all the years they've been allowed to spray whatever chemical they wanted on them, that's why. They created mutant crops. I've seen cabbages the size of armchairs out there, you could feed Africa with 'em.

Oh yeah, I said, cabbages the size of armchairs? (Just because we were blood brothers didn't mean I was just going to swallow his every word.) Same as Keeper's Cottage being haunted, I suppose?

Whooo, he went, in the universal language of spook.

Whooo, I replied.

Okay Radford, the haunting business is just a village legend that I made up, I'll give you that. But this is true. I've seen Brussels sprouts the size of cauliflowers. And the government don't just *allow* that, they actively encourage it. Set-aside my arse. The land's dead anyway. They don't mind poisoning and killing land, bor, they only mind killing foxes.

First Gelling, now Luke. It certainly got into them, this chemicals on the land business. The fox was bouncing slightly with Luke's every stride. Maybe shooting one *without* actually hunting it – with men in red coats on horses and a pack of dogs and all, which I'd seen on television (it was the other main local news story, along with the gang-masters) – maybe that *wasn't* illegal.

Luke picked up his thread. Not that all artificial interference in nature is bad mind you, he said, toking heavily. No, he said, you can't say that; what Amanda achieves with her genetically modified skank, well, it practically aspires to the condition of art.

Amanda? I said, And by the way, Luke, where do you get this lingo?

Amanda is my grower, where we stopped off the night I had to nut Mandela's minder, remember?

Yeah, I said. I remembered okay, I remembered seeing him kiss her.

We're on our way there now, incidentally, he said.

He passed me the joint. A while later I felt the full effects of the genetically modified Norfolk Skank. It gave me a bad headache, and that was all. I don't know why they bothered.

What about the lingo?

I keep my ears open, he said, I pick things up. All part of being a middle man.

I glanced at the fox again. I was drawn to it, it was one of those sights that compelled me to keep looking, like a disaster.

Again I felt sorry for it. In fact, I'd come to the conclusion that I was on the opposite side to Luke in the whole business. I was on the side of the fox. I found it easier to empathise with an animal roughly the size and shape of a dog than I did with a load of birds screeching about in the sky.

Luke, I said, it's your manor and you know what's what, but I tell you what I reckon.

What's that then, Radford? What do you reckon?

I reckon the little terns should learn to look after themselves better, I said.

How?

It's asking for trouble, isn't it, breeding out in the open on the sand like that, I said. Why don't they give themselves a bit of height and camouflage in amongst the leaves and stuff and nest in a tree like normal birds? Why don't they think a bit?

Luke started laughing. Think a bit? What are you on, Radford? Have you never heard the expression 'bird brain'? What d'you imagine it means, eh? *Think a bit?* He shook his head. Birds are the same as any other of God's creatures, he said, they don't have thoughts, they only have *instincts*. That's what separates us from the animal kingdom. Now listen, he said, I've got a busy night ahead.

More missions?

Zackley, he said. Are you with me?

Yes, I said.

# 13.

The day had disappeared; it was beyond dusk as Luke slung the fox over the back of the Land Rover. It landed with a dull clump. He padlocked the rifle in the safe box behind the bulkhead, and started the engine up. I sat up front as we drove along, trying to pick out the sails of the wind farm through the screen, but they had vanished into the night. For a second I thought I heard the sound of a crowd cheering, but it was just an illusion caused by the tiny rush of air through the window which had been left ever so slightly down.

Luke turned into the narrow country lanes that led to Amanda's place. As he took a tight bend, the headlights lit on a hedgehog crossing the road. He braked sharply, in order to avoid flattening it. I didn't ask him why – I'd heard enough about nature for one day – but he told me anyway.

It's unsporting, Radford, to run over one like that. Roadkill, he said. And then he looked at me and said, Sorry, I forgot.

He pulled the Land Rover up the long drive, stopping short as we had done before. The mansion seemed even bigger now than when I was last there. This time I followed Luke round the side. He knocked on the door. Amanda opened it, smiled, and beckoned us in.

Would you like some tea, she asked.

Don't mind if I do, Luke said.

Earl Grey? she said, reaching on a shelf for a tea tin. She swivelled back round, Or normal?

Normal.

And for you, young man? she asked.

Normal, please, three sugars, I said. I noticed her look, the look I always got at first for my accent, but she didn't say anything.

She filled a kettle from a tap which was fixed to the wall high over an old cracked sink. She put it to boil on the ring of a Baby Belling, which was set on a worktop next to an Aga. But don't misunderstand – this Aga wasn't the type you find in Bibendum down Fulham Road where Sally and I used to go shopping sometimes when she was out on her fantasy trips for new things for the flat. Whereas the Agas in Bibendum were displayed like Bentleys in HR Owen, this one was an ancient lump with chips knocked out of the enamel and brown vapour trails streaming from the oven doors, a testament to a hundred years of roasting pheasants and rabbits and stuff for the pot, I guessed. I also guessed that the presence of the Baby Belling meant the Aga was kaput.

You could have fitted a whole house into the rest of the kitchen, which was so vast it had an echo. The walls of the room reminded me of these caves we once visited near Toulouse, when my dad had a couple of days off after an International meeting. They had the same glittering condensation and were just the same shade of green, with paint flaking off. The floor was cast from rough, red tiles which were loose and uneven. There was a long rectangular wooden table in the middle with worn benches either side. The room was cold. In fact, it was colder in Amanda's kitchen than it was outdoors.

I sat on one of the long benches. The table top was obliterated by debris. There were used mugs, milk cartons, plates of half-eaten biscuits, crackers, cheese, pieces of old toast, a bread urn, and an ashtray spilling with detritus and paraphernalia. I picked up a disposable lighter and rolled the flint wheel slowly under my thumb. The food and the smoking materials were the smallest part of the mess. The rest of the surface was scattered with charcoal sticks, pastels, tubes of oil paint and acrylics, a bottle of turpentine, a pile of sugar paper, artists' brushes, and more biscuit plates which had been used as mixing palettes. On a flat wicker basket in the middle there was a selection of loaves and rolls piled up, and on pieces of the sugar paper there were many sketches, studies and paintings of the bread. I looked at them closely. Some were really good, life-like.

Amanda wore a long cardigan that came down to her knees. It was held tight at her waist with a belt and had holes in the elbows. She placed a mug of tea in front of me. The mug was blue and cream stripes, with a handle with two finger-holes.

There you are, she said. Would you like something to eat? She picked a packet out of the bread urn. Here, she said, we have this lovely Soreen.

What's Soreen? I said.

Soreen was a thick, beautiful malt loaf full of raisins and sultanas, a shivery bite in a slice. She coated it with butter. It was excellent.

Is this your work, I asked, picking up a drawing.

Yes. Mmmhmm, she said.

It's good, I said.

Thank you, she replied, as she leaned over me to see the picture I was looking at. Her hair was red and smelt of coconut. You can come again, she said.

He's not a bad kid, Luke said to her. He talks funny, but that's only because he's a Cockney. He's even been out hunting with me tonight; if I didn't know better I'd say he was going native.

Well, you've come to a good place for that, darling, Amanda said. I'm sorry, I didn't catch your name, she said.

Tom, I said, Tom Radford.

Amanda, she replied, extending her hand. I shook it. It was warm, but quite rough.

Are we ready to do business, Lady Amanda? Now we've got the formalities out of the way? Luke said.

Excuse us, Tom, Amanda said, Luke and I have a little matter to attend to.


They crossed the kitchen. At the far end, by these wide conservatory windows, Lady Amanda stopped to pull on some boots before she and Luke went to attend to the matter. She'd been barefoot, which impressed me, considering how cold that floor must be. I picked up a stick of charcoal and a piece of paper and I began to draw a profile of an R1200ST, one of my preferred road bikes at the time. My dad had had the previous model. I rode pillion sometimes when he ripped round the south circular. But regarding wheels he always advised: Stick to four, mate. We visited the Speedway museum at Donington once where there was a board with a list of dead riders. There were well over a hundred, and my dad knew a lot of them too. If I ever got involved he wanted me to be safer and smarter than him, and to work for better wages. Some of the older riders, he said, had only got paid in cigarettes when they first started. The plan, should I feel the inclination, was to go rallying, or touring, or F1, or GP. Stick to four, mate.

I was just about to screw up my drawing, which wasn't working out, when I was startled by a man's voice.

Hello Old Boy, it said. What have we here?

I looked up. He was standing to my left, at the head of the table. How he arrived so quietly I just couldn't tell. You'd expect some warning, with the echo in there, but no, nothing. His hair was unkempt, and curled up over the frayed collar of his un-ironed checked shirt. He wore brown corduroy trousers that had clearly never been washed in their entire existence. They were frayed at the hems too, where they gave onto thick grey socks with holes. I supposed it was the socks that had soundproofed his movements. I'd say he was late twenties. In fact, he was about Lady Amanda's age. In all likelihood he was Lady Amanda's husband. Now my heart started to pump a little, and I had to put my thinking cap on, because I could well imagine that Lady Amanda and Luke were getting into one of their genetically modified clinches in the greenhouse at that very moment.

Let me guess, you're with Mister Luke and he's abandoned you, the man said. Am I warm?

Spot on, I replied.

I'm Will, he said, and offered his hand across the table. Tom, I said, accepting it. It was cold and also rough, rougher than Amanda's.

Well, Tom, Will said, lifting a piece of dry toast from the far end of the table and beginning to eat it, it rather looks like we've been left at a loose end, uhuh?

He sniffed at a carton of milk before downing what remained inside. Then he found an apple and he came behind me crunching his teeth into it, a sound I hate.

What's that you're working on there, Old Boy, he said, leaning in much too close to the side of my head to take a better look. He was one of these cases with no concept of personal space. Ah, a lover of the old two wheels are we? You've come to the right place; I'm a bit of a fan myself.

He pronounced fan, 'fen'. Oh, I said, what d'you ride?

Just a 125 now, he said, to get me about. But I'll tell you what, Master Tom, I've got an absolute beauty in the garage. Would you care to take a look?

I hadn't noticed any garage, so I took a gamble that it would be on the other side of the mansion to the greenhouse. Okay, I said.

Will led us out of the kitchen at the opposite end of it to the conservatory windows, where there was a doorway that I hadn't even noticed; it was covered over with a green curtain, which was as good as a camouflage blanket, the way it blended in with the paint-peeling walls. Will held the curtain back slightly. I brushed through. The other side was a dark corridor with large dusty mirrors hanging on the walls, ancient books on tall bookcases, portraits of old people in huge frames, a cat, and a suit of armour at the end. Like the eggs in the display case at Gelling's, I was once more reminded of the British Museum, but a different part of it, the dungeons part, not the natural history. Will caught me staring at the suit of armour.

We keep the dead bodies in there, Old Boy, he said, rapping his knuckles on the visor and calling, Anybody home?

We took a door opposite the suit of armour, which led into another room that was so cavernous it made the kitchen seem small. You could have fitted a swimming pool in it. At the deep end of this room there were more conservatory windows. Here Will pulled on a pair of Dunlop Green Flash tennis shoes that were manky as hell and falling to pieces. He put them on without undoing the laces.

Excuse the old dogs, he said, they're pretty much pooped-out.

He treadled his heels to get his ankles into the pooped-out old dogs as we crossed a lawn to a wide timber shed, which was his garage.

Will fumbled with a combination padlock. There are too many doors in this place to be carrying keys, he said. Don't want to be my own gaoler, uhuh.

He clicked the tumblers into the combination and slipped the hasp.

Inside it was mint. There were two battered sofas and a dartboard for leisure and lounging, but the centrepiece was an old car with an enormous upright grille, bulbous fenders, big windows and deflated white-walls. It was sitting over an inspection pit.

I'd never seen one like it before, it went even further back in time than the plumber's Morris Minor van that knocked about the village. Will said that she was a 180 saloon out of the

1953 vintage. He said that when she was running she had two speeds – slow, and agonisingly slow. He smiled. But speed isn't everything, he said. The dagos used to run the old girls as taxi cabs, he said, and when they thought they were absolute goners – and one can only imagine the state a vehicle must be in for a Sicilian to consider it finished uhuh? – well, *then* they moved them on, over to Africa. And if you were to visit Syria even today, Master Tom, you'd find them *still* in commission, *still* running as taxis. Can you imagine?

I could see what he meant. The lines of the 180 were prehistoric, like a hippopotamus; the drag factor would be unthinkable. But even though the paintwork had died to matt and there was a big dent in the bonnet and two more cats living in comfort on the back seat, it was a really, really beautiful car, one you'd be delighted to own, even in the condition it was in. I peered inside. It was all cracked leather and walnut veneer, a three-pointed star horn-ring identifying the Mercedes marque ran concentric within the steering wheel. It would be a sight to lift the spirits if you were attempting to flag down a yellow light anywhere in the world, but probably even more so in Syria. I imagined taxis were hard to find, out there in the desert.

Are you restoring it? I said.

Uhuh. He smiled again. It's a long project, he said, practically a lifetime's work Master Tom, and we're always fighting the old enemy, time. Time is money, uhuh.

This uhuh was starting to do my head in, though at least he had quit crunching the apple. He'd stood the core up on a workbench where it joined a colonnade of many other cores in various states of bloom, decay and desiccation. He led me round the other side of the 180. Here, strewn amongst a mass of jumble, lay the skeleton of an old BSA Rocket, the absolute beauty he'd mentioned in the first place. She was stripped down and pulled to pieces, the tank was missing, the chain was off, there were fractures of mudguard, bundles of spokes, the valves were on the floor and the block sat on the oily workbench beside a mechanic's vice alongside a selection of rusty tools. What he needed was a proper kit of Snap-On. He needed to upgrade and modernise, I could have told him that for free. I touched the block. I raised the trace of Castrol oil to my nose, a mistake; it put me right back in Lambeth, with the Lions.

What d'you make of her . . .?

To my mind the set-up was beyond a mess, it was a nightmare, the kind of spread where you could see at a glance that certain components had been lost for ever, never to see the light of day again.

. . . Uhuh?

I shuddered. And then I had the thought: what would I normally be doing on a Friday night? Messing about on the ramps on Acre Lane, not killing foxes and talking with a bloke whose voice was so posh I could hardly tell what he was saying. What had happened to my life?

Uhuh?

She'll never run again, Will. That was what I wanted to say. But I felt like he needed a more encouraging response than this, so I pulled myself together and said, You'll get some torque out of that baby, once you're up and running.

Torque? He smiled once more. Yes indeed. Now listen here, he said, I don't want to detain you . . .

No, no problem, I replied, It's a nice set-up you've got here, Will, it's cushty.

Uhuh, he said, cushty, indeed, well put Master Tom, but we should step back inside, see what gifts Mister Luke has procured for Amanda. He can normally be relied on to turn up with something novel, uhuh, uhuh.

Uhuh. It was okay. He might have been some sort of toff, but that didn't mean I didn't like him, and I had worked out what it was, a nervous tic, a punctuation, a similar sound to a laugh, but with more worry in the throat.

We retraced our steps through the enormous hall of the mansion, and it was here that I had my great idea.

Will, I said, this place could seriously do with re-decorating couldn't it?

Uhuh, uhuh, Master Tom, I see you're not one for standing on ceremony, what? But then again, you are *absolutely* right, things have been allowed to slide a little.

I fished out one of Sally's new business cards from the pocket where I kept things, and I handed it to him.

The card read, 'Keeper's Interiors ~ Contemporary Interior Design, Refurbishment & Decoration.'

What's all this? he said.

It's my mum's, I said, It's her business. She's new round here, but she's quality, she has the touch – you could give her a call, she could do you a consultation? I pointed at the bottom line where it said Free Consultations.

Very well, Master Tom, he said. The touch, uhuh? And free consultations, no less. Splendid.

I peered about. Absolutely everything in sight was shabby and dangerous. There were bulbs missing from the chandeliers, lethal-looking cracks in the ceiling, as though it might cave in at any moment, flock wallpaper peeling apart, and the curtains looked as though if you touched them they would disintegrate in your hand. Fixing up this mansion would be a major gig; in fact, it would probably take longer to restore the house than it would to get the 180 and the BSA back on the road together.

I was hopeful. If I could secure this contract for Sally, that would count as looking after her all right.

Just before we stepped back into the kitchen, I remembered about Luke and Lady Amanda and I coughed loudly, in case they had returned, in case there might be anything going on. I could see now that it was the green curtain as well as Will's socks that meant that I never heard him enter in the first place, there being no opening or closing of a door involved.

Luke and Amanda were standing at opposite sides of the table.

Hey, Will, said Luke. What sort of trouble has my boy Radford been getting you into?

Trouble, uhuh? said Will. Not a bit of it; the young master has simply been examining the fleet, he replied, that's all.

Ah, said Luke, he's a regular grease monkey from what I've seen of him. He could help you out there – if you're looking for an apprentice?

Apprentice, indeed, said Will. Uhuh. Now then Mister Luke, what have we here?

I'd forgotten about the fox. But there it was, laid out in the middle of the kitchen table on fresh sheets of newspaper. I looked at it. It gave me the creeps.

Luke apprehended it earlier, said Amanda, while out on a

mission to save the little terns from extinction. Rather beautiful, isn't it? I'm going to take some studies. More Soreen, Tom? she said.

No thanks, I replied. I felt hungry, but I didn't think a fox ought to lie there amongst the biscuits and the pieces of toast and the Soreen. I wouldn't have eaten anything from off of that table once a carcass was part of the mess. I might catch rabies or something. I put my hand in my pocket, feeling for a shivery bite.

Look, said Will, the young master has delivered a business card.

Lady Amanda took it from him. How compelling, she said.

# 14.

We left the mansion. Luke drove off in the direction of Caesar's Palace, for his next mission. It was the night of Red Star's gig at the campsite bar.

Sally had already left a message, asking where I was. I phoned back. To get my defence in first, for being on the road without letting her know what I was up to (again) I told her how I'd carded-up this rich couple, Will and Amanda, who lived at this huge mansion, and how there was this massive restoration job in the offing, which would really bring some money in and help her get a proper foothold in Norfolk society. She said had I got my key, so I said, Yes. After we ended the call Luke said to me that I shouldn't expect too much on the job score.

Why not, I asked.

It's your shabby chic gentry, bor, he said. I doubt they've got two beans to rub together.

You can't live in a house like that and be skint, I said. How would that work?

I don't know how they manage, exactly, said Luke, but the place isn't the state it's in for nothing, is it?

D'you think they *like* living like that, I asked.

Yes and no, he said. The general grime is part of their image, but they'd probably prefer a roof that didn't leak.

Does it leak?

I don't know, he said, but it's bound to, isn't it.

So interior design and decoration might be low down their agenda?

It's possible. Just don't build your mum's hopes up too high, that's all I'm saying.

I changed tack. Lady Amanda seems to like you, I said.

She's alright, Luke said, We go back. I used to do some gardening round there for pin money, when I was a kid.

And her husband's quite friendly too, I replied.

Husband? said Luke.

Mr Will.

Will's her brother, Tom – that's the family pile they live in.

Oh, I said.

He's a bit fucking simple if you ask me. He'll never fix that car, I can guarantee that.

It's the bike that's history, I said, the car's not beyond repair.

Oh, y'really think you could get that motor rolling?

I think so, yeah. Imagine it in concours condition, I said.

It'd be worth some dough, he replied.


We parked up a little distance from the campsite. We jumped the back gate and weaved in and out between the green and cream caravans, making our way towards a low building that was lit up beyond. Luke paused beside one particular caravan and put his finger to his lips. I listened. There was some talk, occasional shouting, and laughing in foreign voices. He squinted through a crack in the curtain, and beckoned me to follow suit.

Inside, the Bosnian Units were set up in pairs either end of a pull-out kitchen table, playing cards and drinking brandy. In the middle of the table was a pile of matches that they were using for counters. We walked on, into territory from which, I suddenly recollected, Luke and Saff had been warned off.

Only playing for matches, I said. I would have thought they were into higher stakes than that.

Those matches will stand in for something else, Luke said, believe me.

Like what? I said.

A woman, a car, a plot of land back in Sarajevo – that sort of stuff, he replied.

A long queue of punters snaked around the front and side of the campsite bar. The building was painted pink with a neon sign over the main door advertising the venue as The Nelson Room at Legends. A much bigger crowd than I would ever have expected had turned up. I followed behind Luke, who was moving up a gear. He approached the place with a swagger, like he was a combination of Brazil, Jay-Z and Robert Plant rolled into one. He was on his way to work. He cased the queue as if he were choosing what to eat from a canteen at a motorway service station, stopping just short of the front. There was nothing to worry about, only the usual two heavy goons on the door trying to impress the girls. He made his way back and started dealing twists of the Norfolk Skank that he'd picked up from Lady Amanda. Having no part to play in this, I sniffed about, seeing what was what, and I found myself round the back of the Nelson Room at Legends where Tucker was dragging a flight case along.

Hey up, Tucker, I said to him.

Awright kid, he replied, give us a hand with this fucker would you? It weighs a ton.

It was a black flight case, and it did weigh a ton too, because it was full of stands and cymbals. Inside, up on the stage, I helped him unload it. The drum kit itself was more or less already in place, he was nearly finished with his preparations. While he went back to the van for some gaffer tape, I set up a couple of stands, tightening the wing nuts and fastening the cymbals down, and I played the hi-hat with the pedal. It was cool; I wished I was musical. Suddenly the front doors flew open and the crowd started steaming in. The first few ran to the stage as though this were going to be a proper gig, like it was the Milton Keynes Bowl where my dad took me once, to see Bon Jovi.

Tucker returned. He scanned the incoming crowd and looked well satisfied. He tried the hi-hat himself, and seeing that I'd taken care of it properly he said that I could be his roadie if I wanted. I asked him what that would involve.

You manage my equipment and requirements, he said. You make sure I can find vegan food at the venue, and you supply me with chicks, weed, crack and speed. He must have seen my face, because he said, It's okay, only joking. It's just the weed and the chicks I need – I cook my own crack and speed.

I asked him what the pay was.

Pay? he said. Young people today, I ask you. Isn't getting to hang with the hippest band on the planet glory enough in itself? It'll be something to tell your grandchildren.

I'm not going to feed my grandchildren on stories, am I Tucker? I said. Hippest band on the planet my arse, I thought. But then I looked back round.

It's gonna be way more rammed in here than I thought it would be, I'll give you that, I said.

We were on the front cover of *Slash!* last week, Tucker said, that's why. We're a Sell Out, kid. We're going on tour. We're the next fucking mahoosive big thing.

I was into the sound of going on tour, it'd be like travelling to race tracks on Wednesday nights. Okay, I said, I'll tell you what – I get to hang about side-stage while you play your set, right?

Top ligging, he said. Pole position.

I'll do it tonight on a trial basis, see how it goes. How's that?

Before he could answer, some of the crowd who'd rushed the stage started calling him. Not the chicks, but a gang of neds – from North Walsham by the look of them – who were noising him up. I looked around and I found the switch that said Safety Curtain. It guillotined the neds as it faded across their greasy hair and pimply faces and disappeared them from view. Tucker nodded at me. We fine-tuned his kit together, experimenting with cushions, his parka, and a sleeping bag in the bass drum. When we were done he did a run-through, knocking out his rolls and paradiddles. I jumped up on an empty flight case behind the PA stack. I'd get a bird's-eye view from there, it would be sweet. I swung my legs against the side of the stack, feeling good.

By the time the gig kicked off, The Nelson Room at Legends was throbbing. Scanes and Rickenbacker Edwards-Moss had emerged from a changing room at the back accompanied by a posse of village groupies. One of these was Chelsy, wearing a 'Grenade' t-shirt. Grenade? H-bomb, more like, stretched across that chest. I had to smile. I didn't know about going like a train –

Gelling had gone all coy on me about that subject: trains were no longer mentioned now they were an item and he had Chelsy's reputation to protect all of a sudden – but still, she seemed to be stopping off at a few stations. Seeing her made me wonder where Gelling was. I slipped off the stack before I was spotted by the groupies and called him. There was no answer, but that was no surprise, the occasions on which he was running both credit and battery simultaneous were few and far between.

From my concealed position I watched as Scanes and Rickenbacker abandoned the girls, took up their stage positions, one-two'd their mics, tested their wah-wah pedals, tuned their guitar strings and, in Scanes' case, threw a couple of rock-god poses. Suddenly an old guy wearing a biker jacket came from nowhere. He gave the band a little pep talk, and cleared them to my side of the stage so that, in a few minutes when he'd got the signal from the monitors man, they could make their big entrance.

Who's doing the curtain? the old guy asked. The band jigged about as if they didn't even hear him. They were full of nerves, they had the fear, they might even be good; their body-English looked up to it.

I put my hand up, to indicate that I knew where the switch was. In my pocket I had just one shivery bite left, which I popped in and sucked slowly.

The old guy ambled out centre and okayed me for the curtain. He took a deep breath and as the house lights cut, he leaned out into the crowd going:

*Ladeezangenlemeennnboyzzangirlzzz,*
*Your favourite sonzzz, my favourite sonzzzz*

*The biggest band on the Planet,*
*I give you, for one night only . . . Red . . . Star . . . Grenade!*

Scanes and Tucker hit the stage as if they were the biggest thing since Snoop. They went at it like there was no tomorrow – feedback flying all over the place, blow-back off the mics, broken strings, broken drumsticks, spitting, glasses and bottles thrown, stage-diving, the lot. One girl even fainted. I handed it to them, much as their brand of retro '70s glam wasn't for me, they were a lot, lot better than I expected. Scanes had a voice like an engine with a badly slipping timing belt, which suited him. He over-hyped the histrionics, he was worse than Bono, but the hardcore at the front seemed to like it well enough, those that weren't already mooning at Rickenbacker Edwards-Moss with his O-so-cool-ever-so-slight hip-dip and his reluctant demeanour behind his shy curtains of hair. In between songs, Scanes hollered *ThangyouveurymuuchsthisnexonescalledLessThanMinimumWage*, or *ThangyouveurymuuchsthisnexonescalledWeShootBurglars*, which went like this:

*We shoot burglars*
*Burgling scum.*
*We shoot burglars*
*where we come from.*

The stage was lit in tungsten light, primitive but effective. I looked out into the crowd, imagining I was hidden behind the light, the absolute reverse of the truth. I could see Luke jump up on the monitors platform at the back of the hall and start fiddling about with a projector. Suddenly I remembered the film, *The Happening*. He must be setting up for a screening. There was a girl beside him, Saff. First Chelsy, now Saff. Zoë must be here somewhere. I searched the crowd for her face. I couldn't see her, though I did see someone I recognised at the side of the hall, which was Ryan. I stepped into the back of the speaker stacks, which vibrated like road drills, to hide myself from him, and to gain a better vantage point. I must be able to spot Zoë by her hair, at least, surely. It was while I was looking for her that this commotion started kicking up, centering round Luke.

I squeezed round the side of the PA so that my head was right in the cone and my eardrum roared. It was difficult to see what was going on at first, but then I caught sight of the tallest Bosnian Unit, the one who had called Luke an 'omosexual'. He was really laying in. I dived into the crowd. Even above the din, I could hear a cheer, as though I must be part of the entertainment. Raised hands cushioned my drop. I rose and started fighting to the back. People were shoving me out of their way, I was hacking them off, obviously, I was a pest, but I was on a mission, and I was not to be stopped. Everybody needs a mission, like Luke said, and I hadn't lost my upper body strength either, from all the pull-ups I'd been doing on that perpendicular branch in Lion Wood. Some of the crowd followed in behind me, into the gap; some because they wanted to get me, others because I was alerting them. I was a live catalyst oxidant to whatever it was that was happening.

The tallest Bosnian Unit and his gang were piling on Luke. Mandela's minder had turned up, waiting to one side, waiting for the moment, for a glimpse of the sweet spot, so he could stick his boot into Luke's teeth, pay-back time for the head-butt.

I launched myself at him, tackling into the back of his knees. The fat fuck collapsed backwards onto me and nearly broke my neck: rugby moves – I just couldn't get one right to save my life. Another shower of stinking, sweating, kicking bodies came in over the top. I was buried, I couldn't breathe, and for a moment I really thought it was Goodnight Vienna Tom Radford, age fifteen, death by asphyxiation. As I suffocated I heard a loud crack, a sound which I thought I recognised. And then I heard another loud crack, a repeat of the sound, and now I *did* recognise it. It was Luke's rifle being fired. Then nothing. This was it. It *was* Goodnight Vienna.

I lay there, certain I was dead, and then a roar broke the silence. It was a roar which was much louder than the gun cracks. The bodies peeled off me one by one, like sections of an orange. I stood up. Everyone was looking in one direction, and I followed their gaze. Plaster dust was falling from the middle of the ceiling. That must be where one of the bullets went. Saff started screaming, and knelt down over Luke, who was on the floor, twitching like a half-dead fox. The two goons from the front door steamed in and stopped Shorty the Bosnian Unit from legging it out of the side fire escape. One pinned him against the wall while the other shouted abuse inches from his face. Onstage, Rickenbacker Edwards-Moss began to thumb his thick, heavy bass strings and to sing, *What the world needs now, is love sweet love, it's the only thing, that there's just too little of,* and then Scanes kicked in on rhythm guitar, and Tucker found a backbeat, and they turned that hippy old anthem into a riot.

Mandela's minder carried Luke outside and lay him on the grass in front of the Nelson Room at Legends. People came from all sides, hassling and crowding him, but Mandela's minder held them at bay. Now I felt I'd been right to believe him, about Mandela. He might have been about to give Luke a good hiding, but once he'd seen that the boy was in some sort of serious trouble his attitude reversed one-eighty. He took control, he had authority. There was a familiar stink in the air but I couldn't quite place it. I looked around, trying to understand what had happened. I must have missed something while I was buried. I looked again. With the exception of Shorty, the Bosnian Units had disappeared. One of the goons was pinning Shorty down on the ground while the other made urgent calls on his phone.

I pushed in towards Luke. Mandela had ripped his shirt up and was using it to bind Luke's side in attempt to staunch the flow. In the sodium light of the neon sign, Luke's blood was even darker than fox-red, it was black. Gelling shoved in behind me.

Gelling! I said.

What happened? he said.

I don't know, I replied, I don't know, I was buried.

I heard there was this van down the road, Gelling said, and that someone torched it.

That was it, that was the familiar stink.

I heard they were blaming Luke, Gelling said.

Who?

The Bosnian Units. It was their van.

It wouldn't be him, I said, he was dealing twists, he was being an entrepreneur. I saw him.

Mandela looked up at me.

Has he been shot? I said.

No, he said, But he's in trouble. This is no place for you boys, he said. Do yourselves a favour, make yourselves scarce.

I looked down, but I didn't move.

Go on, Mandela's minder said, he's in trouble but he'll be all right. He'll be all right.

The way he said it, you knew it wasn't true.

Chelsy showed up, blubbing. It in't right, it in't right, it in't right, she kept saying, over and over. Now she'd seen for herself first-hand what crime scenes are like, it looked like she had gone right off the idea of boys who'd been inside. She blinked at me through her tears, as though I might be able to explain something.

For the first time in his life Gelling seemed at a loss for words. I pushed him towards Chelsy to look after her. He put his arm round her shoulder, and with his free hand he pulled his inhaler out of his pocket, neglecting to twirl it like it was a Colt 45, and took a mighty toke.

Saff tapped me on my back. She was carrying the spool of film, and had the big old camera slung over her shoulder.

Can you take these to Amanda, Tom? she said. She'll know what to do with them, she'll keep them safe.

She handed me the keys to the Land Rover. I know you can drive, she said, I've seen you moving that pick-up about. Please, she said, It's important. I don't want it lost or used against him.

Okay, I said, but I couldn't figure it out; it seemed to me that these items were a matter of the least importance. I thought maybe Saff must be in shock – it was the only explanation – but I was happy to oblige, because there was something in what Mandela was saying, it was worth slinging it. Don't think it hadn't already crossed my mind that my dabs were all over that rifle, from which shots had been fired at a crowded gig, that was still going on, because it had.

So I made my way through the caravans, over to the edge of the campsite. Gelling's story was right. I ran past the burnt-out van, an old Renault Traffic; just round the bend beyond it was the Land Rover. I jumped in through the open back as two police cars went by with their sirens blazing. Then I sparked the ignition and moved off. Half a mile down the road I nearly got hit by an ambulance travelling towards me half on my side. It missed me by millimetres. What were the idiots trying to do, drum up business? And then I realised why. I'd only got side-lights on. Yet I could see where I was going. My eyes must have gone native, like the old boy's.

Over at the mansion, I parked on the gravel drive, walked round to the side door and knocked. Amanda answered, and squinted. She should have been surprised to see me, but she wasn't.

Oh Tom, she said, it's you. Would you like to come in for a cup of tea?

No, it's okay, I said, I've just brought this round, for you to keep safe. Sapphire sent me.

Sapphire?

Luke's girlfriend?

Oh, Saff, she said, and she paused. Luke has a girlfriend? she said.

I'd let it slip accidentally, but who could blame me? I guess she was bound to find out now, one way or another. I was only the messenger. I made no reply to her question. I just stood there until she said quite absently:

Keep it safe? Why, has something happened to Luke?

Something certainly had happened to Luke, but I didn't want to tell her what, and anyway, I didn't know for certain either, so I gave her a version. I told her there'd been a bit of a rumble at this gig.

Red Star Grenade, I said. D'you know them?

Not really, she said. What d'you mean, rumble?

A fight, I said.

Oh, she said.

She looked worried, so I said I didn't think it was more than cuts and bruises. I mean, I think he's all right, he's just . . . is this camera yours Amanda, by the way? I said, as a way of changing the subject, and getting back to the point. I didn't want to talk about it. I suddenly felt totally fazed, and I was completely out of shivery bites.

It's a shared facility, Amanda said. Luke and I have an arrangement, Tom, you see . . . I don't deal much in cash, I negotiate most of my transactions on the system of barter.

And then she giggled slightly. I could see she had been sampling her own Skank. I pictured her at the long table, sketching the loaves and pulling on a little roach like the actresses in the movies that Nico was always watching in the 10$^e$ – always subtitled, always with a sex scene in a bathroom, the sex scene always featuring a crazy gamine with a flat chest and a gap between her two front teeth. I reckon Nico wanted to become one of those actresses.

Are you sure you won't come in for tea, Tom? Amanda said. I looked at her. Her eyes were dreamy, her hair fell onto her shoulders in ringlets and I could see now that she was attractive and handsome and comely but her breasts were too full for my liking. Those films of Nico's, they were absolutely key to my psychology, I can see that now. Because in fact, here was an offer any young man ought to grab with both hands, here was a possibility to have sex with Mrs Robinson, not just a one-year-ahead Chelsy-type, a genuine mature. You might think my imagination was on overtime, that the incident at the Nelson Room at Legends had driven me hyper, that her offer was actually just for Earl Grey or normal tea and a slice of Soreen. But you'd be wrong.

No, I really ought to be getting back, I said.

Oh, she said, if you must. Then I'll have to lock these in the studio, on my own, she said, taking the camera and the film, Only it's rather dark down there.

Where's Will? I said.

In the pub, she said. I'm all alone, Tom.

I looked down there, where she meant, in the garden. I could smell cut grass, the same note as Gelling's lawn. I remembered the herbs of Zoë. I looked at Amanda's hair, I looked at her eyes, I avoided looking at her breasts. I found the courage to say, Okay, I'll, er . . . (I was searching like hell for the neutral word) . . . I'll accompany you down there. No trouble. Least I can do.

'Accompany,' Amanda said. That's excellent, she said, You're a gentleman.

Amanda led me to her studio at the bottom of the garden. What with the glasshouse for her genetically modified dope, Will's timber garage, a wrecked barn with a collapsed-in roof beyond the garage, and this studio, which was a sort of brick-built summer house, the mansion had more outbuildings than it had main building. She unlocked the summer house with a big key from under a brick next to the door. Inside there were drawings and paintings hanging everywhere, there were several easels and plinths, there were half-sculpted lumps of clay, slices of coloured glass, all sorts.

She locked the camera and the film into a heavy green safe, and then she approached me with her hands extended in front of her. She took my hands in hers and held me at arm's length, appraising me from side to side.

Tom, she said, I wonder if you'd sit for me?

Sit? I said.

Model, she said, indicating a couple of life studies pegged up on the wall in smudged charcoal. I know it's a rather sudden invitation, she said, but, well, you have such a complex and interesting form. I really think you might be a subject.

I thought for a second. Outside these walls there were Dibble and ambulances flying up and down like nobody's business. For the next few hours at least, this was a safe place to be. No one would find me here. There was a screen in the corner. She said I could go behind it to change.

Change? I said.

You'll find a dressing gown, there, she said.

What, you want me to take my clothes off?

Yes Tom, she said, it's perfectly normal.

I stepped behind the screen and did as she required. I came back feeling naked even within the towelling robe, and took up a position on a big low box. Amanda came across, removed the dressing gown, and set me in a pose. Now I was naked. My heart was pattering like a little tern, I felt afraid, but Amanda half-hid herself behind one of the easels and she worked quietly, as though she wasn't really looking at me, and the only noise I heard was the scratch of charcoal on paper, and instead of thinking about what had just happened, and things that had happened recently – all the things I didn't want to think about – and instead of feeling my fear, I stared at a damp spot on the wall and thought about nothing instead. I just listened to the rhythm of the scratch of the charcoal and I found it sooth-ing. We were in silence for a long while until she said, You're well-developed across your chest, Tom. Do you work out?

Some, I replied.

Where do you do that? she said, do you have a gym? She moved about, shifting in and out from behind the easel, sud-denly darting her look back and forth between me and the paper.

No, I said, I exercise in the woods.

In the woods? How bucolic – Luke was right, she said, you have gone native. You're rather elegant, she said, stepping back and looking at her work. You remind me of the Luke of a few years ago. Different colouring, of course.

Has he . . . sat for you?

Oh, yes, she said, all my boys sit for me. In fact, given the news you've brought here tonight, this may mark the end of an era.

End of an era?

Yes, but what must happen when one era ends, Tom?

Another begins, I said.

Exactly. It would make a rather felicitous handover, she said. In fact, it would even be conceptually intact.

For the first time in my life I didn't mind the use of the word felicitous. Conceptually intact? Keeping his ears open,

Luke said. Picking things up, he said. He never mentioned a private tutor.

How would it be conceptually intact? I said.

You'd be following a lineage, she replied, an ancestry, a bloodline almost.

She came over, wet her forefinger, and ran it across my cheek. She turned the finger up to show the red trace, the residue of the fox cross, from earlier. I'd forgotten all about that. She took my hand and led me round the easel, to show me the sketch. It was good, realistic, and I said so.

You deserve a reward, she said.

I looked at her. She slid the belt from the long cardigan and removed it; she undid her skirt and let it slip to the floor. It was only now that I noticed she was still barefoot. She asked me to undo the buttons at the back of her blouse, and she let herself out of it. By the time she had removed her bra I was already losing my sperm. She was just in time to take me in her hand. We had sex three times that night, on a battered sofa, in the studio in the brick-built summer house. When I opened my eyes in the morning, Amanda was asleep beside me, covered only by the towelling dressing gown. I walked to a broken mirror in the corner and examined the scratches where she had scored me. Luke was dead, I knew it in my bones.

Amanda woke up, walked to a corner, where she dropped a record onto an ancient record player. Seeing my face, she wrapped the towelling robe around me. *Breakfast in bed, kisses for free, you don't have to say that you love me.*

Afterwards, I wondered how old Amanda was. Too old for me, that was for sure, having Dusty Springfield in her collection. I recognised the song, of course, from Sally's singles. And

I felt strong, to have given pleasure to a woman of such experience. I felt confident. Not only did I feel strong and confident, I think I *was* strong and confident too, though whether it was the right sort of strength and confidence, I don't know.

Amanda turned, began to tidy up, finding her clothes, handing me my own. You ought to be getting home, Tom, she said.

I drove the Land Rover back towards the village, when suddenly it occurred to me that the vehicle might be evidence. There'd be forensics all over it. I didn't know what stains or particles would incriminate me, but there was bound to be something – gunpowder from bullets or some such trace – so I turned round, and drove to California where I rammed it into the dunes. I set it ablaze, ran back to the track, and walked into the main road nice and slow, as if all I could possibly be guilty of was being an itinerant. After a minute or so there was a sequence of loud bangs, the ammunition exploding in the strongbox. Did that mean that it wasn't Luke's gun I'd heard last night, then? Or did it just mean that ammo had been left behind?

I walked along the main road until I felt numb and then I sat on a wall on a corner opposite a big pink-painted pub and stuck my thumb out. You'd be surprised how many people won't stop to pick up a teenage boy in East Anglia. I sat on that corner until my eyelids drooped. Finally a man in a Ford Focus pulled in just beyond me. I ran to the car.

Climb aboard, chief, he said.

A jet of water hit the screen as he used the wiper arm to

indicate with, as we pulled off. He explained that he hadn't got used to the controls because it was just a hire car. He said he'd tried out several new models lately, a Vauxhall, a Kia, a Toyota, but that none of them somehow suited.

What do you usually drive? I asked.

A vintage Talbot Alpine, he replied. But some low-life had taken it and burnt it out, he said.

Oh, I said, that's too bad.

Yes, too bad, indeed, he said. It was a classic, he said, And it belonged to his father before him, it was his pride and joy, he said.

I heard his voice crack as he said this last. I looked at him. He was pretty old, but he was touched with the same thing I'd got. Here's a fact, a fact that you can only ever find out yourself. The fact is this: it will take years for the penny to drop, when your parent dies. After a certain time, maybe once the first anniversary has come and gone, or the second, or the third, you think you're over it. But four or five years later, or even longer than that, you'll begin to realise the truth: that it's only just sinking in.

How long ago did he pass away, I asked him.

Pass away? he said, What a rare expression for a young man to use. Where did you pick that up?

I don't know, I said.

I remembered the seatbelts in the back of the Alpine. But you've got children, I said, haven't you – to keep the . . . (what was I trying to say?) . . . the lineage going?

Lineage? he said. You've got some patter, he said. Yes, they've grown up now, flown the nest. And it's been some time since their granddad died. I talk to him, quite regularly, he said,

He's buried up in the church yard at Winterton. I find it helps.

I nodded.

I'm on my way back from there now, as a matter of fact. It was his favourite place. But enough of this, chief, he said, what brings you out on the California road, looking for a lift at this early hour of the day?

I've been to an all-night beach party, I said.

Have fun?

Yes, I said.

Enjoy yourself while you're young, he said, But watch out with certain people in the village, he said. There are one or two who'll set you on the wrong path. I think you know who I mean.

Thanks, I said, I'll bear it in mind, I said.

He dropped me outside the school gates, exactly opposite where I'd got into his pride and joy at the outset.

# 15.

The Dibble were round at Keeper's Cottage once more, this time in a pair, because I'd been seen getting into the Land Rover with Luke yesterday, hadn't I, by all the nine-to-fivers. I told the coppers my version of events, about watching the terns and going to the gig. Insofar as shooting a fox, eating Soreen, or picking up genetically modified Skank went, I said nothing. None of it was relevant, in my view.

Watching terns? Are you trying to be funny? one of the Dibble said.

No, I replied, They breed in the sand at Winterton. They're under threat from predators, you know, their numbers are right down, I said.

What predators, the other Dibble asked.

Kestrels, I replied.

They just looked at me.

Then they wanted to know where I'd slept. I said on the beach at California. They wanted to know how I'd got there.

Walked, I said.

I'm warning you, son, the first one said.

Warning him about what? said Sally. Is sleeping on a beach a crime?

218

Ask the photographer, if you like, I said. He picked me up from the corner by a big pink pub. I think it was called the Nelson.

Of course, they wanted information about the 'arson attack' on the Renault Traffic.

But I knew nothing about it. Also I had an alibi, didn't I. In fact I had two alibis, Tucker, and the MC guy, who, as it turned out, was Tucker's dad, could both totally rule me out of any involvement because I was tightening wing nuts on cymbal stands and flicking the switch for the safety curtain at the time any arson attack happened.

Cymbal stands?

Yes, hi-hats.

What did you see, the first one asked, when it all kicked off?

Nothing, I replied.

But you were there.

Yes, I already told you, I was helping Tucker with his drums, trying out as a roadie.

So you were there, but you saw nothing? How's that? You weren't curious about all the frenzy kicking off around your friend Luke?

I got buried in the stage diving, I said. I was under a pile of bodies. I thought I was going to die, actually. Is Luke all right? I said.

We ask the questions, they said.

A few days later Sally and I did our traditional thing following a visit from the Dibble. We went shopping. This time we went to auctions, in barns, in another village called Aylsham, the barns where Luke said he took the fish that he bought from the

Spanish fishermen, and the mushrooms. Sally was looking for a gilt mirror. While she was searching about in the furniture barn, I wandered around looking at the livestock, the chickens and ferrets and rabbits in cages. Next to the livestock was the motor auction, and after that the outdoor barn. In the outdoor barn I bid on a mountain bike, it was only ten pounds, an absolute bargain. Back outside I pushed it over to watch the motor auction. At home I stripped it down in the garden, fitted new tyres and tubes, tightened the spokes, soaked the chain in petrol, upgraded the brake blocks, changed the saddle. When I was satisfied it was in running order, I cycled over to Bungay to swim. It seemed a long way, on a bike, but it was nice, the pool was practically empty. Next I cycled up to Lady Amanda's mansion.

Hello, Tom, she said, as she opened the door, would you like tea? Three sugars, isn't it.

We took our mugs down the garden to the studio. She sat me on the plinth while I drank it, and she did a few quick sketches. She'd accidentally given me Earl Grey tea, but I didn't mention it.

She had been very naughty that night, she said. Taking advantage of me like that. She should be ashamed of herself. But she had felt very sad, because of that news I'd told her about Luke and Saff. Not sad for herself, but sad for Saff, she explained. She said it wasn't fair to her, a young girl like that deserved more respect from her boyfriend. She thought Luke was a free agent. It was a terrible thing, what happened to him, Tom, she said, that night; that very same night. She studied my face intensely for a close-up.

I'll miss him, I said. He was a friend.

You will, but you'll always remember him.

I'd rather have the real people than the memories, I said. I'm a magnet for death, I'm a curse, I said.

No darling, you're not, she said. You have love in you, I've felt it. And you're a survivor, I can see it in your eyes. You'll make someone very happy one day, she said.

So, our affair had been a one-off. I was disappointed, but I said to myself it was okay; I was prepared for things to turn out this way. It often happens like that between an older woman and a younger man, I'd seen it many times before, in Nico's films. I'd prepared ulterior motives for my visit to the mansion in anticipation of this turn of events. I had actually come over to remind her about my mum's business card, I said, and there was also something that I wanted to speak to Will about too.

Amanda dismissed me from the sitting, and I went to the garage where I found him lounging on a sofa, eating an apple.

Uhuh, uhuh, he said. To what do we owe this pleasure, Master Tom?

Fixing up the mountain bike had got my juices flowing again. I circled the 180 and dropped a piston into the engine block while telling him about this very exciting Lot that I'd seen at Aylsham auctions: a Mercedes 180, just like his own.

Never, he said, you're pulling my leg.

No I'm not, I said. And there were no bids for it either, Will. It wasn't even near going under the hammer. It's exactly what you need, I said, for breaking for parts. It's got an un-dented bonnet and two good wings just for starters. I checked them out. Solid, they are.

Solid? Indeed. And she's still there? he said.

Yes.

That's champion, he said. We'll soon have the old girl up and running again, uhuh? He stood up and set the apple core in rank with all the rest, and stroked the bonnet of the 180.

We might, I said.

And the BSA too?

Never in a million years, I said.

Will smiled at me. I know that, he replied. And I appreciate your honesty in saying as much, Master Tom.

I taught Will how to get online, at North Walsham library because, of course, he had no computer or broadband, or anything else that connected to the real world within the walls of the mansion. He needed this access because even with a pair of cars to work with there were still parts that were either common, or too far gone to use – discs and springs and gaskets – so we had to buy them new.

I thought about Luke every day, and I remembered his words: you have to be a good middle man. I became a good middle man. I became an agent for the Norfolk Skank. The dope was the one commodity in which Amanda *did* do a cash deal. Sharing her equipment with Luke was only part of the arrangement; theirs was a relationship in which barter had definitely been supplemented by hard cash. Milo knew the people in London and around the international community of skate rats. And so he would come up, to collect. I took a percentage arrangement fee, because I got him a very, very friendly provincial price. They weren't all that sharp with money, Will and Amanda. Some of my percentage I would plough into the 180 myself, because the restored car would 'fetch a princely sum', as Will put it. I negotiated into a quarter of whatever this princely sum turned out to be, as reward for my investment in the project: parts and labour.

Out of all this middle-man activity emerged a bonus; Milo would stay over at Keeper's Cottage once in a while. I never lost him.

Ryan caught wind of the intimacy that had taken place between me and Zoë. He gave me a warning for it behind the changing rooms. He kneed me in the nuts, threatened to kill me, told me I'd never play for the rugby team again, and to keep my sweet talk to myself, because he wouldn't be this soft on me if it happened in future, and you never knew who might be round the next corner.

He tried kneeing me in the nuts one more time but I held him off by his thick neck, scraping the back of his thick head against the wall. I told him I knew some bad boys myself, from down in my project, and to watch out for his own skin. I expected more trouble for that, but it never came.

So how did he catch wind in the first place? It was because Zoë had spread the news, wasn't it, it must have been: there were girls in the village who'd said stuff, I'd heard it. I came to the conclusion that Zoë was the kind of girl who got her kicks from seeing boys fight over her, and so I took to blanking her. Except for on this single occasion when Nico accompanied Milo to the village on one of his business trips. Nico looked a treat, storming about the place wearing a striped jumper, an attitude, and an air of cosmopolitan short-temperedness. She said the countryside up here was totally, *totall-y merde* compared to the beauty of France. But she liked Sally's pick-up, a *chic camion*, according to her. And she loved Blue. Ah, *le lévrier*, she said, *très, très belle*, baby. Apparently greyhounds were regarded as nobility in the part of France where she originally came from. I took her to the bookshop where she purchased the most expensive coffee-table edition she could find – a huge volume of photographs of Parisian dogs. I let the woman who owned the place follow me round, guarding her sable brushes, so that Zoë had to serve as Nico paid for the luxury item with her Platinum card. I may not have been a heroic local mutant like Ryan, but I had enough about me that I could run around the tiny, *provinciale*, totally, *totall-y merde* village with some exotic eye-candy on my arm.

There were matters outstanding. I felt the need to do something. I took some notes out of my building society and bought a bottle of champagne from the twenty-four-hour shop. It wasn't Dom Perignon, but it was Moët & Chandon, the most expensive they stocked. I got Chelsy to serve me, because I was still well under age.

What's the occasion, Radford? she said.

Who needs an occasion? I replied.

Ooh, get you, she said.

We were okay these days, there were no hard feelings between us now that events had happened.

I tucked the Moët into my carrier, checked Zoë was at work in the shop, and cycled over to visit her sister Saff. There was no one at home. Out in the street, the old man with new hips stopped to talk.

Who you after, bor? he said.

When I told him he said that young Sapphire was living in

Lion Wood, in a Commer van. I seen 'em up there, he said, shaking his head. They wunt git no further than Wensday in that old theng, he said. That dog o' yourn still ketching rabbits?

Yes, I said, she caught two last week.

The old man was delighted by this. Cycling, he said, nodding at the bike. That'll keep the hips in good shape, he said. How many gears hes she got?

Fifteen, I said.

He shook his head. Only get one in my day, that was moren enough, he said.

It's a mountain bike, I said.

The old man laughed his head off. There hint no mountains in Norfolk, he said. Not that I know of.

Red Star Grenade were on the road, on tour. The live dates were pre-arranged before the incident of the Nelson Room at Legends, but that was the sort of publicity money can't buy: the gigs had been transferred to bigger venues, I'd already heard that. *We Shoot Burglars* had become a download sensation. *Shooting Stars Rise* was the headline on their second *Slash!* front cover. There were rumours that Scanes was planning a solo career, rumours he no doubt started himself. All this news meant that they'd seriously upgraded the tour bus.

I knocked on the door of the Commer. Saff came out wearing a cardigan with her hair knotted back in a headscarf.

What's this in aid of? she said, when I showed her the bottle.

It's in aid of you, I said.

That's nice Tom, she said, that's thoughtful, she said, and

she pulled out a couple of plastic glasses and we sat outside drinking it. She'd got herself a dog, a little black lurcher.

What's his name, I asked. Is he a he?

Yes. He's called Black, she replied, He's my Black dog.

We sat in silence for a bit and then I asked her a question: Luke *was* your boyfriend, wasn't he Saff?

What? she said.

I mean, he wasn't just a 'friend friend'?

Saff shook her head. Why d'you ask that Tom? she said.

I was just never entirely certain, I said. I mean neither of you ever . . . said as much.

We went through phases, she said, But we always looked out for each other, always, ever since we were little, we've always been together, that was our thing, the way it was. She said that she wished she could look out for him now, but she couldn't anymore, could she?

You went to Amanda's with him, didn't you, that night. To pick up some gear?

Yes, I said. Why?

She wiped away a tear. Scanes said he'd seen them together, she said. Scanes said that they were at it. Did it look like that to you, Tom?

No way, I said.

No way? Are you sure?

Absolutely, I said.

Thanks Tom, she said. And we clinked our plastic glasses together.

In the aftermath of the incident of the Nelson Rooms at Legends it had been the Bosnian Units who picked up all the sympathy. Whoever torched the Renault Traffic was a wanted man, because one of the units was sleeping in it at the time. They took it in shifts, apparently, to guard it from being stolen. It was the only asset they had. He was just sixteen, the dead man, only a bit older than me. They printed his picture in the paper, smiling with his terrible teeth. It was the boy who had said Zdravo and given me the Juicy Fruit, the boy I had raced in the pool at Bungay.

There were calls for a public enquiry into the gang-masters and associated goings-on. For a time, it was Mandela's minder who had the finger pointed at him, but all he was guilty of, in the end, was non-declaration of taxes to do with the letting of caravans, and some irregularities with the sequencing on his poker machines. It was no surprise to me that his arcade was fixed, given that he had a Porsche 911 parked round the back of Caesar's Palace. I'd noted it as I'd been tying to get a signal to call Sally, but I never mentioned it to anyone at the time especially not Luke because:

One: I admired that model, a lot, it was a Top 3 motor for me, and,

Two: I had no desire to roll onto a beach under 325 brake horsepower with the Turbo locked on and Luke complaining about the 'choice fucking clutch'.

By the time the short Bosnian was let off in court with a plea of self-defence and a rap on the knuckles, most people had almost forgotten what had happened. Luke wasn't the sort of victim to attract public support, on the contrary. A cigarette lighter in the design of the cross of the Union Jack was discovered near to the Renault Trafic. It wasn't a Clipper, it wasn't Luke's, but who'd have believed him? The Dibble would have put it into his hand before he knew what was happening, fitted him up. I'd trust them to do that. Several witnesses claimed to have seen him sniffing around the units' caravan. And he'd been spotted outside on the road too, not far from the Renault – he was waiting for Saff to show up with the film of *The Happening*, of course. With his reputation, I reckon he'd have gone down, though, but he died in intensive care instead. There was no gunshot wound. It was a knife blade that had punctured his liver. The sound of the shot being fired was some clown from North Walsham who'd sneaked an air pistol in down the side of his tan elasticated boot and fired it at the ceiling during *We Shoot Burglars,* as his own personal tribute and special effect. The weapon that caused the wound was never found. Once I heard about it I took my own penknife from the pocket where I kept things and looked at it, considering whether or not I should sling it into the sea. I never did.

Notwithstanding his civil crimes, Mandela was granted the freedom of Hemsby (the nearest village to his amusement arcade and caravan site empire), once it was recognised that he had tended to Luke and attempted to give him the kiss of life.

Saff organised a Service of Celebration in the woods. Everyone was there, even Tiffany Gelling. There was so little of her that she could have hidden behind the sapling that Saff planted to remember Luke by. Tiffany sang the Carpenters' song, *Calling Occupants of Interplanetary Craft*, which she said was the recognised anthem of 'World Contact Day'. Afterwards she accepted an After Eight mint from a box which Chelsy had brought along. Gelling told me it was the first time he'd seen her handle chocolate for years. Tiffany Gelling had been Luke's first girl-friend. Gelling told me that too. They were next-door neighbours, he said, before the business with the cancer collection boxes, when his mum had to sell up and move into the smaller house over the other side of the village.

He hated those Bosnians for that, for the gambling, said Gelling.

He blamed his dad at least as much, I said.

Did he?

Yes, I said.

D'you think he did it? Gelling asked.

What, torched their van?

Gelling nodded.

No, I said, he was busy doing other things. (Of course, no one gave him an alibi saying, Oh it couldn't have been Luke because he was selling me a twist at the time.) He wanted to get that film shown, it was part of his night, part of his mission, maybe even the most important part of it. But d'you know what, Gelling?

What?

I think if he'd have lived he'd have copped for it. Everyone was on his case, weren't they. He'd have spent the rest of his days watching the little terns fly free from the window of his cell. It would have been no life for Luke. It would have killed his pure self.

He's had a lucky escape then, Gelling said. That's the way to look at it, eh?

Stick with you, Gelling, I said.

You won't go far wrong, kid, he replied.

★

On a wet Monday afternoon some time after all this, I took Blue for her run in the field behind Lion Wood. She hit a jagged piece of beer bottle that was half-buried in the ground where someone had chucked it, and she slashed a pad. I had to take her to the vet myself, because Sally was out. In the absence of any other adult, I had to sign a consent, in case anything went wrong with the anaesthetic.

Do you *have* to knock her out? I said.

Yes, the vet said, a dog just won't keep still enough to take stitches without sedation.

We picked her up the following morning, dressed and bandaged. She hopped over to the pick-up and I lifted her in: she still seemed a bit drowsy. At first she wouldn't bear weight on the leg, and for her that was the worst thing, having to hop about on three pins. It was only when she *could* put it back down that she really seemed to notice that she was wearing one of those clear plastic lampshades attached to her collar, the ones they fit to prevent them from worrying at the wound. She'd been wearing it all the while, but at first the soreness in her leg was her main problem, and that was all she noticed. Once the soreness had eased she became properly aware of the collar, and she started to attack it, biting at it round the edges until it was shredded.

That was how it was with me. When it came home that other people die too, as well as Ray, the knowledge gave me something new to concentrate on.

Once I'd got Blue settled I returned to the field behind Lion Wood, found the bottle, and dug it out. I held it up to the light and looked at all the jagged edges. It reminded me of Zdravo and his crooked teeth. Somebody ought to make an effort here, I thought. Somebody ought to clean this mess up.

## Another Summer

Soon after Luke, Amanda phoned Sally to arrange a visit to the mansion for a free consultation. They clicked, as I suspected they would, and they agreed on their system of exchange straight away. Part of the fee Sally negotiated for restoring the main hall was to take a selection of Amanda's prints and paintings. They also agreed that once the job was done, Sally would have exclusive rights to use the room for magazine promotion.

With the help of a number of New Norfolk Buddhists she decorated it in the art deco style of the ballroom at Claridge's hotel. They finished the walls in seven coats of silver leaf varnish. It shone like the sea. There was a grand opening. Sally pulled off a coup by getting Robert Plant to come up, and Alice sorted out a photo shoot for a magazine called *Interior Life* – Alice had had a personal conversion and taken a job in PR out at Holt-next-the-sea, which was Knightsbridge for East Anglia. Sally had read Alice's runes for her, and it seemed that it was this that was responsible for the conversion. I don't believe in runes, but for my money I don't think Alice had ever been a real Buddhist, so the stones did no harm that time. She and Girlish split up, but it didn't seem to ruffle his feathers (because it was all written in the runes), and because one day he would be sailing to Kathmandu on that boat.

*Interior Life* ran a six-page spread on the restoration of the

Grand Hall at The Old House, which was the official name of the mansion. It not only kick–started Sally's business, it brought Amanda to the attention of London too, because certain of her works were hung on the walls for the shoot, and certain art dealers noted them. It was a result for them both, and it was a result for me too, because I didn't have to feel the responsibility of looking out for Sally anymore. I'd done that job, and the relief was immense.

I retired from village life as much as I could. I spent the next two years in my room playing computer games, only venturing out to take Blue for walks, and to see Will. I hung with Gelling less and less. We were all right, but the tighter he got with Chelsy, the less he stuck with me, kid. Once I visited the Fens – Will and I went to Kings Lynn speedway, to watch the All Stars, but I didn't enjoy it and I didn't want to go back. In winter I saw the brown fields glitter under the cover of snow, in spring I saw the masts of boats sail across the fields on those hidden rivers, the broads; in summer I saw marquees balloon up for the fêtes where painted eggs and tin whistles were sold, and in autumn I saw bales of hay littering the landscape like giant spools of rope. I saw the seasons change three times in East Anglia, but one thing I never saw was those ten blades of the wind farm all turning together.

When I was eighteen I applied to study at the North London Free, and I was accepted. It was for a Certificate in Futures which sounded a good course in the prospectus.

For my first base back in town I made arrangements with Milo to stay at his place in Crouch End, where he kept a flat. Quite a few faces from the old days passed through, stayed over a night, had a drink, stacked up zeds, but it was only me who Milo trusted with keys. He was careful about that, he'd been turned over once or twice in his early flush. Things had gone missing.

As it turned out, I didn't much care for the course. I could do it, but I was ambivalent. If anybody had asked me to comment on how it was going in Futures I'd do that thing where you hold your hand out flat and horizontal and rock it from side to side a little. *Comme-ci, comme ça*, as Nico would say. She and Milo were on one of their regular trial separations when I arrived, so I saw nothing of her. Her modelling career had gone slightly flat, so she was on the look-out for a recording contract back in France. Also, and recently, she'd been snapped with some French actor, a Johnny Depp-a-like, but according to Milo that was nothing, it was just to pay him back because he'd been seen drinking in Soho with an England under-twenty-one footballer about whom there were always gay rumours.

Are they true rumours, I asked.

Tom, Milo said, Nico's always had a highly developed sense of drama to go with her overactive psychotic imagination, no point denying it. He's hardly even a mate – I just bumped into him, that was all.

And then he squeezed my arse, in a gesture of safe-in-our-own-manliness-un-gayness-ness.

French girls: you want my advice, give 'em a swerve, he said.

Why don't you just kick the whole thing into touch, then, I asked him. Go clean break. You're like a bickering old couple.

That's probably what keeps us together, he said. We understand each other.

I'd overheard them understanding each other in the middle of the night when they stayed up at Keeper's Cottage. It sounded like they understood each other inside out. I guess you couldn't put a price on that.

Milo was still in demand. He had perfected a unique version of a railside ollie, and he was doing good, in negotiations for an endorsement for a PlayStation game, and fully booked for exhibition work and tournaments as well. As a consequence, I was on my own a lot in the one-bed flat in Crouch End. In fact, I got lonely at times. To my surprise, I began to realise that I missed Norfolk and East Anglia; I'd lie on the bed, close my eyes and see the sky burn blue through the red dawn, smell the graphite sea, hear the terns circle overhead. I even counted down to the holidays at Christmas.

There were only twelve contact-hours a week on my course, so there was plenty of free time. I needed focus, to arrange a timetable. First and foremost I required extra cash to pay my way, so I applied for this flexi-time job working in Community Liaison Outreach for this firm called Netto. The work was advertised on the intranet at the North London Free. It was a good number because the experience could feed back into one of the modules on the course.

Community Liaison Outreach involved visiting and listening to elderly people to see what they thought was most needed to upgrade their areas and projects. I had an A-star GCSE in Citizenship & Practice, and a couple of useful AS Credits, plus a clean driving licence. That got me through the interview easy.

The work was a freelance ruse for a licensed government sub-contractor. I was entitled to precisely none of the old-fashioned employee rights that I'd recently been learning about in a taught-elective option in Futures. My contract with Netto was short-term, renewable every six weeks. There was no holiday pay, no pension, and all obligations to do with personal accident, health, and medical cover were down to me to attend to as I saw fit. In short, I was a self-employed unit. I was even supposed to deal with my own income tax liability. Since it was debatable as to whether I had so much as third-party fire-and-theft on the wheels I was using (I was keeping an old VW Golf of Milo's warm, I fixed it up a bit) there was no chance of that. Like most in my position, I simply didn't have the spare cash to attend to these abstract niceties. But that's the way the world shakes up now, the individual is powerless to do anything about it – not under the conditions of single-party politics where collective bargaining under the umbrella of a trade union or other representative group has been consigned to the dustbin of history (this is straight out of a Future Policy Lecture, by the way; we had them once every six weeks, compulsory attendance). Of course it cuts two ways: when we have no sense of a stake in society, it follows that disaffected groups and individuals can easily develop the sense that they are free to opt out, no obligation. We had this idea unpacked in a follow-up group tutorial to the Future Policy Lecture.

But anyway, in truth, the politics of Future Policy aside, paddling my own boat suits me. It's in the blood, I guess. I wasn't tied down, I was out and about, safe on four wheels, hours to suit. I felt like I was drifting, but it was okay. Once I'd done the field work, I wrote up reports on my findings and sometimes I made recommendations. After a few months of the work I could busk it; it was the sort of task I could complete in the canteen of the

North London Free without the background noise even putting me off. There was a girl there that I liked. She was (you guessed it) a slight gamine with an elfin haircut, beautiful, to me. I looked up from my report-writing very frequently, and finally I caught the girl's eye. I went up to the counter and bought her a banana milkshake, and took it over.

What's this? she said.

It's a banana milkshake, I said. I've noticed you drink them.

Oh, you've noticed, have you? she said.

Her name was Naz. She was from Finchley Central, a second-generation Iranian who lived at home. This was a major obstacle because her parents ruled Naz according to a thousand codes and morally un-wonderful ideas. If you boiled these codes and ideas down to their essence, the point was that Naz should only mix with her own. As a consequence she had a great deal to negotiate out in the real world of cross-cultural intercourse at the NLF. She was bright, of course, so she knew this. Her method of coping was to keep the world at bay as much as possible by the specific means of meeting it head-on with a barrage of chatter.

She accepted the banana milkshake; after her first pull through the straw she told me she loved banana milkshake because it was a forbidden drink at home. Once she had made this initial unguarded remark she seldom stopped for breath. She was quietly spoken, but committed; she had a lot to get off her beguiling, flat chest. Her breasts must be a very delicate colour, I thought, as I sat looking at her and listening and stirring sugar into my coffee.

Sugar, she said, shaking her finger. Very bad. And three tubes? *Tut tut tut.*

Why tut tut tut?

Sugar provokes strange rushes. And coffee too! That's even worse. Banana milkshake only gives natural energy, she said.

She let me drive her home, though, even if my veins *were* pumping full of illicit substances. She never let up all the way to Finchley Central.

I began hanging around when I knew her lessons were at an end, parking down from the main gates, and I noticed that she loitered too, casually checking up and down the road to see if I was waiting to give her a lift. It was only a couple of miles to Finchley Central, but when we neared her road we had to park two streets away – no one was to see us because that would be very, very bad, terrible, even worse than sugar in coffee. Still, she was reluctant to step out of the car because that would only break the rhythm of her spiel. I felt as though the real Naz lived somewhere below all her talk about her friends, what she liked to eat, the battlegrounds of clothes, jewellery, television, music and shopping. I felt as though it was all just a device to keep me at a distance. As the lifts grew more regular, I managed the occasional interjection, to ask a question. I learnt two important details.

First, was that her parents would *not not not* approve of her seeing a white boy occidental like me. It wasn't a hard one to guess, but Naz did actually spell it out in triplicate, and she looked sad about it too.

My skin has a little pigment, I said, I've got Polish blood on my dad's side.

I'd learned this on an internet family-tree thing. Ray's great-grandfather was called Radzinski, our surname got changed to Radford somewhere down the line in Manchester.

Pigment?

Yes, pigment, I said. I tan in the sun. I'm not a complete snowflake, I said.

Polish pigment won't be enough, Tom, she said. As a matter of fact, it'll count against you.

How?

Because my parents like to have someone to look down on, and all these Polacks coming over here eating popcorn and working cheap as plumbers and maids are their latest target, she said.

The second thing I learned was that her inverted-snob racist-fascist parents had a boy lined up for her, the son of an honourable family. In fact, if they heard anything of our friendship, they'd ban it.

Hence, I found myself spending Sunday afternoons in a restaurant called the Isfehan run by Naz-relatives down near Paddington. I didn't like the place, I found its ambience claustrophobic, the décor nauseating, the tables too close together, and the food difficult. I tended to stick to Kateh and Joojeh Kababa – rice and chicken kebab. There was sometimes pressure put on me to try other things, but to my palate all the stews tasted much the same, of saffron, which is a flavour I don't like, it's too overpowering and olfactory. The big deal about going down to the Isfehan, the big extra nuisance that came with it, was that with this restaurant being run by relatives I was required to go out with Naz *plus* a group of her Naz-friends and hangers-on, as cover for our delicate situation, in order that I could be just one of the student boys from the NLF, 'the one who only eats rice and kababa, and dresses funny in the suit and the tie', should it ever occur to the restaurant-owning relatives to come over inquisitive and ask trick questions. I didn't even sit next to her.

Couldn't we just go somewhere else?

No, because she'd always gone to Uncle's with her friends on a Sunday, and to change this routine would arouse suspicion. After the thick Iranian coffees, which were excellent – worth a visit on their own, atmosphere and everything else aside – I gave lifts to the friends and hangers-on, dropping them off in various backstreets of Childs Hill and Hendon. Most of them were a geek-posse from Biology. She, too, was in Biology, and was also geeky, in her chatterbox way, but then with her there was the haircut and the gamine-ness to trump the geekiness.

So, we were dating, after a fashion, though it would be fair to say that our intimate moments were few and far between since we hadn't even kissed on the lips yet. It was a small war, but I felt I was winning it by inches – I *had* been allowed to kiss her on both cheeks, and she had hugged me too. She smelled nice, a bit like basil. I could see what an effort it was for her to allow this forbidden intimacy. It meant a lot to me, it was worth something; it was almost foreplay.

Once every three weeks I was required to meet with my betters at Netto. The meetings were the worst part of the job. There was a condescension to the way I was treated, with me being on the short-term, something of the head-pat, but, with complete regularity, a sum of money was transferred into my account at the end of each month. That was the point of it, for me. The point of it for them was to make sure all our business was conducted transparently. The meetings were simply a device designed to keep the big cheeses happy: seeing that everything was properly minuted and accounted for was the clearest way to allow the external government assessors to record the transparency of Netto's transactions. The external government assessors in their turn completed the virtuous circle by reporting back to their validation panels and group committees, thereby ensuring that the wheels of transparency ran as smoothly as a greased bearing.

Netto's offices were by the river near Pimlico. Afterwards, to cleanse myself of their cloying atmosphere, I would often take a journey to nowhere in the pool at Dolphin Square, which was round the corner, and is one of the sweetest in London, set amongst luxury surroundings in the basement of a residential block full of politicians and other stiffs. After that I might take the Tate Boat down to Tate Modern from the Tate Britain jetty. This was how I came to see those Gerhard Richter paintings, *October 18, 1977*, that time when Milo never showed up. It's the date that the small-time terrorist outfit the Baader-Meinhof gang topped themselves in prison in Stuttgart, because they'd heard that the hijacking of a Lufthansa jet by a party of their colleagues had totally failed. The passengers were supposed to be a ransom, bargaining counters to secure the release of the Baader-Meinhof gang. The hijackers were Palestinians, sympathisers, who were overpowered and killed by storm troopers after putting the jet down on a runway in Mogadishu. I read all this in the pamphlet. Young Germans wearing Bedouin headgear, the international symbol of the nomad, massed up at the funeral in Stuttgart. I looked at my watch. Nearly thirty years ago. Hijacking had changed a lot since then. Twenty-six years after her death, a scientist examined gang leader Ulrike Meinhof's brain and decided that she became a terrorist because of an operation she had on it for a tumour that was sparked by some family crisis when she was much younger. You have to admire them, the lab-dwellers. First of all they have the foresight to keep a brain pickled in a jar, then a quarter of a century later they announce that they've made a new discovery from it. Scientists must be the last genuine optimists, people who can explain the world out the way it used to be.

There was something bothering me. Where had I heard of these Baader-Meinhofs before?

Aside from the meetings in Pimlico, my work took me to the fringes of Greater London. That was where the communities in need and the associated projects tended to be located. The centre, as is normal, and as has been the case for ever, was very effectively governed on the simple basis of wealth. We'd had this in Futures too, in a lecture on Haussmannisation, the process by which the streets of Paris were broadened into those wide boulevards (down which I'd skateboarded with Milo and Nico) following the 1848 revolution. This was to prevent the peasants from barricading themselves in alleys, and to allow passage for the army to get in quick, to prevent any more uprisings.

Someone asked why it was that in Futures we were always studying the past.

The tutor just gave a look as if to say, How dim is that question?

Someone else put their hand up and asked why London had never been broadened like Paris.

We simply don't have the history of insurgency, said the tutor, Though we do have the history of governance by wealth.

★

He was right about the last bit. If there was any outreach worker or external validation committee operating round Berkeley Square, Belgravia, or any of the adjoining postcodes, parks or palaces I'd never heard about it. No, my work took me to places most people don't even know exist, and would be hard-pushed to find on a map; places like Burnt Oak, which is in the north-west section near Colindale and Kingsbury, two other suburbs most people have never heard of. Burnt Oak is seven miles from Charing Cross but when you get there you might as well be in a district of California, Norfolk.

Once I arrived in Burnt Oak, I'd meet up with the elderly, who had names like Flo and Den. Nine times out of ten we'd rendezvous at a supermarket cafeteria (Netto's research showed that supermarket canteens were high on the list of preferred meeting points amongst the elderly). We'd arrange our time by email, or phone, Netto supplied all the contact details. This is them, this is how they really talk:

We'll be at the window table at one o'clock, there'll be the two of us and Den is a bit deaf so you'll remember to speak up?

Okay, Flo.

And I walk a bit sideways because of my op, so you can spot us by my stick, it's pink with a green handle, it makes it easier to find in the dark. All right?

Fine, no problem.

And I'd get there and look out for them, him with the hearing aid, her with the customised stick. They came in battalions; the grey demographic was massively unwieldy, as I'd already come to understand. In fact the more I did this work, the more I wondered why I was doing it. People were living for ever now, and they weren't making any money, they were just a drain on resources. I wondered if my reports didn't contribute to something sinister, a scheme for bringing their numbers down so that they could fit tidily within a transparent quota.

I'd arrive a bit early sometimes, and I'd watch them in the car park, all loading convenient food into those thermo-sensitive bags-for-life. I'd observe as they transferred the shopping from the shallow trolleys into shallow cars in washed-out colours – pale green Nissans, lemon Toyotas. I'd observe the struggle to lift the bag-for-life up over the tailgate. They might be sacks of concrete for the effort it took. The well-equipped opted for a hatchback with the slide-out storage tray complete with anchor-straps, which made the job a whole lot easier.

Stupid key, why do they make it so fiddly? It's never worked properly, we've been back and forth but they can never seem to fix it.

This is Flo.

It's a conglomerate now, this supermarket, it said so in *The Advertiser*. That's the word, isn't it, conglomerate. Merged with the Germans. Makes you think. Who won the war anyway, in the end? Well, that question hardly needs answering.

This is also Flo.

Mods, rockers, punks, we had all that to put up with, and now this hip-hop stuff, coming out of the Sky on ten of the channels. Makes you think.

Flo again.

What's that dear? says Den.

It's a never-ending chatter to rival Naz, deaf husband or not.

Hip-hop? he says. Oh, it's not all bad. Did we get washing powder?

You regard them as they reverse out of the space, barely avoiding the trolley port, or sometimes making contact. Most of these pale little cars are equipped with reversing sensors and parking management systems, but it makes no odds. You imagine they might be concentrating solely on the task in hand, on the reversing, on the positioning of the Nissan or Toyota in relation to the actual trolley port itself, whereas, in fact, their minds are elsewhere, rushing back home to the sofa, to the ice-skating, the free dance programme, live from Trondheim, Eurosport 2, a fiver on the Ukrainian, she's improved innumerably recently, a *very* expressive girl, currently in silver medal position. Evens now, but they backed her in the earlier rounds, a bit tastier at fours on the exchanges. Those barrier machines at the entrance and exit can be very problematical as well, the new ones. They're even *more* temperamental than the old type, which is just typical. The ticket-issuing slots don't work half the time, and it takes an age for them to answer the buzzer.

We didn't forget it, did we?

She looks at him, he looks back at her. One of those vaguely bewildered silent exchanges. If there was ever any rancour between them when they were their younger selves it's entirely spent. It doesn't matter whose fault it was, who did the forgetting; it's done, and the only decision to be made is whether to go back in and out again through the One Basket or to leave it until next time.

I make myself useful, offer to see to it for them.

It's better quality in France, washing powder, washes whiter and not to mention how much cheaper, says Flo, as I return with the Daz. April – the daughter-in-law – she picks up a couple of Géant boxes of 'Blanco' for them when she goes over on the boozer cruiser. April has a mobile hairdressers, a thriving little business. It's not so easy for some to get out of the house, Flo says, and I make a note of this. April comes over once a week, it's a chance to catch up. She does Flo a set, free-of-charge, though Flo won't hear of it, says she always slips some folding into April's handbag.

Forgot the Lottery too, says Den, wiping the lenses of his spectacles.

Heaven help us, says Flo.

I don't think Den catches this. I notice he lip-reads quite well, when his glasses are on, and also that he disguises this ability, as far as he's able, by only watching your lips when he thinks you're not looking. He has the hearing aid switched off too, if he's even got a battery in it in the first place. In this way, he not only denies the deafness, he's also sharp enough to mask the compensatory technique. You have to admire the sequence; it's one of nature's generous touches, designed to ease him into the impending void, make him believe he's keeping ahead of the game, while he's still on his feet, that is. It won't be so nice if he finishes up in hospital. I was sent on a Community Liaison Outreach brief on a ward once. He might want to close his eyes as well as switching off the hearing aid then, or give it the old Baader-Meinhof Goodnight Vienna, farewell cruel world, Burnt Oak, and Stuttgart. They shot themselves, with guns that their lawyers smuggled in, so they say.

Lotto, they call it over there, in France, vertical signs they have, not like ours which are horizontal and easier to read. Of course, they call it Lotto here too now as well, but it's still the Lottery, says Flo.

Den goes to the kiosk.

If you didn't do your numbers that would be the week they came up, guaranteed, says Flo, Sod's Law. Yes, she goes over on the coach, April, with her friend, they make a day of it. Parc de Utilitié it's called, thumping great place just off the Périphérique, the ring road, phenomenal traffic.

Citroëns mostly, hydraulic suspension, says Den, returning. Spheres, he says, filled with fluid. Years ahead of their time.

I like Den. In the way of many an old-timer dawdling about in a 1.1 and generally getting in your way, he demonstrates a serviceable grasp of motoring history.

It's a day out for them too, as well as the saving, he says. Mind you, Flo went once and didn't like it.

*Much* too busy, she says.

Then there's the treble translation, into foreign, Kilos and Euros, he says.

And the piped music on top, piping into the whole place, the walkways and elevators as well as the shops, no escape, even in the toilets, though they *are* at least spotless at any rate (which made her wonder if French disinfectant might not be worth a look), still, at least it wasn't hip-hop they were piping in, so that was something, she says.

French hip-hop it would be too, probably. Though that tends, on the whole, to be more *melodic*, Den says.

He's often at the pop stations, says Flo, studying the form.

Back in the maisonette in Ash Close, Den manoeuvres the pale green Mazda onto the hard standing and opens the hatchback with the stupid fiddly key and slides the shopping out on the storage tray while indoors Flo puts the kettle on. Though he stoops a little, he doesn't need your sympathy and is not struggling so don't go feeling sorry for him because it is not required. He told me that himself. By the time he's dunking a digestive into a mug of tea he's already logged-on to biditup.com, checking the offers for Old Freddie, his trombone. He makes a bit of beer money on the auctions. You can still take your unwanted items down to Qwik$ash on the high street, plenty do, and more would if only it weren't for the insulting offers they make. That's what irks. Den's friend, Trevor, was offered thirty-five for his old horn and yet there they are, bold as, well, brass, displaying one in the window, identical, for as good as two hundred pounds. He only just rediscovered the horn in his loft, friend Trevor. He lost the heart for playing after he knocked that man down.

When was that? I ask.

Ooh, let me think, five, six years back. Funny how the unexpected comes along and affects you in ways you could never predict, says Den. Fate, isn't it?

How d'you mean, 'affects you in ways you could never predict?' I say.

Like losing the appetite for blowing a horn, Den says.

Oh, I say.

Poor chap, Den says.

Who dear? Flo says, coming through to offer more tea.

Trevor.

Oh yes, true enough, she says. He's never been the same since he knocked that man over, that speedway bloke.

The bid for Old Freddie is just a few units short of reserve, we discover, as Den fishes a crescent of biscuit out of the mug using the wrong end of a pencil.

Perhaps I could speak to Trevor, I say. He might be helpful: for my research?

He doesn't have a computer, says Den, that's why he was down Qwik$ash in the first place. So I can't give you an email. Here. He pulls a sheet of A4 out of his printer, and with the right end of the pencil he writes an address in a very tidy hand. That's him, he says.

I sit outside in Ash Close, staring at the sheet.

A few days later Flo calls me on my mobile and says she was back at the supermarket and that as they were leaving an old dog crossed in front of the new barrier – which worked trouble free on this occasion, incidentally – head lowered, claggy coat, whiffed a bit, but, the state of the poor animal, she had Den stop the car and slide him in on the luggage rack. She says they've taken him on and will keep him for a few days while they wait to see if anyone claims him. They might put him in the Lost & Found in *The Advertiser*, though she doubts there'll be any takers – no collar. She says also there's been no ticket-checker on the exit box again, and that if there had been he might have been able to look after the animal, or have seen where it came from, if someone abandoned it, like they do. It's no sort of job for a man, mind, she says, ticket-checking, that's probably why they can't find the staff.

I thank Flo for this additional information and wish her luck with the dog, which I get her to describe: it sounds like a small terrier, maybe a bit of Jack Russell in it. I don't suppose they'll have any dog food, but I haven't the heart to phone her back and say as much. They must have some bacon and titbits around the place. Flo's call makes the report easier to write, provides a little colour. I record that:

i) Supermarket could consider stocking mainland (specifically French) washing powder (and disinfectant) as that was a consumer choice the community would welcome, &

ii) Note, re: ticket-checkers/strays: Suggested recommendation: Post could be assessed and upgraded? Perhaps a new Job Outline could be scaled up to include a Security/dog warden element, the higher salary-weighting this would imply might attract more candidates?

That was all I recorded. Not much, but I'd get away with it. I could have added more, but I didn't. I didn't give the writing-up of that particular report my full attention, if I'm honest, because, of course, I had something on my mind. I drove down to the address on the A4 sheet of paper. I sat outside the maisonettes that Trevor lived in. Nelson Court, it was called, near Queens Park. I drove away, and the next day I drove back again, the same the day after that. Eventually I plucked up the courage to ring the bell.

An old man drew the door ajar, just as far as the security chain would allow.

Yes? he said.

What did I hope to say to him? What was I going to accuse him of? Did I imagine he'd recognise me? I said nothing, I stood there in hopeless silence.

It's too soon for the meals on wheels, he said. What do you want?

I had half a mind to say, Sorry, wrong flat, just to leave it.

And then I had the thought. Your friend Den told me you had an instrument for sale, I said, a trumpet.

Den?

From Burnt Oak. Den and Flo, I said.

Oh, Den, he said.

Has it gone? I said.

Gone?

Is it still for sale?

Yes, he replied. Wait there, I'll just go and fetch it.

I looked around. It was the usual shabby council/housing association scheme. No doubt Netto would find me some work round here one day. He returned with a velvet bag. Now I'd mentioned Den and Flo, he felt safe enough to remove the security chain, but he didn't invite me in.

All the slides are good, he said, and there's a spare mouthpiece, though you've probably got your own. I'll throw the bag in.

How much are you asking? I said.

He started at a hundred, we settled on seventy-five.

I took it back to the Golf, and sat examining it, running my fingers over the cold, shining surface and the little hollows and depressions where it had been bumped and dropped.

Just before Trevor returned to his life inside, latched behind the security chain, I'd had another thought.

How is it that you and Den both have these instruments, I asked.

He told me they used to play together in the Salvation Army band, said they did the backing for 'Penny Lane' by the Beatles. Nice day, that was, he said. I pulled the mouthpiece out and squinted through it like down the wrong end of a telescope.

The Salvation Army band. I had turned over the incident of November 2002, Denmark Hill, many times in my mind, lying in my room at Keeper's, listening to souk music from Mozambique, listening to chess grandmasters talk about dominating space, listening to stories about the re-grouping of the Taliban, imagining them with their beards, in the desert. All these years I had wondered about Trevor, the way he stayed beside my dad, and I had worked up a theory that it was a double-bluff, that it was his own guilt that kept him there, that he was the real killer, that the red Corvette was a red herring, like the dreary Fiat Uno that was never found in the Diana crash, as likely to be a cover story for something sinister as it was a figment of the imagination, and that the only concrete fact about these two mythic vehicles was that no one could ever know the truth about either of them. The papers were once again hyperventilating, re-running the conspiracy theories, with the ten-year anniversary just around the corner. Nico had texted me up from the 10ᵉ saying how *totall-y merde* it all was, the hotels fully booked with *le fucking Diana touristes, the merde bastards.*

Come stay tommy, she texted, Pour remember le good old sk8days nic xx

Le good old sk8days.

I tb: Nostalgie – thats even more merde than fate & destiny, tom x

Fate & destiny? she tb, not knowing what the fuck I was on about.

Even if my theory was true, Trevor was dead man walking anyway. I'd seen that now with my own eyes, and precious little comfort there was in it too. At least he'd once played with the

Beatles. Good for him. I flipped the mouthpiece in the air like a coin, caught it and blew through it. It was a bum-awful sound, and suddenly I remembered where I'd heard about Gerhard Richter's Baader-Meinhof gang before. It was at California beach, wasn't it? It was Klaus Toppmöller, his red army, the friend of the family that hanged.

I drive the Golf down to Dolphin Square. I have the urge to take a plunge. The pool is roped out for a laned swimming session. As I stand making a decision about which lane to join – fast, middle, or slow – I notice this permatanned blonde swimming in the middle. Even through the surface of the water you can tell it's permatan (there *is* a difference between skin tanned just by the sun, and skin tanned by a sunbed, a difference that's harder to define in words than it is to recognise by sight). She wears no cap, her shoulder-length hair drags through the water, pulling into tails as she crawls. As she turns I see her blue-tint goggles. I pull my own over my eyes. In addition to being blue-tinted, mine are anti-mist and optically adjusted too (I have a slight astigmatism now, through playing too many computer games).

The blonde wears a mottled pink-and-green flowered costume which somehow serves to accentuate her main feature – her striking litheness. My astigmatism, in conjunction with the distorting effect of the water, almost certainly causes an elongation of her body, but, these considerations notwithstanding, the litheness is undeniable. The costume, despite its design, is properly cut, like a Speedo, not like something for the beach. Additionally, she swims well, grooved into a crawl that's both stylish and effective. The overall impression as she moves through the water is essentially linear, two dimensional. Unlike breaststroke, crawl doesn't reveal the full three-dimensionality of the body shape; breaststroke is virtually designed to draw attention to symmetry: a stylish execution is as harmonious an action as you're likely to see in human activity. A breaststroke that is not fully co-ordinated, on the other hand, is an entirely different proposition. A leg-kick that's out of plane, out of time, out of kilter, and therefore out of synch not only with itself but also with the upper body is distressing. When I find myself in conditions where such anti-athleticism disturbs my eye-line I change lane or re-sequence myself in the lapping order, depending which is the easier, depending on the crowdedness of other lanes.

But, in any event, the lithe blonde is swimming crawl, and isn't in the lane I'm considering either, so breaststroke leg-kicks are not at issue. The middle lane is busy, as ever, over-populated. In the question of lane-selection, the fast lane is comfortable for me, providing there are just ordinary fast swimmers in it.

But that night there was a butterflying Olympian showing off. I watched him for a second as I emerged from the changing rooms, suppressing my hostility, as far as you *can* suppress hostility when you're only one garment removed from being naked and there are things on your mind: I took the only effective action available to me when I pulled my goggles over my eyes. Headlights crowding into your rear-view mirror when you're already travelling at a hundred miles an hour down the autoroute tend to put your back up – *Vite, vite, out of my way Rosbif* – and butterflying Olympians in public pools have the same effect. If you want to swim butterfly, the pool is open early in the morning for the purpose, the evening lane-swimming session is the wrong window of opportunity.

So, it's as a consequence of circumstances that I select the slow lane, which I have to share with two slow swimmers. Calculating the moment of entry is critical. I step up to the edge, clench my toes into the serrated tile, and wait for the slow swimmers to return to my end before making the dive – *encore une fois, encore une fois* – so I have a clear full length-and-three-quarters ahead of me on entry. I gain on the slow swimmers immediately, but by utilising a mid-length turning strategy I keep clear water in sight and them behind. Even at this I'm still lapping at well under my ideal pace, but when the middle lane is over-congested and the fast lane features the Olympian, it's the best compromise. One slow swimmer leaves the pool. I shift up half a gear. The remaining slow swimmer follows the first one. Suddenly I'm in the slow lane alone, free to swim my natural rhythm. I keep to a low breaststroke, so as not to draw attention to a situation that can't last for long. It isn't the prospect of new slow swimmers joining that concerns me – they tend to be timid in these situations and are likely to sit it out on the side for a while, waiting for a change in conditions. Five minutes isn't much to a slow swimmer, it's probably seventy-five metres. Whereas to me it's two hundred and fifty metres, fourteen per cent of an old metric mile, one-sixth of a reasonable target distance. Calculating percentages and converting to imperial fractions isn't right, multiplying by 0.9, then shifting back to decimals; it's a skewed way of thinking, pointless, but then Dolphin Square is an old pool, twenty yards long, so it has to be done.

So, I keep to the low breaststroke, not to disguise myself from slow swimmers, but to disguise myself from other fast swimmers with the same idea as me. It's by adopting this tactic that the lithe blonde really focuses up in my waterfield. I observe her sidelong each time we pass, like a shoaling seal. And then *she* performs a mid-length turn and slips under the lane divider, joining a full length ahead of me and maintains the gap for ten lengths, two hundred yards, one hundred and eighty metres, one eighth of a reasonable target distance. The lithe blonde turns out to be the first fast swimmer with the same idea as me. So now we're speeding together in the slow lane, swimming in a formation that any cyclist would recognise as a pursuit. We remain at a constant distance for another ten minutes, during which time I lose count of where I am, Trevor, Toppmöller, the hanging man, the Taliban, the red Corvette, everything sliding from my retinal image, my mind emptying. I let her stop first. I do two more then I pull up beside her. She already has her goggles hanging loose round her neck. I drag mine on top of my head, hold onto the gully and lean backwards, stretching. I glance at her. The etiquette in pools is not to take it any further than the single glance. She glances back at precisely the same moment. It's like crossing in the corridors, after the rugby match in the sleet, after the kiss under the fire escape, before events took over.

Zoë?

Tom? Tom Radford? she says. Fancy.

Fancy. Indeed, I say.

*Tom Radford*, she says. She takes a mouthful of water and spits it. What on earth brings you here?

Circumstances. And you?

My career. I'm a PA, for an MP; he lives here. She nods her head back, to indicate the floors above.

I watch her haul herself up onto the edge and turn to sit. Luke was spot on, it's a cute arse all right.

I wait for her outside the changing rooms, watching past the cashier where two men are scraping themselves off a squash court. She emerges from her door playing with her hair, looks me up and down. Christ on a bike, she says.

What?

What you're wearing.

It's only a suit, I say.

It's a dark suit and this – she leans forward and feels it between her fingers – correct me if I'm wrong, but is this your own tie?

Luke's mum wanted me to have it, as a memento. She said that he'd 'spoke well of me to her, and to his brother too, he'd said that I was okay, a grafter'. I suppose if we'd never gone up to Norfolk I might still be hanging in a Hoax zip-up, that in fact my whole life would be different. It's my turn to lean forward to her.

Zoë, correct me if I'm wrong, and beautiful as it may be, but is that your own skin?

What?

It used to be creamy, like milk.

I quit working at the bookshop, remember, and started working at Solar Lab instead.

Oh yes. Why was that? For more money?

In a way. Once Luke was gone, there was no demand for all the tubes of paint I used to slip him out the back. I lost my bit of side-interest.

I watch her fiddle the damp blonde tails into a hair band.

Tubes of paint out the back. For Lady Amanda. He was the middle man's middle man all right. If there was a Middle Man of the Year Award, he could have dominated it for an era, like Tony Rickardsson in the World Championships, or Lance Armstrong in the Tour.

Didn't the woman who owned the shop notice her stock disappearing? I say.

She blamed it on the likes of you, Tom Radford. You were my favourite decoy, being such a thieving Cockney incomer.

I never touched a thing, I say.

Almost not, she says, fiddling her hair some more, and treating me to her knowing Zoë smile.

Tom, she says, are you driving? Have you got a car?

Yes. Why?

I've got this literally really, really heavy bag of stuff and a computer to take back up to Norfolk. I don't suppose you're going up at all, are you? she says. And then does this coquettish thing.

I wait outside Dolphin Square as Zoë brings the literally really heavy bag of stuff and the computer down in the lift, gets the Dolphin Square concierge to bring it to the doors and me to load it in the hatchback while she tells me what a star I am.

We stop and pick up Juicy Fruit, Vimto, the *Evening Standard*, and cigarettes. I take the scenic route to the M11: round the Victoria one-way system, up the back of Buckingham Palace, Hyde Park Corner, Park Lane – where I hang a right to deliberately pass Claridge's – my mum used to work there, I say, and I imagine the Royal stragglers in their Royal clothes falling out into the night, tipsy, like any other guests at any other wedding,

and a fleet of Daimlers standing waiting, with chauffeurs leaning their elbows on the roofs, smoking cigarettes. Along
Mortimer Street, up Tottenham Court Road, through Regent's
Park – where I intend to live one day, in a house in a crescent,
with a wrought-iron balcony and tall windows like we used to
have in Streatham Mansions – on to Camden Town, across
Holloway Road, alongside Finsbury Park, where a Staffordshire
Bull terrier halts the traffic to allow his master to cross, usher-
ing the messed-up hobo to safety on the other side.

Did you see that dog, Zoë?

What dog? she says, chewing and texting.

We pass through the outlying areas, the ghettos where
Netto sends Outreach Units like me, Seven Sisters, Manor
House, Tottenham, Walthamstow – my dad used to race there,
I say, pointing to where the stadium used to be – until finally
the tyres perform their percussive scroll over the cattle gate at
the top of the hill and the road opens out into six carriageways,
all directions home, and the orange oxide lights overhead spit
into life as evening begins to fall.

Zoë continues to chew and to text and to say nothing.
Landing gear swings out of the undercarriage as a jet glides into
Stansted. Still she says nothing, still she keeps chewing, still she
keeps texting. We stop at a deserted service station where I fill
an espresso with tubes of brown sugar and still she says nothing.
We drive through the forest at Thetford and out the other side
where the trees cower low like an African prairie. A deer dives
across the road just in time for us to miss clipping it. Did you
see that?

See what? she says.

Under the permatan her skin remains lightly pockmarked,

the old braille the same. How's Ryan? I say. Is he still your main squeeze?

Ancient history, babe, she says.

So. The MP?

Tom! she says. What happened to the shy boy under the fire escape?

The one you invited to touch you?

Him, the one who told me he loved me, in French.

No, the one who told you what the French words for 'I love you' are, Zoë. When you asked him. Which is quite different. Quite different to the story you put about.

Who says I put a story about?

Who else could it have been?

She says nothing and returns to her chewing and her texting. There's a new by-pass round the big ole city of Norridge, bor, a new roundabout where I put in some very bad cornering to shake her up. I take a certain satisfaction from the sudden fear I see flash across her face as I drop a gear and floor the accelerator. Fasten yourself in, it's going to be a bumpy ride.

How's Saff, I ask.

Off on a project, she says.

What project?

In Asia. Planting trees.

Not with Scanes? (I thought I'd seen something in the papers about him doing that.)

No, she says, with Edwards–Moss.

Well that's something, at least. Sooner than expected we are nearing the village. Outside her mum's old house, I let Zoë take care of her own literally heavy, heavy bag and computer equipment and when she's all done I slam down the hatchback.

Want my advice, I say, turn down the setting on the sunbed Zoë. You're asking for cancer.

Sally is opening the door before I even turn off the ignition. Baby, she says, crunching the gravel, rushing at me and smothering me with her kisses and hugs.

Inside Keeper's Cottage I shake the hand of Girlish, who has made himself a permanent feature. What can I say? I got Tyler Hamilton himself to come up from Devon, more than once, but even he couldn't shift him.

Tea? he says, even though he knows I'm a coffee drinker.

Sure, I say. Thanks.

He brings it in a pot, with a strainer, and soya milk. I don't know what kind of infusion it's supposed to be, it's the colour of piss and smells like a fart. Mixing it in my mouth with the residual tang of Juicy Fruit and Marlboro, it kicks off just about the most repulsive collision of flavours in history.

What a lovely surprise, Sally says. What brings you up, honey?

I bumped into Zoë.

What, Saff's Zoë?

Yes.

Dear Saff, Sally says, hugging me again. I haven't seen her for ages.

No, I think she went travelling, with Rickenbacker.

Oh yes, she says, that's right. So did you drop Zoë off at their old place?

Yes. She needed a lift; she needed a lift, so I took the opportunity to see my mum, and to see you too, old girl: Blue has picked herself up out of her basket and come to nuzzle and say zdravo.

I wake in my old room, late, having dreamt of Gary Kasparov. I press the button on the Galaxy and watch the planets and the UFOs turn. I pull the curtains back. Outside there's a huge Norfolk sky. I take Blue out to Lion Wood; it seems small to me now. She sits and watches as I swing on the rope swing, sits and watches as I do ten pull-ups on the perpendicular branch. I have to curl my knees back underneath myself; it's not as high as I remember. In the fields behind Lion Wood, I can't even provoke Blue into a race. She's getting old.

Later in the afternoon I drive up to The Old House, which I find obscured and obliterated by a skeleton of scaffolding.

Uhuh, Master Tom, says Will, treadling into his indestructible pooped-out old dogs as he comes out to greet. Would you like an apple?

Thanks, I reply. What's with all this? I say, pointing at the scaffolding.

The roof, Master Tom, he says. Leaks like a colander, always has. And now there's this enormous delay of the old enemy, time, uhuh, because they've found these blasted murals on the walls, under the plasterwork in the loft space.

And?

The heritage people want to investigate before we can continue, damn their eyes. They have the law on their side, full rights of trespass, to carbon-date the ink and throw me into the workhouse: the scaffold firm say it'll cost more to take it down and re-assemble it than to leave it up even though it won't see use for *months*. Every minute of every day it costs money. It's a ruination.

Where's Lady Amanda?

She's up there sketching, copying the bloody mural things for her new show.

But that'll bring some in?

Only if she gets the red dots.

The red dots?

You know the drill when a painting's sold, Master Tom: they stick a red dot beside it.

Ah yes. Red dots, same as you get in the sight for shooting at foxes: one for the money, two for the show.

So: you're broke then?

Flat out. My tab at the Nelson is a shocker, he says, shaking dust from the pockets of the rancid corduroys to mime the peril of the situation. Perish the thought, he says, but I think they might really be about to call it in.

Then the time is now, surely. How are we getting on? I say. On the other thing?

That's the one piece of good news, he says. Uhuh.

I feared the worst, because I'd left a sum of cash with Will, for a specific purpose, and in the current climate I reckon there must be every chance it's been swallowed.

Not at all, Master Tom, he says. You left that money in good faith.


I follow him into the timber garage, my old second home, away from everything, where I spent many hours in the inspection pit and under the bonnet when I wasn't ruining my eyesight playing computer games, slashing the tyres of any red Corvette I ever saw, or cycling over to the pool at Bungay to empty my mind. We had her in running order more than a year back, took her on a maiden voyage from The Old House to North Walsham and along the coast road via California. She ran as sweet as a nut, though she wasn't wearing her finest.

Will rolls the tumblers on the combination lock, and pulls the doors wide. There, he says, what d'you make of that, then?

The one job that was beyond us was to give her the re-spray she deserved, none of your everyday two-part: Will has finally had her finished in old-fashioned cellulose paint, by a specialist in Winterton-on-Sea, at a discount, when he could fit us in. I serviced a bike for him ages back, to help oil the wheels of the deal. I do a circuit, and then I open the driver's door. The sills have been flashed in too. It's a proper job.

That's a sight for sore eyes, Will. She'll fetch a pretty penny all right.

Over to you, Master Tom, he says. Over to you.

Inside, the 180 smells of leather and overalls. I pull up round the front of the house, leave the engine ticking over. Lady Amanda emerges from the shadows of the scaffolding, pink, and glowing.

Tom! she says, My, how you've grown, darling (kiss on each cheek), now . . . where are you going to take that?

To fetch a pretty penny, I say.

Down south?

There's funny money in the capital, Amanda, you know that; I've seen your work in that gallery – they stick an extra nought on those prices, don't they?

Yes, she says, but the commission they take is more than enough. The early ones your mother has are becoming collectable, by the way, she does know that?

I'll make sure she does, if not. But it's not just funny money, there's funny goings-on in the capital too, Amanda. How did Luke's film find its way out of your safe and into the Tate? I hand her the catalogue.

We were having a clear-out and one of my curators came across it and drew it to the attention of Damien. *Crush Dates*? she says looking at the catalogue. Is that what the show's called?

Mmmhmm, the theme is the calendar and death and stuff, I say.

She flicks the pages, pausing at the plates that show the stills from *The Happening, California, February 2004*. 'California,' she says, Priceless. What was that band called, Tom, the one you went to see when you brought it round that night.

Red Star Grenade.

Did they do well? Should I really have heard of them?

No not really, they were small-town wonders, Amanda.

As I climb in behind the wheel she stops at a further set of plates. Did you see these Richters, she says, while you were down there?

Yes. They're very realistic, in an obscure way. They remind me of your work.

This portrait of Ulrike Meinhof looks so like you, she says, comparing it side-by-side with my face. Now you've grown your hair. It's uncanny. What's it called, she says, holding it at arm's length, I can't read type at this size.

It's called *Youth Portrait, 1988*. It's a picture of a girl, by the way – I'm not flattered, Lady Amanda.

It's a picture of a very intense face, she says. It's a face on a mission.

It was a face on the wrong sort of mission though; bombing ze departmental stores, and ze people in them.

Yes, they were rather naughty, weren't they? Why did they behave like that?

I've read all the blurb twice Amanda, and I don't even think they knew why themselves. For the same reason Luke was pissed-off, maybe. Because they were mad with their fathers and their forefathers, because older people had let them down.

For the same reason you used to slash tyres on red Corvettes, Tom? She gave me a look.

Maybe, I say. And eighty-four Ford Mustangs to be taken into account too.

Yes, not forgetting the odd Nissan Z, so I've been told.

Oh?

Will always got a kick out of your stories. 'Master Tom's tales', he called them. But look what you've achieved here, darling, she says, patting the bonnet. It's a work of art. Enjoy it for a little while, at least, before you make your pretty pennies.


Back at Keeper's, Sally says, Off? So soon? Why not stay on for the weekend?

I have stuff to do in town Mum, but I won't be long. I'll be back. Got something to show you. Come and see this.

Swoon, she says, surveying the Merc. You've really done it there. It's practically concours.

Yep, I say.

Girlish steps out, getting gravel caught between his big bare toes. As a Buddhist, it goes without saying that he's opposed in principle to the internal combustion engine. He nods a big fat irritating guru-nod of pseudo-approval, in some hopeless effort to be stepfatherish.

Drive carefully Tom, he says. Look after yourself.

As I push out through the village, Zoë crosses the road from Solar Lab to the Nelson. She pauses just long enough to see who's driving the rare machine. I pause just long enough to consider giving her a lift back to the MP, her lover, in order that Gelling won't have to put up with her chewing and her texting; inside the Nelson I can see my old friend puffing out his enormous cheeks while pulling a pint of Razor as Chelsy cleans the butts out of an ashtray with a decorator's paint-brush.

I put my foot down, bring her up to a speed approaching agonisingly slow, and note a strange vision in the rear-view mirror: ten sails of a wind farm all rotating at the same time, a world first. And then I see something else almost equally strange. Blue, rising up off the back seat. She must have jumped in while I went inside to pick up my bag.

Down the M11, out through the wide African Prairie, into the corridor of Thetford Forest. The handling's not the greatest, but the ride is superb, and the view from the driving seat is excellent, fit for a king. At the deserted service station we fill up, and on the shelves I find a loaf of Soreen to keep us going. Through the window of the pay station two truckers in baseball caps circle the 180, admiring her lines.

I pull us up in the street two streets away from Naz's and text her to come outside. She runs down the road wearing fluffy slippers with gonks on top.

Tom, what's up? she says, stepping inside. First I don't see you for days, now you're here at all hours texting me at home. Has somebody died?

Come away with me Naz.

Away? Tom are you insane, don't say this to me. My brother will kill you, and what about all my friends? I have nothing to wear. Away? What do you mean, away? Where's your proper car, anyway?

She looks around, suspiciously.

How far will we get in this thing, Tom – Hendon Central?

The car's sound Naz, I fixed it up myself.

Jesus, she says, laughing. Why on earth would you do that? Look, she says casting her arms around, it's *ancient*. Things aren't even made properly. What's this? she says, touching the walnut dash. *Wood?* Wood will fall apart. What sort of a car is it, anyway?

It's a Mercedes.

No, no, no, she says, It's not a Mercedes. My uncle has a Mercedes. It's not like this.

It's a vintage Mercedes.

I like modern cars. You know the car I like best?

The Mini One Convertible?

Tom, how did you know that?

It's the car all girls like best, Naz.

Blue rises from the back seat. Naz catches the movement in the corner of her eye and screams.

A dog! You've brought me in here with a dog?

She practically springs out and bangs the door. I lean across and turn the handle. After the Greek jeep and the Alpine, this is only the third car I've been in without electric windows. Don't you like dogs, Naz? I ask her.

267

No, she says, They're nasty, dirty animals, urgh! I can't believe you expect me to run away with you in *this* car and with a *dog* too. I thought you were intelligent, Tom.

We take the M2 down to Dover, to cross the channel. It seems cruel, but I hide Blue in the boot, because I have no dog passport for her, though the boot *is* extraordinarily capacious, built to take a lot of monogrammed leather luggage. Once or twice I slip down to the vehicle deck to check she's all right but I don't linger, because of all the places I don't want to die the terror of the cold, black sea rushing into the car deck of a ferry is my second-last choice.

The tang of landed fish and rotten drains is in the air as we disembark. We drive through the city of containers where I pull up, to release Blue. I give her a drink of mineral water from my bottle. On the autoroute south we travel in a pocket of curious Frenchmen and other Europeans. I read the registration plates, they're from all over. Many slow down to take a look at the car and some give us the thumbs up and the O sign, because even those who start by trying to shove us out of the way by flashing their lights in disgust at our two available speeds of slow and agonisingly slow, and wave baguettes like there's no tomorrow, take a different view when they realise they are in company with a thing of beauty, a work of art, a concours.

I follow signs to the Périphérique. Phenomenal traffic, just as Den had said, Citroëns mostly, but many Renaults as well, even Renault 4s like Dad taught me to drive in. The old girl doesn't take kindly to sweating it out in traffic. The temperature gauge rises to red. Perhaps the fan has cut out? I flick the switch for the cabin heater, and slide the control to Max, to help cool the radiator. The night is warm enough and sticky too, and the blast of hot air does me no good, nor Blue, so I take the first turn off the Périphérique, out of the phenomenal traffic and into some tight cobbled streets lined with dustbins and vegetables rolling along the ground, streets that Haussmann must have missed, but the suspension doesn't complain (we spent well on the springs). Eventually we squeeze out of it into a wide boulevard which is very empty, except for the four corners of the first junction, and the four corners of each and every junction thereafter, where four Gendarmes stand blasting on whistles, like in the old films I've watched with Sally on TCM. It's impossible for me to take them seriously or even imagine that their peeps are meant for me, so I keep on going, enjoying all the amazing space, and I even crank the old girl up a bit, and see 55mph on the speedo as the temperature falls back, as air floods in through the intakes.

Apparently there were no fewer than forty-six CCTV cameras along the route we took and every single one stored a grainy image. Why Inspector Clouseau and his army of frog Dibble didn't put a road block across the approach to the Pont de l'Alma tunnel and corner me, only they can tell. For myself, I didn't even know I was going through it until I was, didn't know what route I was taking, no way – it was the only route available, it seemed to me. Once I found myself in the closed-off roads I rolled like water, as if in a dream, looking at all the people, wondering what they all were doing there so late. I looked at my watch, it was midnight. The moment for the crowd to pay its respects. Perhaps Inspector Clouseau and the army of Dibble didn't want to get in the way of the silence. I passed down into the tunnel without even looking sideways at the unlucky thirteenth pillar. It was so cool down there, and calm. I could have stayed longer. The gauge dropped right back to normal. As I came out the other side I wound the window down a touch and for a second I thought I heard a sound like cheering, but it was just a silent echo from behind me; the only note I heard was that whisper of wind.

And then sirens begin to fill the air, French sirens, which have an especially urgent note, almost comical. I'm not so stupid as to not know what I've done, where I've been. Not now. I've made the car famous, like Harry Potter's Anglia. To make it even more famous I stop it outside a hotel called the Ritz, write *À Vendre* on a little sign in the window, and put Will's phone number on it with the (00) as you have to do when calling from abroad. I take my rucksack and Blue off the back seat, and we walk down into the Metro where the trains are running all night. If there is a sign saying *Chien Interdit*, I don't see it.

We disembark at Louis Blanc. At the top of the platform Nico is waiting. She takes my hand. We cross the road and walk down towards the Canal St Martin. We stop outside a bar. Look, she says: It's on television. Bella, she says, I always imagined it was black, you never told me it was white, like a wedding car.

And there it is, footage of a pristine 1953 Mercedes disappearing through a crowd of people who all raise their mobiles and camcorders and flash them off like they're at Jay-Z in Docklands.

Look at *her*, says Nico, taking Blue's lead from me and pointing at the screen. You can see her there, she looks so *jolie* sitting up in the back alert, her ears all pricked. Nico tickles her under the chin. How clever of you, she says, to bring *le lévrier* along.

How d'you mean, clever?

Because of the dog, of course, the dog that was seen in the back of the white Fiat Uno that never existed. Don't you remember? I thought that was part of your plan.

I'd never read or heard about a dog that never existed. Though I was delighted to learn about it now. And a plan? Because what had I actually done, when you analyse it? I'd gone slightly off-track, that's all, got a bit lost along the way.

A dog that never existed? Really, there was one of them?

*Oui.*

Conceptually intact, I said. *Mais un accident,* Nico.

Conceptually *formidable*, Tommy, she says. She squeezes my hand. *Et un 'appy accident.* And for your next trick?

I met this man once, on a beach, soon after my dad, I tell her. He gave me Blue. He gave me Blue and a lecture.

What was the lecture?

He said to be a force for the constructive.

Oh. So: no more slashing le tyres of red cars?

No.

No more boring les Futures Certificates?

No.

No more le Netto?

No more le Netto, no more la Naz; no more la Zoë. No more wrong turns, if you're with me, Nico. I'm going to concentrate on ze good energy, ze creative.

Great, she says, linking her arm through mine, like the gamines always do in her movies. How will you start?

I pull the velvet bag out of my rucksack and take the instrument out. The only thing I know about it is that it makes a sound less dark and less mournful than a flugelhorn. I fit the mouthpiece.

By learning to play this trumpet, I say.

I lift it to my lips, and blow as hard as I can.

*'Youth Portrait' by Gerhard Richter*

*Are You With Me?* is Stephen Foster's second novel. An author of fiction and non-fiction, including the *Sunday Times* Top Ten bestselling *Walking Ollie*, he lives in Norwich with his partner and two hounds.

Praise for Stephen Foster's *Strides*:

'Somewhere between Julian Barnes and Nick Hornby' *Guardian*

'Truthful, perceptive and very funny . . . Exposes the hang-ups, disillusionment and fragility so common in the contemporary male' *Time Out*

Praise for Stephen Foster's *She Stood There Laughing*:

'Stoke's answer to *Fever Pitch*' *The Times*

'A marvellously mordant account of one football supporter's helpless obsession with a team who usually manage to let him down . . . amusing and effortlessly easy to read' *Scotland on Sunday*

'*She Stood There Laughing* by Stephen Foster is the diary of a season experienced by two football supporters, father and son. I actually laughed until I ached, and identified with the raw helplessness that is the lot of supporters. But [also] I cried – because I again identified absolutely why I was one myself' Delia Smith

*Also by Stephen Foster*

FICTION
Strides
It Cracks Like Breaking Skin

NON-FICTION
Walking Ollie
She Stood There Laughing